I0631234

Homersham Cox

Whig and Tory administrations during the last 13 years

Homersham Cox

Whig and Tory administrations during the last 13 years

ISBN/EAN: 9783742838872

Manufactured in Europe, USA, Canada, Australia, Japa

Cover: Foto ©Andreas Hilbeck / pixelio.de

Manufactured and distributed by brebook publishing software
(www.brebook.com)

Homersham Cox

Whig and Tory administrations during the last 13 years

WHIG AND TORY ADMINISTRATIONS

DURING THE

LAST THIRTEEN YEARS.

BY

HOMERSHAM COX, M.A.

BARRISTER-AT-LAW;

AUTHOR OF 'THE INSTITUTIONS OF THE BRITISH GOVERNMENT,' 'ANTIENT PARLIAMENTARY
ELECTIONS,' AND 'THE HISTORY OF THE REFORM BILLS OF 1866 AND 1867.'

LONDON:

LONGMANS, GREEN, AND CO.

1868.

PREFACE.

In the following very concise account of recent Whig and Tory Administrations there is no affectation of historical impartiality. These pages have been written under the influence of earnest convictions; but, at the same time, the obligation of strict fidelity in the statement of material facts has been scrupulously regarded. The references continually cited will afford the means of ascertaining readily whether that obligation has been fulfilled.

LONDON : *November* 1868.

CONTENTS.

— ◦◦ —

CHAPTER I.

Lord Palmerston's First Administration, 1855-8.

Resignation of Lord Aberdeen, Lord Palmerston's Cabinet, page 1.—Sir George Cornewall Lewis, Chancellor of the Exchequer, 2.—Abolition of New Paper Duties, 3.—Resignation of Lord John Russell, 4.—Increase of Estimates condemned by Mr. Gladstone, 6.

CHAPTER II.

Lord Derby's Administration, 1858-9.

Lord Palmerston's Resignation, Lord Derby's Cabinet, 8.—Reform postponed, 9.—Admission of Jews to Parliament, 10.—Transfer of Indian Government to the Crown, 11.—Mr. Bright's Reform Speeches of 1858, 13.—The Conservative Reform Bill of 1859, 15.—Resignation of Mr. Walpole and Mr. Henley, 16.—Defeat of the Bill, Appeal to the Country, and Defeat of the Ministry, 17.

CHAPTER III.

Lord Palmerston's Second Administration, 1859-65.

Reform Bill of 1860, 19.—Withdrawal of the Bill, 20.—Increase of Expenditure, 20.—Mr. Gladstone's Financial Statements, 22.—Commercial Treaty with France, 23.—Duty on Wines, 24.—Paper Duty, 25.—Re-

form and Simplification of Tariff, 26.—Paper Duty abolished, 27.—
Budget of 1863; Reduction of Tea Duty and Income Tax, 28.—Reduction of Expenditure, 30.—Sugar Duties, Income Tax, and Fire Insurance
Duty, 31.—General character of Mr. Gladstone's Financial Reform, 32.
—Legislation during Lord Palmerston's Second Administration, 33.—
Lord Westbury's Expurgation of the Statute Book, 34.—Mr. Villiers's
Parochial Assessments Bill; the Highway Act, 34.—Government Annuities Act; Audit of Public Accounts, 35.—Foreign Affairs; Expenditure condemned by Mr. Cobden, 36.

CHAPTER IV.

LORD RUSSELL'S ADMINISTRATION, 1865-6.

General Election, 1865, 38.—Death of Lord Palmerston, 88.—Franchise
Bill, 1866, 39.—Redistribution of Seats' Bill, 40.—Defeat and Resignation of Ministry, 41.—Mr. Gladstone's Budget, 1866, 42.—Reduction of
National Debt, 42.—Terminal Annuities' Bill, 43.—Tenure of Land
(Ireland) Bill, 44.

CHAPTER V.

LORD DERBY'S ADMINISTRATION, 1866.

Lord Derby's Cabinet, 46.—Reform Resolutions, 47.—Ten Minutes' Bill, 48.
—Reform Bill, 49.—Its anomalies, 49.—Abolition of Small Tenements
Acts, 50.—Liberal Amendments of the Bill, 51.

CHAPTER VI.

MR. DISRAELI'S ADMINISTRATION, 1867.

Autumnal Session, 54.—Lord Derby's Resignation, 54.—Scottish Reform
Bill, 55.—Irish Reform Bill, 56.—Boundaries of Boroughs, 58.—Election Petitions Act, 61.—Registration Act, 63.—Compulsory Church
Rates Abolition Act, 64.—Abolition of Flogging in the Army, 65.—
Abandonment of the 'Balance of Power,' 66.—Irish Church, 67.—Mr.
Dillwyn's Motion in 1865, 68.—Mr. Gladstone's Speech of 1865 respecting the Irish Church, 69.—Lord Russell's Motion for a Commission of
Inquiry, 72.—The Irish Policy of the Conservative Government explained
by Lord Mayo, 73.—Debate on this Scheme, 76.—Arguments for a
State Religion examined, 78.—Mr. Disraeli's repudiation of the Policy
of Catholic Endowments, 80.—Mr. Gladstone's Motion for a Committee
of the Whole House, 81.—Coronation Oath, 84—The circumstances of

the English and Irish Churches distinguished, 87.—The Government defeated, 90.—The First Resolution for Disestablishment carried against the Government, 91.—The Ministers offer their Resignation, 91.—An Appeal to the Country promised, 91.—Suggestions for Limiting the Supplies, 92.—Promise of a Dissolution renewed, 93.—Second, Third, and Fourth Resolutions on the Irish Church, 95.—Address to the Crown, and the Reply, 95.—Established Church (Ireland) Bill carried in the House of Commons, 96.—Rejected by the House of Lords, 97.—Nature of Ecclesiastical Property, 98.—Origin of Tithes, 99.—The Theory of the Sacredness of Church Property, 100.—The Royal Speech at the end of the Session, 103.

CHAPTER VII.

FINANCIAL HISTORY FROM 1865.

Reductions of Expenditure effected by Mr. Gladstone, 104.—Increase of Expenditure by his successors, 107.—The Budget of 1868 announced a Deficit and a Loan, 108.—Mr. Ward Hunt's Apology for Increased Expenditure, 111.—Cost of Army and Navy, 113.—Growth of Admiralty Expenditure, 114.—Reforms of Dockyard Accounts by Mr. Stansfeld and Mr. Childers, 115.—Report of Mr. Seely's Committee, 116.—Instances of Mismanagement of the Admiralty, 117.—Necessity of Reform of the War Departments, 121.

WHIG AND TORY ADMINISTRATIONS

DURING

THE LAST THIRTEEN YEARS.

———

CHAPTER I.

LORD PALMERSTON'S FIRST ADMINISTRATION, 1855–8.

IF we look back upon the actual legislative performances of Liberal and Conservative Administrations during the last twelve or thirteen years, we shall have a tolerably clear view of the relations of the two great political parties towards each other, and of the places which they are likely to occupy in future histories of this country. The existing combinations cannot be considered to have been established until after the year 1855. The Cabinet at the beginning of that year was composed partly of Whigs and partly of former colleagues of Sir Robert Peel. The Earl of Aberdeen was Prime Minister, Lord Palmerston Home Secretary, Lord John Russell President of the Council, Mr. Gladstone was Chancellor of the Exchequer, and Sir James Graham presided at the Admiralty. But soon after the commencement of the Session of 1855, in consequence of an adverse vote of the House of Commons respecting the conduct of the Russian War, Lord Aberdeen resigned. He was succeeded by Lord Palmerston. Lord John Russell was associated with him as Colonial Secretary, but Mr. Gladstone left the Cabinet, and his office of Chancellor

B

of the Exchequer was transferred to the late Sir George
Cornewall Lewis. The following is an extract from a
letter written by that lamented statesman announcing
his appointment. The editor of his Essays on the Administrations of Great Britain from 1783 to 1830 justly
observes with reference to this letter that 'those who
knew him well will not suspect him of any affectation
when he professes his indifference, or rather his reluctance, to accept the high office then placed at his disposal.'

Soon after my return to London after my election, I received
quite unexpectedly the offer of the office of Chancellor of the
Exchequer in Lord Palmerston's Government. I had just
returned from the country. I had had no time to look into my
private affairs since my father's death. . . . . I had to follow
Gladstone, whose ability had dazzled the world, and to produce a war budget with a large additional taxation in a few
weeks. All these circumstances put together inspired me with
the strongest disinclination to accept the offer. I felt, however,
that in the peculiar position of his government, the office having
been already refused by ——, refusal was scarcely honourable,
and would be attributed to cowardice, and I therefore most
reluctantly made up my mind to accept. . . . . . There is an
awkward question about the newspaper stamp which I have
had to plunge into. There are also all the preparations to be
made for the impending budget, and measures to be taken for
providing sufficient sums to meet the enormous extraordinary
expenditure which the war in the Crimea is causing. Gladstone has been very friendly to me, and has given me all the
assistance in his power.*

The attention of Parliament and the country during
the year was occupied principally by the Russian war;
but during the Session the Whig Ministry found time to
carry some most important measures of domestic interest.
Foremost among them was the establishment of a cheap
newspaper press. In the Royal Speech at the end of
the Session Her Majesty was enabled to congratulate

* Essays on the Administrations of Great Britain from 1783 to 1830, by
the Right Hon. Sir George Cornewall Lewis. Edited by Sir Edmund
Head. Preface, p. xvii.

Parliament on the abolition of the duty on newspapers, and to express an opinion that it would 'tend to diffuse useful information among the poorer classes of Her Majesty's subjects.'

In the month of March 1855, it became the duty of Sir George Cornewall Lewis, as Chancellor of the Exchequer, to present to the House of Commons a scheme for the abolition of the compulsory newspaper stamp. The author of this scheme was Mr. Gladstone, and the history of it was thus narrated to the House by his successor. After referring to a Resolution of the previous Session condemning the existing laws with reference to the periodical press, as 'ill defined and unequally enforced,' Sir George Cornewall Lewis proceeded:—

This Resolution having been unanimously agreed to by the House last Session, the question naturally came under the consideration of Lord Aberdeen's Government during the recess, and the subject fell necessarily within the province of my right hon. friend the Member for the University of Oxford. The plan which he submitted to the consideration of the Government is now before the House. It involves substantially the abolition of the newspaper stamp.*

Mr. Gladstone's proposal, which speedily became law, was to allow the proprietors of any newspaper an option of either stamping any portion of the issue or of leaving it altogether unstamped. The stamped copies were to have the privilege of free transmission by post. The project was strongly opposed by the Conservatives, who considered that the effect would be to encourage seditious and immoral publications. When the Bill came on for second reading, Mr. Deedes, Member for East Kent, moved that it should be postponed until after the Chancellor of the Exchequer had made his financial statement. He stated, however, that his opposition to the measure was not exclusively or even principally

* *Hansard*, vol. 137, col. 770.

founded on financial considerations, and anticipated 'the introduction of papers of a low and immoral character.'*

The motion for postponing the Bill was strongly supported by Mr. Disraeli, who argued that the House ought not to be called upon to repeal a tax, when the Chancellor of the Exchequer would not, and possibly could not, state what was the compensation to be afforded to the revenue. Lord Palmerston answered, that though the amendment was ostensibly only for delay, it was intended to prevent the Bill from being passed, and added,

Let every Member know that in giving his vote on this motion he will practically be giving his vote ' Aye ' or ' No ' for the measure.†

After an animated debate, the second reading was carried by a majority of 54—the numbers being, ayes 215; noes 161. The majority included the names of Sir Richard Bethell, Mr. Bright, Mr. Cobden, and Mr. Gladstone. The minority included nearly all the chiefs of the Tory party, and among them were Mr. Cairns (now Lord Cairns), Mr. Disraeli, Mr. Henley, Sir John Pakington, General Peel, and Sir Frederic Thesiger (now Lord Chelmsford).

Lord Palmerston's Government of 1855 was materially weakened by the secession of Lord John Russell, who had taken part at Vienna in diplomatic consultations having for their object the conclusion of a peace with Russia. Lord John found that his colleagues were not disposed to assent to certain proposals which appeared to him acceptable as bases of negotiation with Russia, and when this divergence of opinion became the occasion of a hostile motion in Parliament, resigned his place in the Cabinet.‡

---

* *Hansard*, vol. 137, col. 1100.   † *Ibid.* col. 1104.
‡ *Ibid.* vol. 130, col. 880.

During the following year the Russian war terminated, and under the auspices of Lord Palmerston and his colleagues a treaty was concluded, by which (according to the language of the Royal speech at the end of the Session) 'the objects for which the war had been undertaken were fully attained.' [*]

The period was not favourable for domestic reforms. Less than twelve months intervened between the cessation of hostilities with Russia and the commencement of the terrible Indian Mutiny of 1857. The succession of grave transactions abroad gave full scope to Lord Palmerston's administrative abilities; but the public attention, preoccupied by military events, was directed but languidly towards our internal polity. Royal speeches at the end of a session are at least some criterion of the national progress. If we look at the language of these productions during Lord Palmerston's first Administration, we find them filled with wars and rumours of wars. The people were so much engaged in looking abroad that they had but little time to bestow on their interests at home. In some respects we retrograded. The course of financial economy which Mr. Gladstone had initiated in 1852, when he first became Chancellor of the Exchequer, was not pursued; and, as an independent member of Parliament, he viewed with dissatisfaction the abandonment of some of his most valuable projects for ameliorating the material condition of the lower classes. In 1856 and 1857 Sir George Cornewall Lewis, then Chancellor of the Exchequer, proposed an increase of the duties on sugar and tea—or rather that the successive reductions of those duties for which Parliament, at the instance of his predecessor, had provided, should be suspended. Mr. Gladstone complained much of the estimates which rendered such proposals necessary. He showed that two or three millions of money arising

[*] *Hansard*, vol. 143, col. 1402.

from an expiring income tax, which ought to have been
devoted towards the liquidation of the public debt, in
accordance with a pledge given to Parliament, were
applied to ordinary current expenditure.   He added,

We have not only to look back to the rapid increase of those
estimates extending over several years, but we have to consider what are the prospects for the future ; and I am sorry
to say that in my humble and conscientious opinion those
prospects are still more gloomy and perplexing . . . As
regards the general scale of miscellaneous estimates, it is impossible that they should be effectually cut down in this House.
It is the Government, and the Government only, wisely and
firmly supported by this House, which can possibly cut them
down.   I may, perhaps, be of a censorious disposition, but I
frankly own that the views of the Government with respect
to public economy are not my views . . . The temper of
the public, reflected as it is by this House, is not at the present
moment favourable to economy.*

The observations here made as to the actual control
of Parliament over the public expenditure are of permanent constitutional importance.   The real extent of
the power of the House of Commons in this respect is
very much misunderstood.   Theoretically, the representatives of the people hold the strings of the public purse ;
but in practice, the scale of estimates is determined
mainly by the administrative government.   When the
time comes for voting supplies, it is generally too late to
effect any considerable reduction.   With respect to the
greater part of the expenditure, the nation is virtually
committed to the outlay, by the action of the public
departments, long before the money is voted.   The
estimates which Parliament will have to pass in 1869
are made up in a great measure from the requisitions
of the different branches of the public service in the
latter part of 1868.   Consequently the House of Com-

---

* *Hansard*, vol. 147, col. 1497 (August 12, 1857).

mons considers itself precluded from exercising with absolute freedom its constitutional power of curtailing items of supply.   Economy of the national revenues depends primarily and mainly upon the vigilance of the Cabinet, and its determination to resist excessive demands by the public departments.

CHAPTER II.

LORD DERBY'S ADMINISTRATION, 1858–9.

LORD PALMERSTON's first Administration came to an end in February 1858. The occasion of its downfall was connected with an atrocious conspiracy and attempt to assassinate the Emperor of the French. Some of the conspirators were in this country, but the law was unable to reach them. Lord Palmerston introduced a Bill by which a conspiracy within the United Kingdom to commit a murder abroad was declared to be a felony punishable with penal servitude for life or a limited number of years. The subject had become complicated by diplomatic negotiations and by discussions carried on with needless acrimony on both sides of the Channel. After protracted debates the House of Commons passed, by a majority of 19 (February 22, 1858), a resolution which, while deploring and condemning the attempt on the life of the French Emperor, censured the mode in which the diplomatic communications had been conducted by the Queen's Ministers. Thereupon Lord Palmerston relinquished office, and another Cabinet was speedily formed, in which the Earl of Derby was Prime Minister. Mr. Disraeli became Chancellor of the Exchequer, Lord Stanley undertook the Colonial department, and Sir John Pakington was appointed First Lord of the Admiralty.

The ensuing Session was not very productive. The state of the Reform question at that time is sufficiently indicated by a brief extract from a speech by Lord

Derby on February 11, shortly before the change of
Administration.   The Queen's Speech at the opening
of the Session had stated that the attention of Parliament would be 'called to the Laws which regulate the
Representation in Parliament, with a view to consider
what Amendments may be safely and beneficially made
therein.' *   Referring to this paragraph, Lord Derby
said :—

> If the measure were not brought forward at an early period
> Her Majesty's Government would be open to the suspicion of one
> of two things—either of desiring that the measure should not
> pass at all during the present Session, which he was not quite
> sure that some of them might not desire, as he confessed he
> himself did; or else of hurrying it through without giving
> Parliament and the country time to consider it.†

Of the two species of danger here contemplated, the
second, at least, was extremely remote.   There was no
risk of either Lord Derby or Lord Palmerston 'hurry-
ing' Parliamentary Reform in 1858.

Again, taking the retrospect in the Queen's Speech at
the end of the Session as a guide, we find that all the
ministerial measures to which the speech refers were
of a local nature.   They included a Thames Embank-
ment Act, and other enactments relating to Scotch Universities, the Irish Encumbered Estates' Commission,
and the government of British Columbia.

Two measures of great national importance were
indeed carried during the Session of 1858 ; but the
Conservative Government did not attempt to claim the
credit of them.   Principally through the persevering
efforts of Lord John Russell, a Bill was passed which
settled the vexed question of the admission of Jews to
Parliament.   Respecting this remarkable measure the
Royal Speech was quite silent.

The history of the enactment which first enabled

* *Hansard*, vol. 148, col. 5.   † *Ibid.* col. 1120.

Jews to sit in Parliament is briefly this:—The old
oath of abjuration concluded with the words, 'And I
make this declaration upon the true faith of a Christian.'
Peers and Members of the House of Commons were
liable to heavy penalties if they voted in Parliament
without taking this oath.   This declaration excluded
Jews from the Legislature, though, obviously, the original object of the oath was to maintain the succession
of the Crown against the Pretender.   For many years
the House of Commons agreed to Bills for the relief
of Jewish subjects, and enabling them to take the oath
with the omission of the words to which they had a conscientious objection.   These measures were rejected by
the House of Lords.   At length, after eight or nine
years' struggle, the persistent efforts of Lord John
Russell were crowned with success.   The ultimate solution of the difficulty was due in no small degree to
the astuteness and constitutional learning of Sir Richard
Bethell, now Lord Westbury.   Speaking, on July 13,
1858, Lord John Russell said:—

> The Attorney-General of that day, Sir Richard Bethell,
> enforced with great legal learning, and with great force of
> reasoning, the opinion that this House had the power to ad-
> minister a declaration to a person objecting to take the oath,
> and that declaration would be sufficient to admit him to his
> seat.*

Lord John Russell then referred to the possibility of
such a decision of the House of Commons being con-
tested in the Courts of Law, and gave his preference to
the solution proposed by a Bill then before the House
of Lords, by which either House was enabled by a Resolution to allow any person professing the Jewish religion to omit from the required oath the words 'And I
make this declaration upon the true faith of a Christian.'
The Bill enabling either House to admit Jews by

* *Hansard*, vol. 151, col. 1371.

Resolution* was introduced in the Upper House by the Earl of Lucan, and was ultimately enacted with the reluctant consent of the Government. The spirit in which the concession was made may be inferred from the language of the following 'reason' which, on the motion of Lord Derby, was adopted as a ground for insisting on certain amendments to the contemporary Oaths' Bill sent from the Commons.

Because, without imputing any disloyalty or disaffection to Her Majesty's subjects of the Jewish persuasion, the Lords consider that the denial and rejection of that SAVIOUR in whose name each House of Parliament daily offers up its collective prayers for the Divine blessing on its counsels, constitutes a moral unfitness to take part in the legislation of a professedly Christian community.

This 'reason' was adopted on July 12, 1858, on the motion of Lord Derby, by a majority of 8; and on the very same night his Lordship voted for Lord Lucan's Bill, which enabled Jews, by the contrivance above described, to enter Parliament!

Lord John Russell did not forego the temptation of an obvious retort. On July 21, 1858, the Commons, upon his motion, resolved

That this House does not consider it necessary to examine the reasons offered by the Lords for insisting upon the exclusion of the Jews from Parliament, as by a Bill of the present Session, intituled 'An Act to provide for the Relief of Her Majesty's Subjects professing the Jewish Religion,' their Lordships have provided means for admission of persons professing the Jewish religion to seats in the Legislature.†

The other great legislative measure of the year 1858, to which reference has been made, was the Act by which the government of India was transferred to Her Majesty. The measure was originally introduced in February 1858, by Lord Palmerston, then Prime Minister, who urged that

* 21 & 22 Vic. c. 49.   † *Hansard*, vol. 151, col. 1005.

India, with all its vast and important interests, should be placed under the direct authority of the Crown, to be governed in the name of the Crown, by the responsible Ministers of the Crown sitting in Parliament, and responsible to Parliament and the public for every part of their public conduct, instead of being as now mainly administered by a set of gentlemen who, however respectable, however competent for the discharge of the functions entrusted to them, are yet totally irresponsible.*

The projected change was strenuously resisted by Mr. Disraeli ; but the first stage of the India Bill was carried by a majority of nearly two to one, the numbers being, ayes 318, noes 173. This emphatic expression of the opinion of the House of Commons induced the Conservative Ministry, which was constituted shortly afterwards, to relinquish their opposition to the transfer of the Indian Government to the Crown. The subsequent history of the measure was thus narrated by the Earl of Derby, on moving the second reading of the Bill ultimately passed. After adverting to the resignation of his predecessor, he observed :—

The noble Lord the Member for London (Lord John Russell) made a suggestion, which was, I think, as wise and patriotic as it was certainly just and conciliatory, and it tended to relieve Parliament from what might have been a very serious embarrassment. Lord John Russell suggested—and the Government at once adopted the suggestion ; indeed to a certain extent it had been already anticipated by us—that instead of proceeding to match one Bill as a whole against the other, we should enable the House to consider one by one in Committee, resolutions, the principles of which were involved in each, and out of those resolutions to frame a measure which might receive the sanction of the Legislature . . . The result of that course of proceeding is that there has been sent up to your Lordships' House a measure, not depending for its success on this or that political party, but a measure to a great extent the work of the House of Commons itself, and

* *Hansard,* vol. 148, col. 1282.

to which all parties concurred in giving their tribute of praise.*

In the autumn of 1858 it became known that the Conservative Ministry would propose a Reform Bill during the ensuing Session. In 1852, and again in 1854, Lord John Russell had unsuccessfully introduced Bills to amend the Representation. A great number of notices, having reference to the same subject, or parts of it, had been brought forward by independent members of the House of Commons. The public interest in the question was stimulated by a remarkable series of orations delivered by Mr. Bright, in the autumn of 1858, in several of the most important towns of England and Scotland. In addresses to enormous and enthusiastic audiences in Birmingham, Manchester, London, Edinburgh, Glasgow, and other places, he explained the existing disparities in the distribution of political power; and showed, by statistical evidence, that the majority of the House of Commons were returned by one-sixth part of the electors. On November 5, at a conference of several Liberal members of Parliament and active Reformers, at the Guildhall Coffee-house, London, it was resolved that Mr. Bright should, in consultation with others, prepare a Bill to amend the Representation. This scheme was fully explained by him at several of the subsequent political meetings, to which reference has been made. It is remarkable, that his plan for extending the suffrage was almost identical with that adopted nine years later by Mr. Disraeli. In his speech at Manchester, December 10, 1858, after citing the authority of Fox and Lord Grey in favour of a rated householder's suffrage, Mr. Bright said:—

Now, what is it that I propose? That every householder—of course, because every householder is rated to the poor—shall

* *Hansard,* vol. 151, col. 1450.

have a vote; and if a man be not a householder strictly, but if he have an office or a warehouse, or a stable, or land, if he shall have any property in his occupation which the Poor Law taxes, out of which he must contribute to the support of the poor—then I say that I would give that man a vote.*

There are passages in the speeches of Mr. Disraeli and Lord Derby, nine years afterwards, which are identical in effect with the foregoing extract. But at the time when Mr. Bright delivered his Reform addresses there existed in the minds of many persons the utmost alarm and indignation. He was going to bring in 'the floods of democracy,' and to 'Americanise our institutions.' Why those disastrous results should follow from his scheme of 1858, and should not follow from the same scheme when reproduced by the Conservative Ministry of 1867, has never been explained. Certainly, Mr. Bright, in his orations, said hard and bitter things of the aristocracy; but many of them were, at least, equally severe on him. The contest was a mere strife of tongues; and, of course, the more skilful word-fencer got the best of it. At Bradford, for example, he said, January 17, 1859,

One Scotch lord told a great audience that I was afflicted by a visitation of Providence, and that I was suffering from disease of the brain. His friends can tell whether that is a complaint with which he is ever likely to be afflicted.†

In his speech at Edinburgh in December 1858, after describing the efforts of various governments to pass Reform Bills, he thus foreshadowed that which was expected from the Minister then in office:—

Thus you see that all the leading holders of office among the Whigs and amongst those statesmen who composed the Government of Sir Robert Peel — all these men have declared in

---

* Mr. Bright's Speeches (revised by himself) at Birmingham, &c. London, 1850, p. 20. Speeches by John Bright, M.P.; edited by James Thorold Rogers. London, 1868, vol. 2, p. 45.
† Mr. Bright's Speeches (revised by himself), p. 57.

favour of the object for the promotion of which we are met to-night. But more than all this, more amazing still, we have the only Government possible representing what is called the Conservative party in the country making—without pressure too—making the same declaration in the country. We know that at this moment they are engaged in putting one ingredient after another in the hope of giving something to us, as soon as Parliament meets, which Parliament and the country may approve of. I hope to the bottom of my heart that it won't be that sort of a feast which it is said that a Spanish host sets before his guests consisting of a very little meat and a great deal of table-cloth.*

But the apprehension was speedily realised. Parliament met in February 1859, and the Royal Speech directed attention to the representation, and expressed a hope that Parliament would give the subject 'calm and impartial consideration.' When Mr. Disraeli came to unfold his plan the 'table-cloth' proved to be of almost interminable length. The history of the question was narrated in many words. Many elevated sentiments were uttered in that pompous language which recalls the period when debates were interlarded with frequent references to 'the noble lord in the blue ribbon,' and Pitt and Fox were Mr. Pitt and Mr. Fox. The scheme now described was of almost microscopic dimensions. There was not to be any lowering of the franchise in boroughs. Mr. Disraeli objected altogether to 'the coarse and common expedient of what is called "lowering the franchise in towns."'† But there were to be lateral extensions of the franchise: for example, persons holding a certain amount of property in the Funds or savings-banks, and graduates and certificated schoolmasters, were to have votes. The grand feature of the scheme was the equalisation of the county occupiers' qualification with that of occupiers in boroughs. The occupier of a house of the annual value of 10l. in a county was to be entitled to

* Mr. Bright's Speeches, &c., 1850, p. 32.   † Hansard, vol. 152, col. 985.

be registered. With respect to the distribution of seats, the Chancellor of the Exchequer expressed himself principally concerned for the counties. He said:—

Why, Sir, it is notorious that if you come to population in round numbers, 10,500,000 of the people of England return only 150 or 160 county members, while the boroughs, representing 7,500,000, return more than 330 members. Admitting then the principle of population, which is the principle of the new school, I say you must disfranchise your boroughs and give their members to counties. Sir, I never heard an answer to that argument.*

And yet the answer is simple and obvious. The 'new school' would be perfectly content to embrace Mr. Disraeli's proposal of disfranchisement and redistribution according to population if carried out uniformly. When he said that the counties were inadequately represented, he omitted to mention that they include a vast number of petty boroughs which are under the influence of large landowners and really formed part of the county representation. The 'new school' would very readily consent to an equal partition of power in the House of Commons between urban and rural populations, but the county interest has uniformly rejected that arrangement.

Mr. Disraeli's proposal to lower the county occupiers' franchise to the borough level was opposed by some of the most conscientious of his colleagues. Mr. Walpole offered his resignation in a letter to Lord Derby, in which he said:—

The reduction of the county franchise to a level with that which exists in boroughs is utterly contrary to every principle which the Conservatives as a party have always maintained. . . . . I cannot help saying that the measure which the Cabinet are prepared to recommend is one which we should all of us have strongly opposed if either Lord Palmerston or Lord John Russell had ventured to bring it forward.†

* *Hansard*, col. 978.   † *Ibid.* vol. 152, col. 1002.

Mr. Henley, the President of the Board of Trade, re-signed his office on the same grounds.

One of the chief parts of the ministerial scheme was the elimination of the owners of property in boroughs from the county registers. Mr. Bright pointed out that the effect of this innovation would be to transfer 'one hundred thousand votes on a franchise that had existed for 400 years from counties to boroughs.' This part of the Reform Bill, and the absence of provisions for lower-ing the franchise in boroughs, rendered it extremely objectionable to the Liberal party. Lord John Russell offered a Resolution strongly condemning the measure, and with the strenuous support of Mr. Gladstone, Mr. Bright, Lord Palmerston, and the whole strength of the Liberal party, defeated the Government by a decisive majority. Mr. Disraeli had previously made it known that if the vote proved adverse he should appeal to the country. This threat is one of the favourite weapons of his armoury. He has been thrice in office, and on each occasion has advised a dissolution. He took this course in 1852, then in 1859, and now again in 1868. The experiment failed in the two earlier instances, and will probably fail again. After the election of a new Parlia-ment in the summer of 1859, the Conservative Cabinet was ejected by a vote of want of confidence, and a new Ministry was formed, which comprised Lord Palmerston, Lord John Russell, Mr. Gladstone, Sir George Cornewall Lewis, and Mr. Sidney Herbert.

The debate on the vote which led to this change of Government gives a fair idea of the actual work which the Conservatives had accomplished during their term of office. It is simply a matter of fact, that during that period not one great legislative measure was passed of which the new Ministry could claim to be the authors. It is remarkable that, in his elaborate defence of his government (June 7, 1859), Mr. Disraeli does not take

c

credit for one solitary legislative achievement. His
speech is a series of able apologies. He admits that
the principal Bills which he had proposed had been
unsuccessful—but that was the fault of his opponents.
He acknowledges that the diplomatic efforts to maintain
peace between France and Austria had failed—the
failure was no fault of his. It might have been so; but
that the Tory Government of 1858–9 did not effect one
important amendment in our laws and government is a
mere matter of history.

CHAPTER III.

LORD PALMERSTON'S SECOND ADMINISTRATION, 1859—65.

LORD PALMERSTON'S talents for administration were almost unrivalled, but he certainly was not a great legislator. He left the business of proposing legislative changes to colleagues whose zeal for Reform was much greater than his own, and the chief labour of preparing and defending the Reform Bill of 1860 devolved on Mr. Gladstone and Lord John Russell. It is not intended to narrate minutely the history of this measure, which failed partly through the energetic opposition of the Tories, and partly through the known indifference of the Prime Minister. The chief feature of the Bill was the proposed reduction of the occupiers' qualification in boroughs from 10*l.* to 6*l.* per annum. Lord John Russell computed that this extension of the suffrage would add rather less than 200,000 votes to the burgess lists.

It is amusing to observe the alarm with which the Tories at that time regarded a proposal which sinks into insignificance compared with the change sanctioned by them seven years later. Mr. Disraeli described the projected enfranchisement of the working classes as 'class legislation, with which, considering its power and probable consequences, no class legislation that has hitherto, though only partially prevailed, can for a moment be compared.'* Mr. Walpole asked whether the effect of the contemplated change would not be

* *Hansard,* vol. 157, col. 844.

'wealth and intelligence placed at the mercy of poverty and passion.'*

The Bill was read a second time without a division, but the motion for going into committee upon it was carried by such a narrow majority (13 in a very full House), that Lord John Russell was compelled to abandon the attempt as hopeless. Thenceforward, during the remainder of Lord Palmerston's career, all Parliamentary efforts to amend the representation were initiated by private members exclusively. The apathy of the Prime Minister and the state of public feeling compelled Lord John Russell to reluctantly abandon, for a season, his zealous and meritorious labours to improve our Parliamentary institutions.

A far more satisfactory issue awaited Mr. Gladstone's Financial Reforms. His comments on the growth of expenditure after the Russian war have been already noticed, but the evil went on increasing until it became appalling. If any statement could win popular attention to the wearisome subject of finance, it would be such an alarming calculation as the following, which is to be found in his budget speech of 1860 :—

We have at our command a tolerably accurate and tolerably complete comparison between the rate of growth in the wealth of the country, and the increase of its expenditure. Between the years 1842 and 1853, the increase of her wealth was apparently at the rate of 12 per cent., and the growth of her expenditure at the rate of 8¾ per cent.; while between 1853 and 1859 the national wealth grew at the rate of 16½ per cent.; *but the public expenditure, so far as it was optional and subject to the action of public opinion, rose upwards at the rate of 58 per cent.†*

Very few people have an adequate idea of the rate at which the national burdens have increased since 1853. The actual cost of government in that year was

* *Hansard*, vol. 158, col. 620.
† Financial Statements by the Right Hon. W. E. Gladstone, p. 120.

55,7(9,000*l*. In 1859 it was 70,123,000*l*.* That i
the annual amount had increased in six years by tl
enormous amount of about *fourteen millions and a ha*
sterling.

But even this result does not fully show the imme
sity of the change—the enormous strides which tl
nation has taken in the path of financial extravaganc
We are to remember that a very large part of the annu.
burden of the country is inevitable, and beyond Parli:
mentary control; the interest of the national del
must be paid in full, and it forms a very large iten
The true measure of modern lavishness is obtained b
excluding such fixed obligations. The result is thu
stated by Mr. Gladstone:—

The increase in this expenditure which, as I before said,
under the control of Parliament, and whose amount is in tl
main determined by public opinion . . . during the peri
from 1853 to 1859 (a period of six years) increased fro
23,361,000*l*., at which it stood in 1853–4, to 36,898,000.
or at the rate of 58 per cent.†

In those half-dozen years the annual amount of volu
tary disbursements had received an addition of thirtee
millions and a half sterling!

It is very remarkable that this prodigious lavishne
has been confined almost entirely to the last fiftee
years. In the previous decade (the period of Sir Rober
Peel's and Lord John Russell's administrations) th
expenditure was nearly stationary.

Unhappily, the study of public finance is never likel
to be popular. Except by a few earnest and diliger
students of politics the significance of the series o
'financial statements' which Mr. Gladstone made whil
he held the office of Chancellor of the Exchequer is bu
dimly appreciated. People understand in a vague wa

* Financial Statements, p. 110.
† *Ibid.* p. 120.

that the public burdens are greatly increased in modern times—that there is a prodigious waste in the military and naval departments—that during the last ten or twelve years we have been committed to what a French Minister happily termed a policy of emulation; but how few are able to investigate the real nature of the evil, and to discover practicable remedies! The budgets of which Mr. Gladstone is author are characterised by a quality which, for want of a better word, may be called thoroughness; but that very characteristic renders them necessarily intricate, and there are not many persons who are willing to devote to them the requisite amount of study. Year after year, the late Chancellor of the Exchequer explained with admirable precision and clearness the state of the Imperial accounts; but, it must be allowed, that his expositions are unavoidably abstruse. They are indeed 'caviare to the general.' In this place it is not intended to give even a summary of the remarkable series of 'financial statements' commenced in 1860. All that will be attempted is to select some of those particulars which are nearest to the surface of a profound science.

In 1860, after demonstrating the prodigious rate at which the annual cost of Government had increased, Mr. Gladstone said:—

With what views, then, and upon what principles, are we to face this state of circumstances? I may at once venture to state frankly that I am not satisfied with the state of the public expenditure, and the too rapid rate of its growth. I trust, therefore, that we mean in a great degree to retrace our steps by watching for, and by turning to account, every opportunity of retrenchment. The process of retracing our steps in such a matter, however, even where it is resolved upon and begun, is one which must necessarily be gradual. For, if it be not pursued with circumspection and with caution, it will but serve to aggravate the very evils which it may be intended to remove.[*]

* Financial Statements, p. 121.

It may be objected that, entertaining these sentiments, Mr. Gladstone ought to have insisted upon a
reduction of the Estimates. The sufficient answer is,
that they were, to a great extent, beyond his control;
that they were framed by departments over which he
had no direct authority; and, above all, that public
opinion, as expressed by the House of Commons, did
not enable any statesman to enforce severe economy.
The Chancellor of the Exchequer is, by the nature of
his office, restricted to the duty of adjusting burdens so
that they may be borne with as little inconvenience as
possible. His task is not unlike that of a skilful mule-
teer, or camel-driver, who arranges the load which his
cattle have to carry, so as to equalise the pressure. But
while the nation silently tolerated the load, while the
people of England—to use his own language—were
distinguished by an 'ignorant patience of taxation,' * he
had no more power to diminish their burdens than to
alter the tides and seasons.

Among the great financial achievements of 1860
must be reckoned the Commercial Treaty with France.†
By that agreement, France engaged to reduce largely
the duties on some of the most important products of

* Financial Statements, p. 126.

† The Commercial Treaty with France was strongly opposed by the
Conservative party, and was the occasion of protracted debates. To a motion
expressing approval of the Treaty, an amendment was unsuccessfully moved,
which declared that it contained 'unnecessary and impolitic restrictions to
which this House cannot assent.' The following short extract from Mr.
Disraeli's speech (March 9, 1860), will sufficiently show the part which he
took in the discussion:—

'Sir, I have stated shortly my objections against this Treaty, financially
and diplomatically. Financially it affects injuriously a revenue which is in
a dilapidated state. Diplomatically it has produced an instrument which
does not clearly provide for British interests, which ought to have been provided for in perfect consistency with our commercial system.' He further
objected that, in a critical state of Europe, 'we are called upon to approve
this Treaty with a Power which the noble lord, the Secretary of State, himself has described as a Power of disturbance and distrust.'—*Hansard*, vol.
157, col. 207, 300.

British industry—coal, coke, iron, steel, machinery, and various textile manufactures.   From a system of prohibition our continental neighbours agreed to pass to a system of duties not exceeding 25 per cent. *ad valorem.* England, on her side, undertook to diminish the customs' duties on various foreign commodities, and especially upon wine.   One of the effects of these changes has been the introduction of cheap and wholesome foreign beverages into the English market.   For a while 'Gladstone claret' was a favourite subject of ridicule, which he anticipated thus:—

> You find a great number of people in this country, who believe, almost like an article of Christian faith, that an Englishman is not born to drink French wines.   Do what you will, they say; argue with him as you will; reduce your duties as you will; endeavour even to pour French wine down his throat; but still he will reject it . . . Taste, I say, is mutable. It is idle to talk of the taste for port and sherry, and the highly brandied wines as a thing fixed and unchangeable. There is a power of unbounded supply of wine if you will only alter your law; and there is a power, I will not say of unbounded demand, but of an enormously increased demand, for this most useful and valuable commodity in all its various descriptions.*

Time has slowly proved the correctness of this anticipation.   English people have lost much of their ancient faith in liquids which, by a mere fiction, were described as the products of Spain and Portugal, and every day the relish for light and wholesome wines becomes more general.   It may be safely predicted that, ultimately, this change of social habits will have a most material effect in diminishing the national disgrace of intemperance.

The Chancellor of the Exchequer did not omit to pronounce an eloquent eulogium upon the principal authors of the French Commercial Treaty.

---

* Financial Statements, p. 153.

I cannot pass from the subject of the French Treaty without paying a tribute of respect to two persons at least, who have been the main authors of it. I am bound to bear this witness at any rate with regard to the Emperor of the French; that he has given most unquivocal proofs of sincerity and earnestness in the progress of this great work—a work which he has prosecuted with clear-sighted resolution, not, doubtless, for British purposes, but in the spirit of enlightened patriotism, with a view to commercial reforms at home, and to the advantage and happiness of his own people by means of those reforms. With respect to Mr. Cobden, speaking as I do at a time when every angry passion has passed away, I cannot help expressing our own obligations to him for the labour he has at no small personal sacrifice bestowed upon a measure, which he, not the least among the apostles of Free Trade, believes to be one of the most memorable triumphs Free Trade has ever achieved. Rare is the privilege of any man, who having fourteen years ago rendered to his country one signal and splendid service, now, again, within the same brief space of life, decorated neither by rank nor title, bearing no mark to distinguish him from the people whom he loves, has been permitted to perform a great and memorable service to his Sovereign and to his country.*

Another important recommendation of the Budget of 1860 was the speedy abolition of the Paper Duty—one of the chief obstacles to the diffusion of cheap literature; this impost was not, however, actually remitted until the next year. The total amount of taxes remitted in 1860 was 2,900,000l., or, in round numbers, three millions sterling. But this statement by itself does not

---

* Financial Statements, p. 155. In this amply merited eulogium of Mr. Cobden for his services in negotiating the French Treaty, Mr. Gladstone characteristically omitted to mention his own share in that achievement. It is well known now that he was closely associated with Mr. Cobden in it, was in constant communication with him throughout the negotiations, and by his counsels and co-operation contributed in a most material degree to their final success.

Some idea of the extent of that success may be inferred from the statement in the Budgets of 1864 and 1865, that in 1863, three years after the Treaty was established, the exports to France had risen from nine millions and a half sterling to twenty-three millions sterling, and in the following year to twenty-four millions sterling.—*Hansard*, vol. 174, col. 561; vol. 178, col. 1007.

adequately show the amount of benefit conferred upon
the commerce of this country.   Mr. Gladstone effected
what he most justly termed a Reform of the Tariff—
an extensive revision and simplification of duties—which
had a great effect in promoting trade.   The number of
customable articles in 1842 was 1,052.   In 1859 the
number had been reduced to 419.   By the reforms recommended by Mr. Gladstone in the next year the
whole number of articles remaining on the tariff became
48 nominally.   But many of these were retained merely
as means of protection against frauds at the customs;
and, in reality, the only articles retained on the tariff
for the purposes of revenue were *fifteen.*[*]

It is very remarkable that the large remission of duties
was attended with comparatively little loss of revenue,
while, of course, the importation of valuable commo·
dities largely increased.   The import on four articles
of food set free from duty in 1860—butter, cheese, eggs,
and rice—rose in one year to an enormous amount,
namely, from 4,694,000*l.* in 1860 to 7,393,000*l.* in
1861.   Reviewing in the latter year the observed results of his policy, Mr. Gladstone was able to announce
that, while the foreign trade in the articles on which the
duties were left untouched remained stationary, the
imports of commodities the duties of which were partially remitted, rose by 17½ per cent.; and of commodities the duties of which were wholly remitted, rose by
40½ per cent.[†]

But the picture was not all rose-coloured.   The estimated expenditure of the year 1861-2 was largely increased by the Chinese war, and amounted in round
numbers to nearly 70,000,000*l.*; the revenue was calculated at about 71,800,000*l.*   This immense sum Mr.
Gladstone pronounced to be 'if not the very largest, one

* Financial Statements, p. 170.
† Financial Statement (1861), p. 228.

of the largest estimates of revenue which has ever been presented to the country in times of peace.' It was equivalent to about 200,000*l.* per diem.

From the figures just given it appears that the estimates of this year 1861 showed a surplus of nearly two millions sterling. Mr. Gladstone advised that a portion of this balance should be disposed of by a remission of taxation. But he held out no hope of a speedy abolition of the Income Tax. Upon this subject he made an observation which is important as an indication of the extent to which he believed it possible to reduce the expenses of Government.

Looking forward into the future, and desirous to afford such indications of it as I can venture to give, I should hazard an opinion that if the country is content to be governed at a cost of between 60,000,000*l.* and 62,000,000*l.*, or even 64,000,000*l.* a year, there is not any reason why it should not be so governed without the Income Tax, provided that Parliament shall so will it to be. If, on the other hand, it is the pleasure of the country to be governed at a cost of between 70,000,000*l.* and 75,000,000*l.* a year, it must in my judgment be so governed with the aid of a considerable Income Tax.[*]

He proposed, however, on this occasion, the remission of the impost by one penny in the pound; and he also effected the abolition of the Paper Duty.[†] The speech concluded with another emphatic warning against the mischiefs of public waste.

When in an extended retrospect, we take notice of the rate at which we have been advancing for a certain number of years, we must see that there has been a tendency to break down all barriers and all limits which restrain the amount of public charge. For my own part, I am deeply convinced

---

[*] Financial Statement (1861), p. 244.

[†] The remission of this tax was followed by an immense importation of Foreign paper and an increase of the manufacture at home. The importation in 1859, before the repeal of the duty, was 18,000 cwt.; in 1864 it had risen to the enormous amount of 107,000 cwt. Paper not only became cheaper, but was lowered in price by an amount exceeding the amount of duty abolished.—Financial Statement, 1864; *Hansard*, vol. 174, col. 552.

that all excess in the public expenditure beyond the legitimate
wants of the country is not only a pecuniary waste—for that,
although an important, is yet a comparatively trifling matter—
but a great political, and above all, a great moral evil.   It is
a characteristic, Sir, of the mischiefs which arise from financial
prodigality, that they creep onwards with a noiseless and
stealthy step; that they commonly remain unseen and unfelt
until they reach a magnitude which is absolutely overwhelming.*

It is this aspect of the effects of national extravagance which is most commonly overlooked. The burden
of the taxpayer is only a part of the evil. Lavish grants
of public money have a demoralising effect upon almost
everybody concerned in spending it.   In the public
dockyards, for example, there is naturally a desire to
obtain large grants.   They increase the consequence
of those establishments, and the staff, from the highest
officer down to the humblest artificer, regard the amount
voted not as a matter of national interest, but as it affects
themselves individually.   It is notorious that if the sum
assigned to a particular dockyard happens to be more
than is wanted, the establishment nevertheless invents
ways of exhausting it.   The superintendents prefer the
interests of the 'service' to those of the public, and act
on the principle of spending all the money they get. ·

Again and again the Chancellor of the Exchequer
reiterated his complaints of the enormous growth of
public burdens.   In 1862 he was enabled to give a remarkable vindication of his policy of remitting duties.
He showed that, in the four preceding years, the annual
revenue—principally under the effect of such remissions,
without extension of the sources and apart from any
change of taxation—rose from sixty-four to sixty-eight
millions, or by a sum of four millions in the course of
those four years.   Among the prominent characteristics
of the Budget of 1863 may be mentioned another large
reduction of the duty on Tea. and an alteration of the

---

* Financial Statements (1861), p. 257.

Income Tax, by which incomes under 200*l.* and above 100*l.* were to be charged at a diminished rate. Of the effect of lowering the duty on tea he gave the House ocular demonstration in a curious manner, by exhibiting two parcels which had been forwarded to him by a member, the one labelled 'a pennyworth of tea at 1*s.* 5*d.*' and the other 'a pennyworth of tea at 1*s.*' The Committee was asked to observe the considerable difference in their respective bulks. It was now proposed to reduce the tea duty from 1*s.* 5*d.* to 1*s.* a pound. Ten years previously — namely, in 1853 — the duty stood at 2*s.* 2$\frac{1}{4}$*d.*, and Mr. Gladstone procured the reduction, first to 1*s.* 10*d.*, and, in the course of three years, to 1*s.* a pound; but the public charges subsequently necessitated a postponement of this ultimate reduction.[*]

One more extract must suffice to indicate the general character of the remarkable volume from which the foregoing particulars have been taken :—

It must always be borne in mind that when we speak of the expenditure of the Government, we speak of that which is taken in great measure out of the earnings of the people, and which forms in no small degree a deduction from a scanty store, which is necessary to secure to them a sufficiency, I do not say of the comforts of life, but even of the prime necessaries of food, of clothing, of shelter, and of fuel. Scarcely in any country, scarcely in any period, have the earnings of the labouring community availed to secure to them in these primary respects even real sufficiency, much less general abundance. And if we have been enabled, by proceedings of ours taken within these walls, to raise the standard of comfort, and to diminish, if not to do away with, the fearful gap which existed half a century ago between the absolute necessities of the labouring man and his means of supplying them, we have accomplished a work for which the name of the Parliament of this our age will be blessed to the latest generation. It was about twenty years ago when Sir Robert Peel, Prime Minister of this country at the time, referred with the greatest authority

---

[*] In 1865 Mr. Gladstone procured a further reduction of the duty to 6*d.* per pound. The effect of this change will be considered in a subsequent page.

to the devouring effects of the Naval and Military expenditure then maintained by the Governments of Europe. I am afraid, Sir, that since the period at which he felt called upon thus to speak, the evil has grown not less, but more intense. In no quarter have those establishments diminished, in few are they stationary, in almost all they have increased. The natural consequence has appeared in the financial condition of almost every country; and, speaking generally, it might be said, without any gross exaggeration, that deficit has become a rule. Nor need I dwell upon the evils, political and social, and not financial only, which permanent or even frequent deficit entails.

After referring to a recent speech of the Finance Minister of France, condemning what he termed the expenditure of emulation, Mr. Gladstone proceeded:—

I trust I may also say—both on my own behalf and on that of my colleagues—it is to us matter of additional satisfaction, after reading the eloquent denunciation of the Finance Minister of France, if, while we submit a plan which offers no inconsiderable diminution of the burdens of the people, we can also minister ever so remotely to the adoption of like measures in other lands; if we may hope that a diminished expenditure for England will be construed beyond the Channel as the friendly acceptance of a friendly challenge, and that what we propose, and what Parliament may be pleased to accept, may act as an indirect yet powerful provocative to similar proceedings abroad.*

The last two years of Lord Palmerston's second Administration showed that these doctrines had begun to take effect, and that a sensible diminution of expenditure has been produced. In the Financial Statement of 1864 Mr. Gladstone showed that the annual amount of money spent was upwards of three millions less than in 1859, which he designates the first of the years of high expenditure.

In 1859 the expenditure was £70,017,000
In 1860 (including heavy charges for
   the Chinese war) 72,504,000
In 1864 (including 1,125,000l. for fortifications). 66,731,000

* Financial Statements (1863), p. 406.

At the same time at which this satisfactory statement was made, Mr. Gladstone was in a position to announce a surplus income amounting to rather more than two millions and a half sterling.* With this balance he dealt as follows:—The Sugar Duties were largely reduced; and the Income Tax, which stood at 7*d*. in the pound, was altered to 6*d*.; and lastly, the Fire Insurance Duty was lowered by half its existing amount—that is, from 3*s*. to 1*s*. 6*d*.,—so far as stock in trade was concerned. With regard to the Income Tax, Mr. Gladstone observed:—

My growing belief is, that if it is the desire of the House to see re-established in public administration those principles of reasonable thrift—I do not speak of wholesale changes, or wholesale reductions, in which I have little faith—but those principles of reasonable thrift which directed the Government of this country from about the period of the Duke of Wellington's Administration until the time of the Russian war, it is most questionable whether that object can be accomplished compatibly with the affirmation of the principle that the Income Tax is to be made a permanent portion of the fiscal system of the country.†

The very large reduction of taxation in this year, it was reasonably supposed, would produce a considerable loss of revenue. Mr. Gladstone estimated the loss at 3,080,000*l*.; but the next year he had the gratification of finding his prediction completely falsified. So far from suffering a diminution of three millions, the revenue for which he gave account in the budget of 1865 was actually slightly larger than that of the year before. He was again in the agreeable position of a Chancellor of the Exchequer with a large surplus in hand. The total estimated income of the year was just over seventy millions sterling, while the expenditure was slightly more than sixty-six millions; consequently there was a balance of four millions to be disposed of. During three years in succession there had been a surplus amounting in the average to three and a half millions annually. The

* *Hansard*, vol. 174, col. 587.   † *Ibid.* col. 587.

duty on tea stood at 1s. in the pound, which was at least
40 per cent. of the price of the commodity as sold by
the chest.   This duty Mr. Gladstone now reduced by
one half—that is, to 6d.; and he considered the effect of
this change would be to reduce the price by at least 20
per cent., and to place 'this most valuable and most
healthful of all the luxuries of the poor within the reach
of many who now do not enjoy it at all, or who only
enjoy it in a very limited degree.' *

Another considerable relief of the taxpayer, proposed
by this budget of 1865, was the reduction of the Income
Tax from 6d. to 4d. in the pound, which is by far the
lowest point which that tax has ever reached.

Lastly, the diminution of Fire Insurance Duty, which
had been confined in the previous year to stock in trade,
was now extended to all insurances alike.

This very superficial and imperfect review of the
financial changes effected in the five years from 1859 to
1865, will serve to indicate the character, but not the
extent, of the services rendered to the country during
that period by the Chancellor of the Exchequer.   Many
of the important changes which he effected in the collection and management of the public revenue have been
here left unnoticed.   It is impossible to read the five
budgets of this period without perceiving that they are
the result of unwearied industry and most minute and
careful investigation.   Anyone who is accustomed to
difficult researches will at once recognise the thoroughly
solid workmanship of these annual expositions.   They
are the productions, not of an author who has merely
'got-up' his task for the occasion, who has hastily
'crammed' information obtained at second-hand—but of
one who has thoroughly digested his knowledge and
elaborated his conclusions.   The innovations were many of
them bold, and would have been audacious but for the

* *Hansard*, vol. 178, col. 1120.

extreme care with which they were considered. There is a courage of ignorance, and there is a courage of knowledge. Mr. Gladstone, in many of his reforms, trod upon new ground, but he trod upon it firmly and confidently, because it had been well surveyed.

Time has vindicated the wisdom of measures which promoted economy in the collection of taxes, increased trade with foreign countries, and largely reduced the price of commodities valuable to all classes of the community. The most adverse critics have not been able to show that any one of the great changes introduced by the budgets of 1860–5 have injured the revenue or credit of the country; and in no single instance has a reversal of Mr. Gladstone's financial reforms been even suggested by his successors.

Passing now to a survey of the Legislation of Lord Palmerston's Second Administration, we find that it comprised many permanently beneficial changes, though few of them were adapted to excite much popular applause. The parliamentary history of Lord Palmerston's time—it must be admitted—was not brilliant, and there has been a fashion of unduly depreciating the labours of the Legislature during that period. The value of new laws is not always directly proportional to the noise which accompanies the enactment of them. A review of the Statute Book during the five years commencing with 1860 would show that Parliament was not only not idle during that time, but that it accomplished a large number of important, though unostentatious, improvements of our laws and institutions.

The technical and utilitarian character of these amendments would, however, render any extended account of them very tedious and uninteresting. A very rapid enumeration of some of the principal improvements must here suffice. In 1861 a series of Statutes was

D

passed for the purpose of consolidating and condensing the Criminal Law. This great work, which had the effect of substituting a Statutory Compendium in the place of a heap of Enactments which had been accumulated for upwards of two centuries, was carried through Parliament principally by the exertions of the Lord Chancellor, Lord Westbury. In 1862 an excellent Act, with which the name of Mr. Villiers is honourably associated, provided a greatly improved system of Parochial Assessments, and established a machinery by which the rateable value of property throughout the country is fairly and impartially estimated. The Highway Act of the same year was another development of the principle of local self-government: that Statute took away the management and maintenance of roads from petty officers of individual parishes, and constituted representative Highway Boards, which manage the roads throughout districts which usually include several parishes. One of the most useful, though certainly not brilliant, performances of 1863 was a Revision of the Statute Book, consisting of a repeal of an enormous number of obsolete Enactments. This excision of superfluous matter is obviously the first step towards obtaining a compendious Digest of Statutes. Contemporaneously, considerable improvements were made in Election Law; and in order to restrain undue expenditure at elections, candidates' accounts of their election expenses were required to be published by the returning officers.

In 1864 Mr. Gladstone introduced and carried, notwithstanding great opposition, the Government Annuities' Act. The general object of this measure was to enable persons, principally of the working-class, to effect Life Assurances with a Public department for small sums of money. The premiums were to be received, and the sums insured were to be paid, by the National

Debt Commissioners, through the agency of the Post-offices. It was objected, that this measure would enable the Government to enter into active competition with Friendly Societies and Assurance Companies; but such associations do not afford the same security and facilities for investment as a national institution can do. The obvious advantages which Mr. Gladstone's scheme offered to the working-classes secured for it the approval of Parliament.

Another measure which he originated in 1865 had reference more especially to his own department. The office of Comptroller-General of Exchequer was constituted by an Act of the last reign, for the purpose of providing an independent and impartial supervision of national expenditure. It was the duty of this officer to see that the Treasury did not draw out of the Bank of England larger amounts of the public money than the grants of Parliament authorised. But the office had become almost a sinecure, and Mr. Gladstone showed that its duties might be safely and economically transferred to another department—that for Auditing Public Accounts. An Act of 1865 accordingly provided that the two departments should be consolidated.

Still, it must be allowed that the retrospect of the latter years of Lord Palmerston's Administration does not show a list of magnificent legislative achievements. The period was one of transition, during which public opinion upon many great issues was becoming matured by frequent discussion; but the ultimate solution of questions of the highest moment seems to have been postponed by common consent. There were several reasons for this pause in the progress of Reform. One was the influence of Lord Palmerston himself. Another was the great interest excited by foreign affairs. In 1861 public attention was much occupied by the war in Italy, which resulted in the establishment of the

Italian kingdom. This country regarded with intense anxiety the civil war in America, and the consequent cessation of supplies of cotton produced, in 1862 and subsequently, an unparalleled amount of distress in our manufacturing districts. The Chinese war of 1862, carried on by combined British and French forces, occasioned a large increase of the public expenditure. In 1863 a series of minor foreign complications arose—a dispute with the Japanese—a rupture of diplomatic relations with Brazil—and troubles with respect to the Ionian Islands. In 1864 the diplomacy of the English Government with reference to the war between Denmark and Germany became the subject of protracted debates, and votes of censure upon the Ministry were moved in both Houses of Parliament. In the House of Lords the vote was carried by a majority of 9. A similar vote in the House of Commons, moved by Mr. Disraeli, was, after four nights' debate, rejected by a narrow majority of 18.*

The most severe critics of Lord Palmerston's policy were found amongst the advanced section of the Liberals. They especially objected to the increased expenditure required for military and naval purposes, and to the Prime Minister's indifference to Reform. In a review of the Session of 1862 Mr. Cobden said:—

I have sometimes sat down and tried to settle in my own mind what amount of money the noble lord had cost the country since he had been in office; and I think that from 1840, dating from that Syrian business which first occasioned a permanent rise in the estimates; judging by the way in which he, in conjunction with others, continually stimulated the late Sir Robert Peel into increased expenditure; taking into account his Chinese wars, his Affghan war, his Persian war, his expeditions here, there, and everywhere; taking into account his Fortification scheme, which I suppose we must now accept with all its consequences of increased military establishments;—

* *Hansard*, vol. 176, col. 1300.

the least that I can put the noble lord down as having cost the country, must be 100,000,000*l.* sterling. I think the noble lord, with all his merits, is very dear at such a price.*

Adverting to the omission of the Government to propose a Bill to amend the Representation, to the opposition of the Prime Minister to the Ballot, and to the abolition of Church Rates, and his indifference to other reforms, Mr. Cobden added, ' the conduct of the whole party becomes slack, and the principles advocated by the party lose ground.'† It was notorious, however, that the political apathy of Lord Palmerston was not shared by the most eminent of his colleagues, and that especially Lord Russell and Mr. Gladstone were dissatisfied, both on account of the large expenditure and the unprogressive policy of the Administration.

* *Hansard,* vol. 168, col. 1101. † *Ibid.* col. 1114.

CHAPTER IV.

LORD RUSSELL'S ADMINISTRATION, 1865—0.

THE Royal Speech at the close of the Session of 1865
announced that 'the Electors of the United Kingdom
will be soon called upon again to elect their Representatives in Parliament.' The Eighteenth Parliament
of the United Kingdom had so nearly reached the sep-
tennial period of its existence that a dissolution was
considered desirable. The election resulted in the
return of a computed majority of seventy members in
favour of Lord Palmerston's policy. But the accuracy
of this computation was not tested by experience; for
the Prime Minister never met the new Parliament. He
died in October 1865, and was succeeded in his office
by Lord Russell, Mr. Gladstone retaining his place of
Chancellor of the Exchequer.

The change in the Administration immediately made
a great difference in the prospects of Reform. The
newly constituted Government during the autumn collected a large mass of invaluable electoral statistics of
boroughs and counties. The volume compiled from
this information by Mr. Lambert has furnished the principal *data* of the subsequent Reform Bills.

The 'History of the Reform Bills of 1866 and 1867' *
has been narrated by the present writer, and it is not
intended to repeat it. For the very succinct account

* London: Longman, Green, & Co., 1808.

here to be given authorities will not be cited, for they
are stated with great minuteness in the former work.
Mr. Gladstone, in March 1866, submitted to the House
of Commons a Bill to extend the Rights of Voting in
England and Wales. The principal features of this
measure were as follows:—It did not include a redistribution of seats, which was to be left to a subsequent
measure. The borough occupiers' qualification was to
be reduced from 10*l.* to 7*l.* A lodger franchise was
given to persons occupying rooms of the annual value of
10*l.* The condition of payment of rates annexed by the
Reform Act of 1832 to the borough occupiers' qualification was to be abolished entirely; and all compound
householders—that is, persons whose rates were paid by
their landlords under a composition—were to come
upon the register, supposing the qualification to be
sufficient in other respects.

The county occupiers' qualification was to be reduced
from 50*l.* to 14*l.*; and the county franchise of leaseholders and copyholders in boroughs was extended. It
was computed that the total addition to the number of
electors would be about 400,000, of whom rather more
than one-half would be new borough voters, and the
rest new county voters.

The Bill was persistently opposed; not only by the
Tories, but also by a large section of members who
had been elected as Liberals. They objected to the
measure as too democratic, and they objected also
to the severance of two questions of extending the
franchise, and redistributing seats. Mr. Gladstone
had separated these questions for two very sufficient
reasons: first, because they were in their nature
essentially distinct; secondly, because the suffrage
question was quite sufficient work for one Session. Subsequent legislation has amply proved the accuracy of
these views; but very soon after the commencement of

the discussion he was compelled by the pressure put upon him to promise the Redistribution Bill.

Mr. Disraeli contended that the increase of the number of voters by 400,000 was excessive, and warned the House against reconstructing 'their famous institutions on the American model.' During the next twelvemonths, as we know, his ideas as to the limits within which additions could be safely made became greatly enlarged, until they went beyond those of Mr. Gladstone, and even of Mr. Bright.

The Seats Bill of 1866 provided for the transfer of forty-nine seats to counties, boroughs, and the University of London. The counties were to receive twenty-six additional members. No existing borough was to be extinguished; but a number of the smaller boroughs were to be arranged in groups, returning their members collectively. To this method of grouping great objections were made; but it was the only method then feasible for obtaining seats for redistribution among the larger constituencies. The reforming zeal of the House of Commons in 1866 was not sufficiently aroused to render any scheme of total disfranchisement practicable.

It is not necessary to enumerate the successive attempts to defeat Mr. Gladstone's Reform Bills. Amendments after amendments proposed for this purpose were defeated by small majorities. The House of Commons, as a body, had not then any real desire to amend the representation. At length, in June, an adverse motion was carried, which proved fatal to the further progress of the measure. This amendment proposed that the value of qualifying tenements in boroughs should be estimated by their 'rateable' instead of their 'clear yearly' value. There is indisputable proof that the proposal was founded in a sheer mistake as to a matter of fact. The most common argument for the amendment was that it would 'make the rate-book the register;'

in other words, that the parish books would be evidence of the value of qualifying tenements. This view is unobjectionable, but the absurdity of the amendment consisted in this, that the very principle on which it was founded had been already effectually adopted in the Bill. Mr. Gladstone was quite as much in favour of the principle as his opponents were. The valuation proposed by him, and that which the supporters of the amendment preferred, are *both* contained in the ratebooks in parallel columns, and as far as the object of making the rate-book the register was concerned, it did not matter an iota which column was chosen. From the debate it is manifest that many of the speakers were ignorant of the provisions of the Bill, and of the forms in which parochial assessments are kept. The majority against the Government was due to a notable blunder as to a matter of fact.

But, in truth, almost any other amendment would have answered equally well the purpose of the Opposition. Their real objects were to get rid of the Reform Bills, and as a necessary consequence to eject the Ministry. Read with the light of the subsequent debates of 1867, the objections that Mr. Gladstone's measures of Reform were too democratic, are now seen to have been mere excuses.

The Liberal Ministry at length refused to continue the contest with an Opposition the most unscrupulous of which there is any example in the recent history of English politics. On June 26, 1866, Earl Russell and Mr. Gladstone announced to the two Houses that their Administration was at an end.

The account of Lord Russell's Administration would be imperfect without some notice of the Financial Statement of 1866, and one or two important measures originated by the Liberal Government of that period.

Mr. Gladstone produced his budget in May 1866. He again announced a surplus of considerable amount, though smaller than those of the three previous occasions. The total expenditure of the year under review was sixty-five millions and three' quarters—a reduction of three millions from that of the year 1859-60, the year in which, as he remarks, 'the most important changes in the scale of our expenditure were made.'*

The surplus now announced as the estimated difference between the income and expenses of the ensuing twelve months, amounted to 1,350,000*l*., with which the Chancellor of the Exchequer proposed to deal by a remission of several minor taxes. Among them he selected the mileage duty on omnibuses — a tax upon locomotion affecting principally the large and rapidly increasing class of inhabitants in large towns who are obliged to live at a distance from the area of their daily labours.

But the principal interest of the budget of 1866 relates to the development of an elaborate scheme for gradually reducing a considerable part of the National Debt. By a very remarkable review of the finances of this and other countries, Mr. Gladstone showed that the enormous and increasing accumulation of national obligations had a serious effect in restricting industry and retarding the growth of wealth. The great bulk of the public debt of Europe, which he estimated at no less a sum than 1,500,000,000*l*., 'has been accumulated in a time of peace, and has not been thrown upon the several countries during a struggle of life and death.'† He emphatically drew attention to the 'stealthy manner in which the practice of borrowing in order to meet the ordinary charges of Government is becoming the standing vice of almost every Government of Europe.'

* *Hansard*, vol. 183, col. 307.   † *Ibid.*, col. 308.

For the purpose of reducing the public debt of England, he proposed to convert 24,000,000*l.* of that debt into Annuities, terminable in 1885, and computed that at an annual cost of about half a million, thirty-seven millions of the National Debt would be cancelled in 1885. The Terminable Annuities Bill for carrying this provident scheme into effect passed the second reading, but was withdrawn in July 1866, at the request of the incoming Conservative Government. Mr. Disraeli, when he became Chancellor of the Exchequer, brought in supplementary estimates, which made fresh demands upon the public purse. In answer to his appeal, Mr. Gladstone said (July 27, 1866):—

Finding himself, owing to the introduction of supplementary estimates, in a small deficiency of 250,000*l.*, he proposes to make good that deficiency, and to restore the balance of income and expenditure to the point at which we left it—namely, a surplus of about 300,000*l.*—by abandoning the measure we had proposed for the reduction of the National Debt by the creation of Terminable Annuities. Were I entirely satisfied as to the nature of the supplementary estimates proposed by the right hon. gentleman and his colleagues, I do not know that I should object to his method of meeting the case. I shall certainly offer no opposition to the discharge of the order on that Bill. The right hon. gentleman is therefore free, so far as I am concerned, to follow the course he has indicated; but I say this on the ground that while I reserve my judgment in regard to a portion of these supplemental estimates, I feel that in the present state of political affairs any advantage to be gained by seriously questioning them, would be less than the disadvantage which might result from disturbing the proceedings of the responsible Ministers of the Crown . . . It is important that it should be recollected that until 1860-1, we had for a length of time been paying in the shape of Terminable Annuities—a very large portion of which went, not to satisfy the claim of interest, but for the liquidation of the capital debt—a sum about, and sometimes above, 4,000,000*l.* annually. In 1860-1 that amount was reduced to a little more than 2,000,000*l.* Since that period we have been endeavouring by various measures which have received the assent of Parliament gradually to raise it again, but by no measure so important as to the scope of its operation, as that which the right hon. gentleman now proposes to relinquish.*

Another measure of the Liberal Government, which met the same fate as the Terminable Annuities Bill, and for similar reasons, was the Tenure and Improvement of Land (Ireland) Bill, introduced by Mr. Chichester Fortescue, Chief Secretary for Ireland. This measure proceeded on a principle different from that on which former attempts at legislation on the subject had for many years been founded. The Bills of former years did not give a right to compensation for improvements made without the landlord's assent. Some advocates of tenant-right proposed that the tenant should have the right of calling on the landlord to execute required improvements himself, or to consent to their execution; and, if the landlord refused assent, the tenant, subject to the adjudication of some tribunal or authority, was to have the right to make the improvements in spite of that dissent, and to charge the landlord for them. The Bill of 1866, however, was founded on a different and more practical principle, and was intended to bring the law of the land in Ireland into accordance with the actual circumstances of the people. It proposed to create by law *implied contracts* between landlord and tenant, in the absence of special prohibitions or stipulations by the landlord to the contrary; and to introduce, with reference to permanent improvements of land in Ireland, a custom analogous to the obligations which in England are enforced, not so much by strict law, as by hereditary confidence between landlord and tenant and by agricultural usage.

The Bill was vehemently opposed. It was declared to be founded on a principle almost sufficient to create a revolution, and tending to an ultimate redistribution of land. After the advent of the Conservative Govern-

* *Hansard*, vol. 183, col. 1200.

ment, Mr. Chichester Fortescue found himself compelled
to withdraw the measure (July 25, 1866); but both he
and Mr. Gladstone, who followed him in the debate,
insisted that the Bill was based on a rule which prevails extensively in England—that of allowing tenants
compensation for unexhausted improvements.*   Mr.
Gladstone quoted, in support of this assertion, a passage
from a speech of Lord Derby—certainly a very high
authority on the subject of agricultural usage in England.   Mr. Henley combated the assertion, but his
contradiction amounted to this—that 'there was no such
right either by custom or law in England in regard to
buildings.'   But the difference was somewhat minute.
It could not be disputed that for other kinds of improvements outgoing tenants in this part of the kingdom
commonly receive compensation; and Mr. Fortescue's
Bill, so far as it related to structures, was but an extension of an idea which in England has long been recognised as consonant with justice.

The times, however, were not favourable to the consideration of domestic reforms.   Two parties stood
opposite each other in hostile mood.   The Tories, with
the sudden aid of deserters from the Liberal camp, had,
after a fierce party conflict, won the coveted citadel of
the Treasury Bench.   The mass of the people were
bitterly disappointed at the loss of the Liberal Reform
Bill, and indignant at the unworthy devices by which it
had been defeated.   Immediately after the Tories came
into power, the battle of Reform raged more furiously
than ever.   It was no time for philosophical inquiry and
dispassionate consideration of minor improvements of
our social institutions.

* *Hansard*, vol. 183, col. 1400.

CHAPTER V.

LORD DERBY'S ADMINISTRATION, 1866.

Upon Lord Russell's resignation, the Earl of Derby was—to use the common phrase—'sent for' by the Queen, and desired to form a new Administration. Among the principal members of the Cabinet were Mr. Disraeli, Chancellor of the Exchequer; Mr. Walpole, Home Secretary; Lord Stanley, Colonial Secretary; Lord Cranborne, Sir John Pakington, and Sir Stafford Northcote, at the India Board, the Admiralty, and the Board of Trade, respectively. Lord Derby made a ministerial statement in the House of Lords, July 9, 1866. He held out no hope that the Government would introduce another Reform Bill. He said :—

I hold myself and my colleagues entirely free and un-pledged upon the great and difficult question of Parliamentary Reform.   It is said —

> Felix quem faciunt aliena pericula cautum.

But we have had experience, not only of the dangers incurred by others, but of dangers incurred by ourselves—dangers too which had a very fatal termination; and I certainly shall consider well and carefully, before I again introduce a Reform Bill, the wise advice laid down by the noble Earl, my imme-diate predecessor, that no Government is justified in bringing forward such a measure without having a reasonable and fair prospect of carrying it.*

There was here no presage of that great exten-sion of the suffrage which the Tories sanctioned, at

* *Hansard*, vol. 186, col. 730.

least, in the following year. It is now well ascertained that not only the form, but even the substance, of the Reform Bill was undetermined by the Cabinet at the end of February 1867 ; for, with reference to that period, we find a statement of the Prime Minister in March that, 'two schemes were under the consideration of the Cabinet, varying from each other in that very essential particular—the amount of the extension of the franchise.' *

There is abundant evidence, both internal and external, that the Reform Bill of March 1867 was adopted by the Ministry and prepared with extreme haste. It was preceded by several abortive schemes, proposed by Mr. Disraeli to the House of Commons, and almost instantly withdrawn. First, he proposed (February 13, 1867), a string of Resolutions as a basis of legislation. They were condemned on both sides of the House as hopelessly vague and impracticable. Next he recommended (February 25) a scheme of which the most remarkable feature was a 6l. household suffrage in boroughs. The project acquired the name of the Ten Minutes' Bill. In a speech at Droitwich, March 13, 1867, Sir John Pakington told the story with a candour and amplitude of detail which can hardly have won the gratitude of his colleagues.

They knew already how on Saturday, Feb. 23, the Cabinet Council came to a conclusion on the Reform Bill, which it was intended should be proposed to Parliament. On Monday the 25th, at two o'clock in the afternoon, Lord Derby was to address the whole Conservative party assembled in Downing Street. In the afternoon of the same day, at half past four—he gave them the hour, because they would see presently that time was an important thing—the Chancellor of the Exchequer was to explain the Reform Bill to the House of Commons. When the Cabinet Council held on the previous day rose, it was his belief that they were a unanimous Cabinet on the Reform Bill then discussed and determined upon. As soon as the Council

* *Hansard*, vol. 185, col. 1285.

rose, Lord Derby left London, and went down to Windsor to communicate with Her Majesty on the great measure which the Ministry was about to introduce to the country.   He (Sir J. Pakington) heard nothing further on the subject till Monday morning, when they were informed that Lords Cranborne and Carnarvon had seceded and objected to the details of the Bill, which they thought they had adopted on Saturday.   They might imagine the difficulty and embarrassment in which the Ministry found themselves placed.   It was then past two; at half-past two, as he had told them, Lord Derby was to address the Conservatives.   At half-past four Mr. Disraeli was to unfold their Reform scheme before the House of Commons. Literally they had not more than half-an-hour—they had not more than ten minutes—to decide what the Ministry were to adopt.   The public knew the rest.

It is not often that the proceedings of a Cabinet are so completely disclosed to vulgar gaze.   A thoughtful critic may, perhaps, object that the word ' Council,' or any other word which implies deliberation, is not applicable to a knot of politicians who take ten minutes to decide upon a new constitution of the Imperial Parliament.

After the Ten Minutes' Bill was withdrawn, the Cabinet, or at least the most influential members of it, resolved, at the commencement of March, to revert to the scheme which appeared to three of their colleagues —the Earl of Carnarvon, General Peel, and Lord Cranborne—so democratic, that they withdrew from the Administration.   Lord Carnarvon considered that the measure would ' effect an enormous transfer of political power, and alter the character of five-sixths of the boroughs of this country.'   Lord Cranborne considered that the contemplated changes were such ' that with respect to very large numbers of boroughs, they would scarcely operate practically otherwise than as a household suffrage.'

The scheme launched in such discouraging circumstances proposed to give a vote in boroughs to every

man who occupied a house for two years and was rated
for that period and duly paid his rates.

The hopeless defect of the plan was that while it
trebled and quadrupled some constituencies, in others it
produced no appreciable effect. The reason of this irre-
gularity of operation was that in some boroughs occupiers
were personally rated and paid their own rates, while in
other places the landlords, under the Small Tenements
Acts or by local arrangements, paid commuted rates on
houses of which they were owners. In the latter instances, under Mr. Disraeli's scheme, the tenants would
get no votes.

Mr. Gladstone instantly detected the utter absurdity
of the project, and exposed it with a merciless amplitude of statistical information. Sir Roundell Palmer
also devoted his great abilities and profound legal
knowledge to the same service; in several speeches,
remarkable for logical power and perspicuity, he dis-
sected the Bill, and showed that it involved gross
mistakes of law. When the fantastic incongruities of
his scheme were detected, the Chancellor of the Exchequer excused them on the ground that they produced variety in the constituencies. 'The Small Tenements Acts,' he said, 'absolutely though unintentionally
give us that variety which the country requires, and
which I believe is an admirable quality.'*

This reply is a magnificent specimen of that audacity
which is the chief cause of Mr. Disraeli's success. Almost anybody else would have been compelled to have
acknowledged the palpable blunder. However, the pre-
posterous irregularities of the Bill were too much for the
patience of the country or even of his own followers. It
soon became evident that the plan must be amended.
Various methods were suggested by Mr. Disraeli for
getting the non-rated householders on the register, but

* *Hansard*, vol. 185, col. 1349.

E

they were successively rejected as palpably inadequate
for their purpose. At last, by a proposal of Mr. Hodgkinson's, the difficulty was solved. His argument was
virtually this—the only way of making Mr. Disraeli's
rate-paying test work with tolerable uniformity is to
abolish the Small Tenements Acts with reference to
boroughs, and to insist that within their limits all
tenants shall pay their own rates.

There were many reasons for accepting this suggestion, though it involved a great sacrifice. The Small
Tenements Acts have been found very convenient. They
enable poor tenants to pay rates in the easy form of in-
stalments included in their weekly rent. The parishes
also have the advantage of getting the rates from a comparatively small number of solvent landlords instead of
a very large number of very poor tenants. The composition for rates was just one of those useful contrivances
which worked well for everybody concerned. But the
credit of the Administration was staked on the 'rate-
paying principle.' If that principle were rejected, Reform would be delayed for another year. In this dilemma
Mr. Gladstone recommended that the economical benefits of composition should be sacrificed to the political
exigencies. When Mr. Hodgkinson's Amendment was
proposed (May 17), the leader of the Opposition said :—

I am sorry that in deference to what seems to me an unwise
judgment of the House, it is necessary to interfere with the
scheme of composition which exists throughout the country.
But if the practical considerations are to prevail, my duty is
plainly to choose the lesser of two evils.*

Shortly afterwards he told a deputation at his own
house that he had assented to the abolition of Compounding, 'as I would assent to cut off my leg rather
than lose my life.'

But Mr. Disraeli felt no difficulty in the matter. He

* *Hansard*, vol. 187, col. 717.

never feels any difficulty about any matter. He accepted Mr. Hodgkinson's amendment with alacrity, and said that he regarded it as a 'signal corroboration' of the excellence of the rate-paying principle. The amendment, he added, 'was the policy of their own measure—a policy which, if they had been masters of the situation, they would have recommended long ago for the adoption of the House.' *

This statement is not easily to be reconciled with the fact that, at least, on two previous occasions during the Session he had opposed the repeal of the Rating Acts. On May 9, 1867, he stigmatised that proposal as 'rash counsel,' and said the difficulty of Reform 'must be infinitely enhanced if we should attempt to carry a measure which should at the same time deal with all the Rating Acts of England.' † And he had spoken to the same effect on the second reading of the Bill.

Mr. Hodgkinson's amendment was a revolution. It extended the franchise four times as much as the original measure would have done. By the abolition of the system of compounding in boroughs every householder becomes, after twelve months' residence, entitled to the suffrage, if his rates are not more than six months in arrear.

The allegation that the Reform Act of 1867 is mainly or substantially the work of the Conservative Government, is one of the most impudent falsifications of history that was ever attempted. Neither in form, nor in substance, does the Statute actually passed agree with the measure introduced by Mr. Disraeli. The Act comprises sixty-one sections, and of them there are but *four* ‡ which are the work of the Conservative Ministry. The Bill originally consisted of forty-three clauses; of

---

* *Hansard*, vol. 187, col. 724.   † *Ibid.* col. 354.

‡ These are, sect. 1, The Title of the Act; sect. 12, Disfranchisement of Reigate and three other Boroughs; sect. 49, Penalty for Corrupt Payment of Rates; sect. 54, Temporary Provisions respecting Registers.

these twenty-one were subsequently omitted or materially altered.   Of the twenty-two which have been
retained eighteen have been taken from Mr. Gladstone's
Franchise Bill and Seats' Bill of 1866. Of the sixty-one
sections of the Act, forty-one are additions to, or com-
prise material variations from, the original Bill.

Again, these extensive alterations changed the character of the Bill fundamentally. Originally it provided
an extremely unequal suffrage, and an extension less in
the aggregate than that proposed by Mr. Gladstone in
1866.   Moreover, the Bill of 1867 contained a clause
giving double votes to certain wealthier classes of electors.   Taking into account the dual votes and the other
alterations, it has been demonstrated that Mr. Disraeli's
measure actually would have increased the voting
power of the wealthier moiety of the electors.* Instead
of being an advance towards democracy, it was a step in
the contrary direction.   Instead of adding to the power
of the lower classes, it would have diminished that which
they possessed already.   But the amendments forced
upon the Government by the Liberal party gave an
essentially new character to the Bill. The dual vote was
speedily abandoned.   Mr. Hodgkinson's amendment—it
has been already said—quadrupled the aggregate extension of the borough suffrage.   An alteration moved by
Mr. Ayrton reduced the qualifying term of residence
from two years to one year. This was one of the many
points which the Government declared to be 'vital,' but
subsequently surrendered.   The county copyholders'
and leaseholders' qualification was lowered, notwithstanding the resistance of the Government. Yielding
to the pressure of a motion of Mr. Locke King, the
Minister consented to a substantial reduction of the
occupiers' qualification in counties. The lodgers' franchise was conceded to the influence of the Liberal party

* History of the Reform Bills, p. 118.

upon the motion of Mr. Torrens.   A clause, giving a third seat to each of the boroughs of Manchester, Liverpool, Birmingham, and Leeds, was forced upon the Government, and the schedules relating to the redistribution of seats were materially altered.   The Reform Act of 1867 is a palimpsest.   The first draught has been almost entirely erased, and so much new matter has been written over it that the skill of a Cardinal Mai would be needed to decipher the original.

This passage in the history of legislation inculcates a lesson of permanent importance.   It shows the value of established rules in Parliamentary procedure, and the extreme danger of heedless departure from them.   The conduct of measures to amend the representation was undertaken by the Conservatives with avowed repugnance, and without the support of a majority of the House of Commons.   Consequently they were compelled at every step to submit to the dictation of their opponents; and to accept, with declared reluctance or feigned readiness, proposals utterly inconsistent with their original plans.   Ordinary rules of ministerial responsibility fell into abeyance, and Parliament was committed unawares to a policy which, at the commencement of the Session, neither party desired or considered possible. The recorded opinions of the most eminent speakers in both Houses show that after their work was done they regarded it with dissatisfaction and apprehension.   Whatever merits the Reform Act of 1867 possesses, it certainly did not express the deliberate opinions of the Legislature.

CHAPTER VI.

MR. DISRAELI'S ADMINISTRATION, 1867.

AN autumnal session was held at the close of the year
1866 on account of the necessity of voting supplies
for the Abyssinian Expedition. The Queen's Speech
(November 19) referred to the detention of several
British subjects in captivity in Abyssinia and the means
about to be adopted to enforce their release. The
speech also stated that the report of the Commission
appointed to inquire into the Boundaries of counties
and boroughs would be submitted to Parliament, and
that Bills would be proposed for amending the Representation in Scotland and Ireland. The principal business of the sittings before Christmas was the vote of
supplies for the expedition to Abyssinia.

Shortly after the Christmas recess, Lord Derby re-
signed his office of First Lord of the Treasury. This
important change in the Ministry was announced (February 25, 1867) in the House of Lords by Lord Malms-
bury, who stated that, 'not from any of those changes
and chances in political warfare to which we are all
accustomed, and to which we cheerfully resign ourselves—but from failing health,' Lord Derby had been
compelled to secede from public life, and from the
management of public affairs.* Lord Stanley made a
similar announcement in the House of Commons. On
March 5 the two Houses were informed that Mr. Disraeli had, by Her Majesty's command, reconstituted the

* *Hansard*, vol. 100, col. 1905.

Administration. The principal changes in the Government consisted in the appointment of Mr. George Ward Hunt, Member for Northamptonshire, to the place of Mr. Disraeli as Chancellor of the Exchequer, and of Lord Cairns to the place of Lord Chelmsford as Lord Chancellor.

A few days previously to the retirement of Lord Derby the Scottish Reform Bill was introduced into the House of Commons by the Lord Advocate. The provisions for extension of the franchise were to follow the English model. All registered householders who had been duly rated and paid their rates were to be entitled to vote in burghs. The occupiers' qualification in counties was fixed at the same standard as in England, namely, the rated value of 12*l.* In accordance with the proposal of Mr. Gladstone, in 1866, seven additional seats were given to Scotland; two to the Universities, three to large counties, one to a new group of burghs, and an additional or third seat to Glasgow. The seven new seats were to be obtained by an equivalent increase of the total number of members of the House of Commons.

A very material alteration was made in the scheme before it became law: seven small English boroughs were disfranchised in order, as the Scottish Reform Act states, 'to provide for the seats hereinbefore distributed.' * It was enacted that Arundel, Ashburton, Dartmouth, Honiton, Lyme Regis, Thetford, and Wells should cease to return any members. Mr. Gladstone and other Liberal members strongly objected to any increase of the House of Commons, already inconveniently large. Mr. Baxter moved (May 18, 1868) that it be an instruction to the Committee that, instead of adding to the number of members of the House, they have power to disfranchise boroughs in

* 31 & 32 Vic. c. 48, s. 43.

England having, by the census returns of 1861, less
than 5,000 inhabitants.   This motion was opposed
by the whole strength of the Government, but was
carried by a majority of 21; the numbers being, ayes,
217; noes, 196.

The section relating to the occupiers' qualification
in burghs provides that no man shall under that section be entitled to be registered who 'shall have been
exempted from payment of poor rates on the ground of
inability to pay.'   This proviso establishes a material
distinction between the English borough suffrage and
the suffrage in Scottish burghs.   In this country householders, irrespectively of their means or the value of
their tenements, are liable to the payment of rates.   In
Scotland a different system prevails.   A large proportion of the poorer householders are exempted on the
ground of poverty, and in many towns a rule prevails
by which persons rated on dwelling-houses at a rent
under 4l. are relieved from poor rates.   In Glasgow,
for example, this practice exists, and one-third of occupiers of dwellings under a 10l. rental are thus excused.
In many other districts the proportion is still higher.*
Consequently the proviso in the Scottish Reform Act,
which disables persons who are not liable to poor rates,
renders the borough qualification in that kingdom
higher than in England.

The 'Representation of the People (Ireland) Act,
1868,' may be conveniently noticed in this place.   On
March 19 the Earl of Mayo, Chief Secretary for Ireland,
submitted a Reform Bill for that part of the kingdom.
The most material features of the project were these:—
The borough occupiers' qualification, which by an Act
of 1850 had been fixed at 8l., was to be reduced to 4l.;
the county occupiers' qualification, which stood at 12l.,

* Return, Poor Rates (Scotland), No. 467 of 1867

was to remain unaltered; six small boroughs were to be disfranchised, and the six seats thus rendered disposable were to be allotted as follows—one additional member to each of the three counties of Down, Tyrone, and Tipperary, one to the city of Dublin, and two additional members to the county of Cork.

The clauses relating to the redistribution of seats were subsequently struck out of the Bill, and it was reduced to the very narrow dimensions of a measure for lowering the borough franchise and making some incidental technical alterations. During the progress of the Bill through Committee, Mr. Disraeli announced that, 'under all the circumstances, Her Majesty's Government are not disposed, after the expression of opinion that has been made, to insist on the 11th and 12th clauses,' which related to the distribution of seats.

The section of the Act relating to the borough occupiers' franchise provides that the 'occupation of lands, tenements, or hereditaments rated at the net annual value of more than four pounds,' * shall constitute a qualification. In Irish boroughs, the rates in respect of houses of a net annual value not exceeding 4*l.* are paid not by the tenant-occupiers, but by various statutory provisions † are collected from the landlords or 'immediate lessors' of such tenants.

When Mr. Gladstone's Reform Bill of 1866 was under discussion, the Conservatives strongly objected to the 'hard and fast line' of his 6*l.* franchise. That was perhaps their most frequently repeated argument against the Bill; but here, in their own Irish Reform Bill, the 'hard and fixed line' was distinctly drawn. All tenements below the arbitrary 4*l.* standard were to be disqualified. Lord Mayo argued in defence of this provision, that persons occupying such houses did not pay rates; and that, consequently, the

* 31 & 32 Vic. c. 00.　　† 6 & 7 Vic. c. 92; 31 & 32 Vic. c. 00, s. 10.

'rate-paying principle'—the distinguishing characteristic
of the English Reform Act—was maintained. This
answer is clearly insufficient. The Conservative maxim,
with respect to English boroughs, was, that every householder who chose to pay rates might come on the
Register; and, accordingly, Mr. Disraeli's English
Reform Bill provided that even non-rated occupiers
might get votes by claiming to be assessed. But in the
Irish Reform Act there is no analogous provision;
there is no option of paying rates to secure a vote; the
4*l.* barrier is immoveable and impenetrable.

For the sake of perspicuity, it will be desirable to
disregard strict chronological order in reviewing the
Session of 1868, and to consider together the several
Acts of the year which affect the Representation. The
English Reform Act of the previous year appointed
certain commissioners to inquire into the temporary
boundaries of boroughs constituted by that statute, and
into the boundaries of all other represented boroughs,
'with a view to ascertain whether the boundaries should
be enlarged, so as to include within the limits of the
borough all premises which ought, due regard being had
to situation or other local circumstances, to be included
therein, for the purpose of conferring upon the occupiers
thereof the Parliamentary franchise for such borough.'*
Under the authority so constituted, a large number
of assistant commissioners during the autumn of 1867
visited the various represented districts, and made
minute inquiries respecting the Parliamentary areas of
counties and boroughs. Upon information thus obtained
the commissioners based a Report, which was laid before
Parliament in March. Many populous towns have
within these last few years largely outgrown their Parliamentary limits, and are surrounded by extensive

* 30 & 31 Vic. c. 102, s. 48.

suburbs.   The commissioners proceeded on the general
principle that these suburbs should be united to the
towns for electoral purposes, and accordingly very
numerous and important alterations of the existing
boundaries were recommended.   If the Report had been
carried out in its integrity, the political topography of
this country would have been materially altered.   The
contemplated transfer of a large number of voters from
the county register to those of boroughs, tended to render the artificial and impolitic distinction between agricultural and urban interests more strongly marked than
ever.   Several places which it was proposed to annex
to adjacent towns were beyond the municipal as well as
Parliamentary limits, and under different systems of
local government.   The only pretexts for the enforced
connection were, in many cases, the mere accident of
contiguity and a specious or ambiguous use of the word
' suburb' to suggest a dependence which did not really
exist.   The annexation was in several instances contrary
to the wishes of the persons who had most right to be
heard on the subject—the inhabitants of the districts
affected.   For instance, Mr. Gladstone referred, in the
debate of May 14, to a petition from 5,000 out of the
6,000 rate-payers of Aston who opposed the contemplated union of that place with Birmingham.   Mr.
Bright, in the same debate, said :—

Nothing could be more contrary to the practice of Parliament than that general bringing in of people from one constituency to another; for it was a fact that some 400,000
people were to be dragged from the counties to be put into the
boroughs.

With reference to the case of Birmingham and Aston,
he said :—

The 350,000 within the borough were apparently almost
unanimous in wishing them not to come in, and the 30,000
who were proposed to be brought in appeared to be absolutely
unanimous in wishing to remain out.

He concluded by recommending that the Report should be referred to a select committee of the House. Mr. Disraeli thereupon expressed his assent to such a reference, and proposed that the committee should have power to confer with the commissioners, and that the evidence should be purely documentary.

By thus yielding to the pressure of the Liberals, Mr. Disraeli gave great disappointment to his own supporters. The Tories wanted to get the suburbs annexed to towns in order that the shire constituencies might be more exclusively rural. Their opponents, from opposite motives, adopted the opposite policy. But it may be reasonably doubted whether the division of a county for electoral purposes should not depend upon higher and more permanent considerations than the temporary objects of political warfare. The division between towns and counties, if carried out strictly, tends to perpetuate the mischievous delusion that their interests are antagonistic. That of itself is almost a sufficient objection to such rearrangements as the commissioners contemplated. Another minor objection is, that their scheme aggravated the existing confusion arising from multiplicity of boundaries. Anciently a borough had but one boundary for all purposes; the municipal area and the Parliamentary were conterminous. Mr. Gladstone's Bill of 1866 would have restored this principle; and it appears to be the only one which affords a safe solution of a problem of no ordinary difficulty.

The Boundary Bill, introduced by Mr. Henley to carry into effect the Report of the commissioners, was referred to a select committee of five members, who reported in favour of changes much less extensive than those originally recommended. Mr. Hibbert moved (June 11) a clause adopting the revised scheme, and this motion was carried upon a division by a majority of 36—the numbers being, for the motion, 184; against it, 148.   Liverpool, Manchester, Birmingham, and other large towns were omitted from the schedule of boroughs subjected to revision of boundaries.   The Boundary Act * ultimately passed alters the Parliamentary limits of upwards of fifty of the old boroughs of England, but the list does not include many large towns, and the changes are not extensive.

The history of the Election Petitions Act is a curious and instructive exemplification of the accidents and vicissitudes to which legislation is subject in this country.   A Bill was introduced by Mr. Disraeli in 1867 by which the jurisdiction of controverted elections was transferred from committees of the House of Commons to a tribunal of lawyers to be chosen by the Speaker.   This Bill was submitted to a select committee, which approved of the removal of the jurisdiction from the House, but recommended that investigations of disputed returns should be conducted by the superior judges of common law, and that each trial should take place with the formalities of an assize, in the county or borough to which the complaint related.   Mr. Disraeli introduced another Election Petitions Bill in February 1868.   He stated that the Government at the commencement of the Session was prepared to give effect to the opinions of the committee of the previous year, but an unexpected obstacle had been interposed.   He said :—

It became our duty—not to consult them, Her Majesty's Judges, whether they would undertake a duty which the wisdom of Parliament would put upon them—but as a matter of courtesy, to inquire of the Judges the most convenient manner to themselves in which the provisions of the Act, if it passed, might be carried into effect.   But I regret to say, that instead of receiving from the Judges information upon the particular point upon which we sought to be instructed, we received from that most eminent and exalted body—conveyed by their most august member—an expression of opinion upon

* 31 & 32 Vic. c. 40.

the proposed Bill so entirely condemnatory of its provisions
that it became absolutely necessary for us to consider the
course we should adopt . . . Although the highest authority
has told us that even in Olympian dwellings there are those who
are not superior to the infirmities of human nature, I may say
on the part of Her Majesty's Government that we feel that
we can no longer attempt to influence the Judges in this
matter, and that we have received their decision with mortifi-
cation and disappointment.*

Mr. Disraeli then proceeded to offer in lieu of the
relinquished plan another, by which a Parliamentary
Election Court was to be constituted consisting of three
salaried judges, to whom the jurisdiction of controverted
elections and also of appeals from revising barristers'
decisions was to be assigned.

The objections of the Common Law Judges to the
plan of the select committee of 1867 were mainly these:
a dislike to be associated with political strifes, and a
belief that the proposed addition to their labours would
interfere with the regular business of their Courts.

The House of Commons, however, insisted upon
transferring the new jurisdiction to the Common Law
Judges. Mr. Lowe said (July 6):—

The tribunal to be created should not only be upright, but
unsuspected and undoubted, and therefore he made an appeal
to the Government to give effect to what appeared to be the
almost unanimous opinion of the House and of the Select
Committee. There was every reason why they should re-
consider the matter, and, considering its vast constitutional
importance, they should not allow themselves to be influenced
by such notions as the dangers to be encountered in another
place. It was for this House to do its duty, and for the House
of Peers to do theirs. If the Judges were great in their
Courts, they were great in their Court; and when they gave
their decision, it was the bounden duty of the Judges to carry
out the decision. He maintained that the House was bound,
in consideration of the public interests, not to surrender its
deliberate opinion at the request of any men, though they
should be the fifteen Judges of England.

* *Hansard*, vol. 190, col. 600.

Upon a division, an amendment to the Bill in this sense was carried by a majority of 65.   Mr. Disraeli correctly observed that this decision brought the question back very nearly to the position in which it stood in the previous year.   A few days later (July 9), he offered another plan, and proposed that the number of Judges should be increased, and that they should, at the beginning of every Michaelmas Term, select from their own body judges to try election petitions, sitting without a jury.

As a matter of some constitutional importance, it should be observed that an uncontrolled power of deciding upon the validity of returns is thus given to judges appointed by the Crown, and consequently, by a circuitous process, the power of the Executive over the Legislature is seriously increased.   The innovation is, however, temporary and experimental, for a section of the Act ultimately passed provides that it shall remain in force only until the expiration of three years and the ensuing Session.

The Act provides that election petitions shall be tried in England and Ireland by puisne judges of Westminster and Dublin respectively.   The Common Law Courts are to select such judges according to a rota.   The trial is to take place in the county or borough to which the petition relates.   The judge is to sit alone in open court, without a jury, and is to determine who has been duly elected or whether the election is void, and to certify the Speaker accordingly. ' Such determination shall be final to all intents and purposes.'*

Circumstances which will be narrated hereafter induced the Government to bring in a Bill for accelerating the Electoral Registration of 1868, and to make provision for a general election and autumnal Session in this

* 31 & 32 Vic. c. 125.

year. The preparation of this measure was facilitated by several preliminary discussions, in which the methods of expediting the election were investigated with great research and knowledge of election law by Mr. Forster, Mr. Bouverie, Sir Robert Collier, and the Home Secretary, Mr. Hardy. These members also served on the Select Committee to which the Bill was referred (June 23), and contributed materially to improve its details.

The 'Parliamentary Electors' Registration Act, 1868,' contains two sets of provisions—the first temporary, the second permanent. In order that the Registration of 1868 might be finished at an earlier period than usual, the Act provides for an extraordinary increase of the number of barristers, and abridges the time within which their labours are to be completed. The legal interval between the proclamation of dissolution and the meeting of the new Parliament is also shortened. The permanent provisions of the Act relate to technical details of Election law.

Early in November 1867 Mr. Gladstone brought in a Bill to abolish the compulsory payment of church rates. These levies for the reparation of churches have been for many centuries imposed upon parishioners in respect of lands and houses occupied by them in their respective parishes. The charge was seldom heavy; but it has been for years a frequent occasion of most mischievous disputes, tending to impair the just influence of the Clergy and create an inveterate hostility to the Church itself. Many dissenters objected to the rates on conscientious grounds, and this ecclesiastical revenue, comparatively small in amount, has been raised at a lamentable cost of local animosities. The principle of Mr. Gladstone's Bill, which was read a second time (February 19, 1868), was simply to retain the existing machinery for assessing and collecting the rates by the agency of vestries and parochial officers, but to render the payment voluntary. The Government reluctantly abstained from resistance to Mr. Gladstone's measure. Mr. Gathorne Hardy said, ' I still adhere to my opinion that church rates are not a grievance to the country, and that they might still be levied by resolution of the vestry without being such a grievance.' * Other members of the Ministry, during various stages of the Bill, criticised it in a hostile spirit, but the Cabinet prudently refrained from an active opposition which would have merely added to the number of ministerial defeats. Mr. Gladstone's measure had, therefore, a comparatively tranquil passage through the House of Commons. When it reached the Lords it was referred to a Select Committee, which modified the details but retained the principle of the measure—that of rendering the payment voluntary. The Act ultimately passed † provides that no suit or proceeding shall henceforth be taken in any Court to enforce such payment. Rates may, however, be made, assessed, received, and applied by vestries as heretofore : but with respect to the expenditure of the money, defaulters who do not pay the sums for which they are assessed are not to have any voice or control.

The Session of 1867-8 deserves to be memorable in the annals of humanity for the abolition of corporal punishment in the army in the time of peace. Upon the consideration of the Mutiny Act, which regulates the government of the army, Mr. Otway, the Liberal member for Chatham, moved (March 26, 1867) an amendment of the clause which authorises corporal punishment. The amendment was carried, upon a division, by a majority of 25, and is now incorporated in the Act as follows :—

* *Hansard*, vol. 190, col. 978.
† 31 & 32 Vic. c. 109.

No court martial shall for any offence whatever, committed under this Act during the time of peace, within the Queen's dominions, have power to sentence any soldier to corporal punishment; provided that any court martial may sentence any soldier to corporal punishment while on active service in the field, or on board any ship not in commission, for mutiny, insubordination, desertion, drunkenness on duty or on the line of march, disgraceful conduct, or any breach of the Articles of War; and no sentence of corporal punishment shall exceed fifty lashes.

There is a section to the same effect in the Marine Mutiny Act.* Consequently, except in time of war, soldiers who wear epaulets are no longer authorised to inflict bodily torture on soldiers who do not wear epaulets. Flogging is retained as a legal punishment of garotters and the sons of gentlemen at public schools.

The honour of effecting another important amendment in the Mutiny Acts is also due to Mr. Otway. The preamble of these Acts has heretofore stated that a standing army was necessary for the purpose of maintaining 'the balance of power in Europe.' Mr. Otway said (March 26) that these words were untrue, and moved that they should be omitted. Sir John Pakington assented. On a subsequent day (March 30) Lord Elcho moved † that they should be reinserted, but the motion was negatived, Sir John Pakington observing that it was unimportant because the words 'meant so very little.' There was a time, and that recent, when they meant a great deal. That Moloch, as Mr. Thorold Rogers ‡ aptly terms 'the balance of power,' has now ceased to be an object of national worship, but not until it had cost us an almost immeasurable national debt, and the sacrifice of uncounted myriads of human lives. The pernicious superstition was first recognised by law in 1727: up to that

---

* 31 Vic. c. 14, s. 22; 31 Vic. c. 15, s. 27.

† *Hansard*, vol. 191, col. 557.

‡ Preface to 'Speeches by John Bright, M.P.'

time the Mutiny Act gave a reasonable ground for maintaining a standing army—' the safety of the Kingdom.' It was not until the reign of George II. that Parliament, by inserting the phrase 'balance of power' in the annual Mutiny Act, formally recognised the idea of emulating the military establishments of Continental Powers. The distinct abandonment of that principle constitutes an epoch in the foreign policy of this country.

But the subject of paramount interest in the debates of 1868 has yet to be considered. Discussions respecting the Irish Church occupied preeminently the attention of Parliament, occasioned a serious conflict between the two Houses, caused a succession of defeats of the Government, compelled the Ministers to offer the resignation of their seats, and to promise, as an alternative, an appeal to the country.

To form a correct and just estimate of the conduct of political leaders with reference to this discussion, we must go back a little in parliamentary history, and refer to some anterior proceedings affecting the relations between the State and the Church in Ireland. We may conveniently take our starting-point at the year 1835, when the House of Commons, mainly at the instance of Lord John Russell, passed a Resolution, declaring,

That this House will resolve itself into a Committee of the whole House, in order to consider the present state of the Church Establishment of Ireland with the view of appropriating any surplus revenues to the general purposes of education without distinction of religion.

The Resolution has never been carried into effect. The Act of 1838 for the Commutation of Tithes in Ireland * was passed 'to abolish compositions for tithes

* 1 & 2 Vic. c. 100.

in Ireland, and in lieu thereof to substitute rent-charges payable by persons having a perpetual estate or interest in the lands subject thereto, a reasonable allowance being made for the greater security of collection arising out of such transfer from the occupiers to the owners of lands.'

A somewhat earlier statute of 1833—the Irish Church Temporalities Act[*]—made a considerable reduction of the Episcopal Establishment.   The number of bishops was altered from twenty-two to twelve.   Ten bishoprics were abolished as separate sees and united with other dioceses which were retained.   An Ecclesiastical Commission was also instituted for the purpose of applying the revenues of the suppressed bishoprics and the crown revenue from 'first-fruits' to various ecclesiastical purposes, including the erection of churches and the augmentation of small livings.   Neither of these Acts appropriated any revenues to general education.

In more recent times Mr. Dillwyn, Member for Swansea, has on several occasions proposed to the House of Commons resolutions with reference to this subject.   On the 28th of March, 1865, he moved—

That in the opinion of this House, the present position of the Irish Church Establishment is unsatisfactory and calls for the early attention of Her Majesty's Government.[†]

Mr. Dillwyn adduced statistics showing that the number of members of the Irish Church had largely decreased between the years 1834 and 1861, and accounted for a slight increase in the proportion of Churchmen to Roman Catholics, by showing that the extensive emigrations of modern times had taken place among Roman Catholics principally.   He referred to instances of gross nepotism among Irish Ecclesiastical dignitaries, and concluded that

Whether they looked at the Irish Establishment as a

* 3 & 4 Will. 4 c. 37.   † *Hansard*, vol. 178, col. 384.

missionary institution, or whether they looked at it as a national institution, it must be admitted to have failed in both respects.

The most remarkable feature of the debate was the divergence of opinions expressed by different members of the Cabinet then in power—that of Lord Palmerston. Sir George Grey opposed the motion in the name of the Government. He admitted that the creation of an Established Church for the benefit of only a small minority was 'theoretically indefensible.'

I have often said that I think the establishment of an endowed Church in any country where that endowed Church is the Church of a comparatively small minority, no provision being made by law for religious worship in accordance with the views of the majority, is a course which viewed as a theoretical and abstract question cannot possibly be defended. If we were now for the first time considering what should be done, I should think it unwise to take such a course as that which was taken in Ireland.

But he added—

We have the Irish Protestant Church established as an existing institution in Ireland. It is not of recent creation; it rests upon the prescription of centuries, and, to use the expression of a distinguished Roman Catholic layman, is rooted in our institutions. The firm belief of the Government is that it could not be subverted without revolution, with all the horrors which attend revolution.[*]

That is, the only excuses for the existence of the Establishment were the fact of its existence and the fear of a revolution. The latter argument, at all events, is shown by later experience to be unfounded. Mr. Gladstone, then Chancellor of the Exchequer, spoke in very different tones:—

I am bound to say that in the times in which we live, it is not too hastily to be assumed that the exclusive and peculiar position of the Irish Established Church is to be regarded as necessarily useful to the progress of Protestantism. No

* *Hansard*, vol. 178, col. 400.

doubt it relieves members of the Protestant Church in a great
degree from the duty and business of making provision for
their own spiritual requirements; but it is a great mistake to
suppose that the exclusive establishment of one religion is in
all circumstances favourable to the progress of that religion . .
. . It has been said that the exclusive establishment of the
Protestant Church in Ireland is necessary for the maintenance
of loyalty and order in that country. We have not heard that
argument to-night, and I believe we shall not hear it. There
can be no more fatal error on the part of those who are
charged with the Government of a country than to do acts or
make provisions which imply that loyalty to the laws, the
throne, and to the institutions of the country, is the particular
and exclusive property of a small minority of the people.*

Mr. Gladstone then proceeded to deal with an assertion that there was no surplus revenue of the Establishment, and showed that with reference to the number of
members the endowment was about 1*l.* per head,† where-
as in England the quota was about 7*s.* or 8*s.* per head.
The following passage from this speech is very remarkable, for it demonstrates the identity of Mr. Gladstone's
views in 1'65 and at the present time with regard to
redistribution of ecclesiastical revenues.

You have towns in Ireland presenting, perhaps, not in the
same degree, but still I apprehend to a certain degree, the same
deficiencies in the means of spiritual instruction as compared
with the Church population as are to be found in this country,
and, on the other hand, you have large portions of the country
in which there are equally large and liberal endowments while
the Church population can hardly be said to exist at all.   It is

---

* *Hansard*, vol. 178, col. 428.

† The Report of the Established Church (Ireland) Commission in 1868
states, p. vi., that the number of persons returned by the census of 1861 as
belonging to the communion of that Church was 693,357, and that its net
annual revenues amount to £581,000, of which 'upwards of £204,000 a
year consists of income derived from lands' (p. xiii).   But the calculation
of revenue is founded partly on returns made by dignitaries and incumbents,
who are not likely to have exaggerated their own incomes, and partly on
estimates for lands in the hands of the incumbents 'taken from the valuation made for their assessment to poor rates' (p. xxxviii).   This valuation
'is somewhat, but not disproportionately, below the full improved value '
(p. xiv).

sometimes the practice to call this an abuse, and to say that there would be a remedy if you would adopt the principle of re-distribution—if you would take the tithes and estates of the Church in Ireland, throw them into hotch-poch, and then dis-tribute them substantially according to the proportions in which the Church population is distributed over the face of the country. I must confess, it appears to me that there are the greatest difficulties, not only in practice but in principle, to the application of any such remedy. I can hardly imagine that the population of Ireland—especially of the provinces of Munster and Connaught, where the Church population is about 5 per cent. of the whole—would be content to see the tithes and endowments of those provinces abstracted in order that they might be carried into Ulster where the Church has one-fifth of the population, or into Leinster where it has one-eighth of the population. If that can be done, at least I know of no Government that has ever been bold enough to propose such an act. Some steps, some slight steps, have been taken in that direction ; but in the main the tithes still remain locally applied ; and I do not hesitate to say that I believe it would be not only inexpedient but unjust, especially in the circum-stances of Ireland, to interfere with the general application of the principle of local endowments. But if the principle of local distribution and enjoyment of endowments and tithes is sound, then *the Church in its present exclusive possession of endowments is doomed, I fear, to the perpetual exhibition of a painful anomaly*. For what can be a greater anomaly than that of a clergy appointed to do the work of shepherds of souls, while in many parishes of Connaught and Munster their flocks are to be reckoned, not by tens, but by units ; thus pre-senting a most painful contrast—painful I am convinced to those clergy themselves—the contrast between the actual state of things and a National Church endowed for the spiritual wants of the country . . . All this appears to me to indicate in the present position of the Church of Ireland inherent elements which show that her difficulties cannot be surmounted by the wisdom of her rulers, or by the piety and devotion of her clergy, and that *they are essential elements of a false position*.

When Mr. Gladstone reiterated the same opinions in 1868, upon a distinct challenge from a Conservative Government, he was said to have advanced a novel doc-trine merely for factious purposes, and for his own poli-tical interests. The speech of 1865 has been cited copiously, not merely for its intrinsic value, but also because it shows that the condemnation of the Irish Ecclesiastical Establishment in 1868 was not a mere after-thought, suggested by the hope of weakening or overthrowing the Ministry.

The speech of 1865 openly and manifestly avowed a policy of Disestablishment. It was so understood by the hearers in the House of Commons. Mr. Whiteside, who followed in the debate, said :—

We now gather from the Chancellor of the Exchequer that the whole question is to be re-opened, and that, not for the purpose of carrying out any definite plan, but of encouraging all that mischief which the right hon. gentleman the Secretary for the Home Department (Sir George Grey) so graphically described. The speech of the Chancellor of the Exchequer is, I may add, calculated to separate him from the policy of the noble Viscount at the head of the Government.*

The next important Parliamentary proceeding, with reference to the Irish Church, was the issue of a Royal Commission to inquire into the Ecclesiastical Revenue. In June 1867, Lord Russell moved in the House of Lords—

That an humble Address be presented to Her Majesty, praying that Her Majesty will be pleased to give directions that by the operation of a commission, or otherwise, full and accurate information be procured as to the amount and nature of the property and revenues of the Established Church in Ireland, and as to the means of rendering that property more productive.

Some time after notice of this motion was given, Lord Russell proposed to add the words—

And to their more equitable application for the benefit of the Irish people.

The House of Lords, after considerable discussion, passed the resolution in its original form without the addendum, and the Government appointed a Commission of Inquiry accordingly.

At the commencement of the Session, in November

* *Hansard,* vol. 178, col. 448.

1867, it became generally understood that the condition of the Irish Church would occupy a large share of the attention of Parliament.   In the debate on the Address in reply to the Royal Speech, Mr. Gladstone referred to the issue of the Commission, and to a rumour that the Commissioners were not merely to collect facts, but also to propose plans for dealing with the Established Church in Ireland.

I own it appears to me that it would be an error to refer to the Commission the preparation of plans for dealing with a national question of that order.   And in the circumstances with which that question is surrounded, I do not think the House would consent to consider as exempted from its own jurisdiction the question of the Church of Ireland during that period that such a Commission might fairly claim to spend in the deep deliberations that preparation of these plans would involve.*

Shortly after the Christmas recess, the Government announced that they were prepared with an Irish policy. During a debate (Feb. 24, 1868) on the Habeas Corpus suspension (Ireland) Act, in answer to Lord Russell, who insisted that it was imperative to satisfy Ireland with regard to the Church, an institution which, he said, the people regarded with 'a feeling of humiliation and degradation,' and 'as a badge of conquest,' the Duke of Richmond replied on the part of the Ministry, that on the next evening 'their policy was to be promulgated in the House of Commons.'†

The revelation was, however, postponed by Lord Derby's resignation the following day.   In announcing, however, on the 5th of March, the reconstruction of the Cabinet, Lord Malmesbury said :—'Within four or five days from this time an ample declaration of our Irish policy will be made in the House of Commons.' Mr. Disraeli made a similar statement the same evening.

On March 10, 1868, the promised exposition was given by the Earl of Mayo, Chief Secretary for Ireland.

* *Hansard*, vol. 190, p. 171.   † *Ibid.* col. 1008.

The occasion was a motion by Mr. Maguire for a Committee of the whole House to consider 'the condition and circumstances of Ireland.'

The Earl of Mayo, in a very elaborate speech, examined the social and material condition of the people. The proposals which he made on behalf of the Government were mainly these:—The issue of a Royal Commission to inquire into the laws and customs affecting the tenure of land, and the institution of a Roman Catholic University, to be endowed by the State. He said:—

We therefore propose to advise Her Majesty to grant a Charter to a Roman Catholic University, to be constructed in the following manner. The institution which it is proposed to create will not resemble the existing Roman Catholic University in Dublin. It is proposed that, in the first instance, a Charter should be granted in the same way that the Charter was granted to the Queen's University; that the governing body under the original constitution should consist of a Chancellor, Vice-Chancellor, four Prelates, the President of Maynooth, six Laymen, the heads of colleges to be at first affiliated and five members to be elected so as to represent the five educational faculties—all being Roman Catholics. . . . With regard to endowment, it will be essential, of course—if Parliament agree to the proposal—in the first instance to provide for the necessary expenses of the University—that is to say, the expenses of the officers of the University, of the University Professors, and also to make some provision for a building. It is possible that if Parliament approves of the scheme, it may not be indisposed to endow certain University scholarships. But with regard to the endowment of colleges, it is impossible to make any proposal at present; and to that extent the question will be left open to future consideration.*

Lord Mayo then approached the question of the State Church, which, he said, 'after a slumber of nearly thirty years, had again become a subject of first-rate political importance.' The following extract will sufficiently indicate the opinions on the subject which the Government then entertained:—

* *Hansard*, vol. 190, col. 1385.

For my own part, I believe that if the Irish Church is over-thrown, that overthrow can only be effected after a long and painful struggle—a struggle which must inevitably tend to the increase and aggravation of those discords and religious hatreds which have produced such evils in the community. The voluntary system is proposed in the interests of peace. There are parts of the country where the voluntary system is established in connection with the Established Church, and I am not aware that those regions are especially characterised by concord among the people. The question must be dealt with in a very different spirit from that which the advocates of entire abolition profess. *The Presbyterians now receive a grant from this House which is miserable in amount and wholly inadequate to their requirements.* The Protestants of Ireland are content with the system which prevails; but are not averse to *improvements and to such alterations of ecclesiastical arrangements* as would make their Church better fitted to meet the wants of modern times. But we must not pre-scribe hastily. Of all the schemes which have been proposed, I object preeminently to that known as the process of levelling down. It is said if you cannot elevate and raise institutions so as to make them equal, the only thing is to abolish them alto-gether. I object to that policy. I think that proposals for universal levelling down are the worst of all propositions. . . . *If it is desired to make our Churches more equal in position than they are, the result should be secured by elevation and restoration, not by confiscation and degradation.*

There is a remarkable variation in the different re-ports of this passage. *Hansard's Debates* copy this particular speech from an authorised edition of it. The newspapers give a materially different version. In the *Daily Telegraph* it appears as follows:—

There is no disinclination on their part to put other Churches in a favourable position; but equality must be realised by elevation and restoration, not by confiscation and degradation.*

In the *Times* the passage stands thus:—

There would not, I believe, be any objection to make all Churches equal; but the result must be secured by elevation and not by confiscation.†

We may take it, therefore, as well ascertained, that

* *Daily Telegraph*, March 11, 1868, p. 5.
† *Times*, March 11, 1868.

Lord Mayo announced to the House of Commons, on
March 10, that there was no 'objection,' or no 'disinclination,' on the part of the Conservative Government,
to make all Churches in Ireland 'equal,' or to put other
Churches besides the Establishment 'in a favourable
position.' In the revised report, and upon subsequent
reflection, the announcement has been softened down
into the mere supposition which compromises nobody—
'if it is desired to make our Churches more equal.'

The debate upon the state of Ireland lasted three
nights. Mr. Gladstone condemned the Government plan
of 'levelling up,' and declared that the Church could
not be satisfactorily reformed without a dissolution of
its connection with the State.

I am not going to discuss the relative merits of 'levelling
up' and 'levelling down.' I am not for levelling up nor for
levelling down. But 'religious equality,' understood in the
sense of grants from the Exchequer in order to bring the
general population of Ireland up to the level of the Establishment; or understood in the sense of plans for dividing and
distributing the income of the Establishment in salaries and
stipends to the clergy of the several communions—these
are measures which, whether beneficial or not, might at other
times have been possible, but in my opinion they have now
passed all bounds of possibility. And it is vain and idle for us,
as practical men charged with practical duties, to take them, or
keep them in our view. My opinion is then, that 'religious
equality' is a phrase which requires further development.
And I will develop it further by saying that, in this religious
equality in Ireland, I for my part, include in its fullest extent of
the word—a very grave word I do not deny, and I think we
cannot be too careful to estimate its gravity before we come to
a final conclusion, the very grave word DISESTABLISHMENT.
If we are to do any good at all by meddling with the Church
in Ireland, *it must in my judgment be by putting an end to
its existence as a State Church.*[*]

Mr. Disraeli commenced his reply by complaining
that his Government should be called upon to produce

---

[*] *Hansard*, vol. 190, col. 1766 (March 10, 1868).

measures equal to the exigency of Irish affairs. He said :—

As the right hon. gentleman proceeded it appeared that the crisis of Ireland at which it has just arrived was the culminating point of a controversy which had lasted for 700 years. I could not but feel that I was indeed the most unfortunate of Ministers since, at the moment when I arrived, by Her Majesty's favour, at the position I now fill, a controversy which had lasted 700 years had reached its culminating point, and I was immediately called upon with my colleagues to produce measures equal to such a supernatural exigency.

The exigency was not supernatural—it was invited by himself. The Ministry had spontaneously undertaken to apply a remedy for the ills of Ireland. Lord Mayo's statement, announced beforehand with much pomp and ceremony, by several Ministers, on several occasions, in both Houses, was the Government programme, and we may suppose that it was submitted to Parliament in order that Parliament might pronounce an opinion upon it. Lord Mayo, on the part of the Cabinet, proposed various measures—a Commission of Inquiry respecting tenant-right—an endowed Catholic University—and, with reference to ecclesiastical affairs, a process vaguely described by the terms ' levelling up ' and ' religious equality.' The Irish Church, he had said, ' had become a subject of first-rate importance;' the grant to the Presbyterians was ' miserable ' and ' inadequate;' there was ' no disinclination ' on the part of the Government ' to put other Churches in a favourable position.' Surely here was a distinct challenge of the opinion of Parliament. The expedients proposed by Lord Mayo, on the part of the Government, might be wise or unwise, adequate or inadequate ; but there could be no question about this—that the Cabinet of its own accord submitted them to the judgment of the House of Commons. What were those members to do, who, like Mr. Gladstone, believed the expedients to be

either futile or impolitic? Were they to feign acquies-
cence, or were they to sit silent? Mr. Disraeli invoked
criticism, but when it was found to be adverse, complained of it as an impertinence.

With respect to the maintenance of the Irish Establishment, he offered the following argument:—

The Established Church in Ireland is, I frankly admit at
once, not in the condition in which I should like to see a
national Church. The condition in which I should wish to
see a national Church would be this—that the whole population of the country should be in communion with it. That
would be a perfect and completely national Church. But in
a land where complete toleration fortunately flourishes that is
not an ideal of a Church which will probably be ever realised.
Well then, we must advance to the position of an Established
Church which is not supported by the whole population of the
country, but by only a part of it. That in my view will still
be a great advantage. I think that there is nothing which we
should be more deeply impressed with, than the importance of
connecting the principle of religion with Government. If
you do not connect the principle of religion with Government,
you must reduce the power and character of Government. If
you once divorce political authority from the principle of
religion, I do not see what you can come to but a mere affair of
police. If you admit that it is wise to connect the principle of
religion with Government, the mind is naturally brought to
endowment. It is the practical mode of bringing the system
into operation.*

This plea for a state religion has been frequently
expressed in various forms, and has great influence
with many persons of strong and earnest religious convictions. But it may be well considered whether the
argument does not involve a confusion of thought and
language. In what sense can we speak of 'connecting
the principle of religion with Government'? Religion
is personal. The individual persons who compose a
government may be religious; but how can the government or system under which they act be said to be

* *Hansard*, vol. 190, col. 1781 (March 16, 1868).

connected with religion? If our Christian profession be sincere we must believe it to be for the advantage of the country that statesmen should be actuated by religious principles; but that is an entirely different proposition from the one under consideration. It is supposed that in some unexplained way the Constitution itself—that is, the contrivance or machine by which the country is governed—shall be religious, or connected with the 'principle of religion.' Mr. Disraeli deprecates 'divorce of political authority from the principle of religion.' He might as well complain of the divorce of the principle of religion from the Binomial theorem. It is not worth while to inquire whether the union be desirable, for it is simply impossible. Persons possessing 'political authority' may also be influenced by a 'principle of religion.' It were much to be desired that statesmen avowed that principle more frequently and more distinctly. But, even if they did so universally, that circumstance would not serve to combine political authority with religion. The two phrases represent two distinct ideas which have no relation to each other. People who are content with inexact language are accustomed to personify the State, and to say that the State ought to be religious, when they really mean that statesmen ought to be religious. We may have a union of State and Church in this sense—that the State may invest the Church with peculiar privileges. We may also have a system of government which promotes religion; but that does not make the system itself religious. The union of religion with the State is as much beyond human power as the arithmetical addition of quantities which are not of the same kind. To talk of an institution or the machinery of government being religious is to talk mere nonsense. The attempt to identify a collection or code of rules—for that is what is meant by the State—with spiritual

belief is as absurd as the attempt to add yards to
ounces, or a number of acres to a number of shillings.

Mr. Disraeli, in the course of his speech, repudiated
the idea that the Government proposed to endow a
Catholic University.

The first thing to which the right hon. gentleman directed
our attention was, the measure—but I should not call it a
measure, for it may not be necessary to legislate upon it—the
intention which we have intimated to Parliament of recommending Her Majesty to grant a Charter to a Roman Catholic
University in Ireland. The right hon. gentleman raised an
argument against that proposition, which, no doubt, may
have had some effect on the House, upon the assumption that
we had announced our intention to ask the House to endow
that University. I certainly never heard of that intended endowment before . . . Certainly my noble friend the Chief
Secretary for Ireland made no such proposition, nor was there
any necessity of making any communication to Parliament
except the honourable engagement which the Government was
under of not moving in the matter without communicating with
Parliament. It is perfectly true that when the right hon.
gentleman opposite (Mr. Monsell) asked my noble friend
about endowment, my noble friend said he would ask the
House to pay the university expenses such as are paid for the
London University. It is perfectly legitimate for the House
to decide whether they will pay them or not. They are of no
great amount; the charge for the London University being
about 8,000l. a year.*

The hearers of this remark must have distrusted
their own ears. Only six days before Lord Mayo had
declared that it was an 'essential' part of the Government scheme that Parliament should pay the 'officers'
and 'professors' of the University, and make provision
for a building. He suggested that Parliament should
'endow certain university scholarships' and the 'endowment of colleges' was to be left 'open for future
consideration.' But in that period of six days a chorus
of disapprobation had shouted down this plan of adding
to Catholic endowments. So Mr. Disraeli says that

* *Hansard*, vol. 190, col. 1774.

endowment even of a University was never intended, only some expenses were to be paid as in the case of London University.   But what analogy was there between that case and the proposed endowment of professors and scholars of the Irish University and the prospective en-dowment of colleges?   The Prime Minister has a rare talent for courageous explanations.

On the 30th of March 1868, the principal work of the Session began.   On that day Mr. Gladstone moved that the House resolve itself into a Committee to consider the Acts relating to the Established Church in Ireland. Whatever might be thought of the principles which he avowed on this occasion, no one, friend or foe, could deny that they were distinctly expressed.

If it is asked what it is, that in endeavouring to put an end to the present Establishment, I renounce for the future, I would again say that what I renounce for the future, is the attempt to maintain in association with the State, under the authority of the State, or supported by the income of the State, or by public or national property in any form, a salaried or stipen-diary clergy.*

With regard to the details of the arrangement, Mr. Gladstone proceeded—

We should begin by a recognition of every vested interest; and I am bound to say, in speaking of vested interests, that it appears to me, at least, a matter for argument and considera-tion, whether we can strictly and absolutely limit the phrase to those who are in possession of benefices, or whether some re-gard ought not possibly to be had—though it would be prema-ture to give an opinion upon the point—to the case of those who have devoted themselves to an indelible profession that separates them from the great bulk of profitable secular employ-ments, in expectation of the benefices which we have kept in existence by law under our authority, even though they may not actually have entered upon them. . . . I apprehend that if the Irish Church were disestablished, none would propose to deprive those who have worshipped in its sacred fabrics of the future possession and use of those fabrics, provided they are

* *Hansard*, vol. 191, col. 472.

willing to maintain them, and to apply them to religious purposes. On that subject I feel the utmost confidence, and I feel
almost an equal confidence that the very same lenient judgment
which goes to the Church, would go likewise to that which is
inseparably connected with the Church—I mean the residences
of the clergy. In addition to this we are told, and fairly told,
that the great bulk of the proprietors of the soil of Ireland are
members of the Established Church of Ireland. I apprehend
I am not wrong in assuming, first, that the proprietors of advowsons would have the strictest and most absolute claim to full
compensation for the value of their property; and, secondly,
that these proprietors of advowsons who, I am aware, are not
nearly as numerous, relatively to the whole number of benefices,
as they are in England—the benefices in private gift in Ireland
only amounting roughly to one-sixth of the whole—are in the
vast majority of cases members of the Established Church, and
to them would be paid the money which the State would find to
be the value of these advowsons. There is another class, I am
afraid not a very extensive one, the category of recent endowments by persons, some of them even now living, some of them
but lately gone from among us, who have out of their own
means and liberality built churches and devoted funds for the
purposes of the Established Church in Ireland. Such endowments, I apprehend, would under all circumstances be respected.
Now, putting together these various items—and this is but an
imperfect sketch—it has no pretence whatever to be a definite
statement—I believe that the effect of the much dreaded disestablishment of the Church, conducted as I have endeavoured
to describe it, would be this; that if the full money value of
the entire possessions of the Irish Church fairly sold in open
market were estimated, certainly not less than three-fifths,
possibly two-thirds, would remain in the hands of members of
the Anglican communion.*

Lord Stanley followed in the debate, and replied to
this proposal by a dilatory plea. He moved—

To leave out from the word ' house ' to the end of the question, in order to add the words ' while admitting that considerable modifications in the temporalities of the United Church in
Ireland, may, after the pending inquiry, appear to be expedient,
is of opinion that any proposition tending to the disestablishment or disendowment of the Church, ought to be reserved
for the decision of a new Parliament.'†

The language of this carefully considered amendment shows that the Government regarded disestablishment, cr disendowment, not as a measure which could never be entertained, but as one which ought to be reserved for the consideration of a new Parliament. Lord Stanley argued that the discussion raised by Mr. Gladstone was premature, as he did not propose to legislate in that Session with respect to the Irish Church. Mr. Gladstone explained that he should recommend immediate legislation 'to prevent the growth of new interests.'[*] Lord Stanley made the important admission, that the next Parliament would have to consider the subject, and that the ecclesiastical arrangements of Ireland were unsatisfactory.

It appears to me that the real question which the next Parliament will have to consider, will not be whether anything ought to be done as regards the Irish Church, but what the particular thing to be done shall be. Probably there is not one educated person in a hundred who will stand up and pretend that the Irish ecclesiastical arrangements are of altogether a satisfactory kind. I am certainly not that one.[†]

Lord Cranborne, who had seceded in the former year from the Conservative Ministry, on account of his objections to their Reform Bill, severely criticised the amendment now proposed. He said :—

I admit that the right hon. gentleman opposite has spoken to-night with perfect candour and openness in expressing his opinions, and I would reciprocate that candour by telling him that I shall meet his motion with a straightforward and direct negative. But I cannot support an amendment of which the object, as it appears to me, is merely to gain time—merely to retain the cards in the hands of the Executive that they may shuffle them as they like—merely to repeat on the Irish Church the process which they last year applied to Reform—merely to enable them to utilise great questions of public policy and matters which excite the feelings of people out of doors to the utmost, for the purposes of party and the maintenance of a

* *Hansard,* vol. 101, col. 500 (March 30, 1868). ·   † *Ibid.* col. 423.

Government in place. I think that such tactics are not honourable to the House of Commons, nor honourable to the Government which resorts to them.*

The Solicitor-General (Sir William Brett) argued that the Coronation Oath precluded the Queen from assenting to disestablishment.

The Coronation Oath, and the law with respect to it, have been very frequently mis-stated. The Statute 1 William and Mary, sess. i. cap. 6, entitled ' An Act for Establishing the Coronation Oath,' gives a form which contains the following passage—the only passage relating to the Church and religion :—

Archbishop or Bishop.—Will you to the utmost of your power maintain the Laws of God, the true profession of the Gospel, and the Protestant Reformed Religion established by law, and will you preserve unto the Bishops and Clergy of this realm, and to the Churches committed to their charge, all such rights and privileges as by law do or shall appertain unto them or any of them ?

King and Queen.—All this I promise to do.

This form was prescribed before the Union of England and Scotland. The Act of Union of the two countries (5 Anne c. 8) directs (article 25) that the sovereign shall ' take and subscribe an oath to maintain and preserve inviolably the said settlement of the Church of England and the doctrine, worship, discipline, and government thereof, as by law established, within the kingdoms of England and Ireland, the dominion of Wales, and town of Berwick-on-Tweed, and the territories thereunto belonging.'

Since this enactment was made, the form has been modified by combining that prescribed by the Act of William and Mary with words intended to give effect to the clause just cited from the Act of Union with Scotland. It appears that at the coronation of Queen

* *Hansard*, vol. 191, col. 540.

Victoria the oath, so far as affects the Church, was as follows:—

Archbishop.—Will you to the utmost of your power maintain the Laws of GOD, the true profession of the Gospel, and the Protestant Reformed Religion established by law? And will you maintain and preserve inviolably the settlement of the United Church of England and Ireland, and the doctrine, worship, discipline, and government thereof, as by law established within England and Ireland and the territories thereunto belonging? And will you preserve unto the Bishops and Clergy of England and Ireland, and to the Churches there committed to their charge, all such rights and privileges as by law do or shall appertain to them, or any of them?

Queen.—All this I promise to do.*

The sovereign swears to maintain the settlement of the united Church, but with that important qualification, overlooked by the Solicitor-General, which is contained in the words ' as by law established.' That the word ' established' is not merely retrospective but prospective also, appears plainly by the context, for immediately afterwards the Queen promises to preserve to the bishops and clergy all such rights and privileges ' as by law do *or shall* appertain to them.' It would be a most violent construction to regard one part of the oath as contemplating possible alterations of the law, and another part as binding the sovereign to an absolute and unconditional pledge to resist such alterations. Those who ask us to adopt that interpretation, ask us to believe that the Parliament which imposed the oath, voluntarily put limits on its own power, and wished to preclude sovereigns from assenting, even with the advice and consent of both Houses, to any further legislation affecting the united Church.

Before we pass from this subject, it may be added

---

* Return to an address for copies of the Coronation Oaths—Number 191 of Sess. 1868. There is a statement in this return which is not quite accurate, for it represents the existing oath as founded upon the Act of Union solely, and omits all reference to the earlier Statute of William and Mary.

that other parts of the oath recognise the power of Parliament. The sovereign promises to govern 'according to the Statutes in Parliament agreed on.' Will anyone maintain that the words 'agreed on' are used in the past tense only? If not, why should the words 'as by law established,' which relate to the Church, be supposed to be used only in the past tense?

Mr. Gathorne Hardy, the Home Secretary, resisted Mr. Gladstone's motion for a committee, with that earnest conviction which always commands respect, even where it does not procure assent. Mr. Hardy principally relied on the argument that disestablishment in Ireland would lead to a similar result in England. He said:—

I do not know why in one country it is to be considered advantageous to be without endowments, and in another country to possess them. And if religion in this country can exist, although cumbered, as the right hon. gentleman would have us think, with large endowments, why do you object to our Protestant friends in Ireland retaining that to which they believe they have a right?

In another part of his speech he reverted to the same topic as follows:—

The main arguments which have been used by the right hon. gentleman and hon. member who sit below the gangway, and with perfect consistency by the latter, in support of these Resolutions, are in favour of religious equality. Now, religious equality I do not understand, either in principle or practice, to apply to only one part of the empire. I say, therefore, it is not unreasonable in us to object, if you are going to touch part of our Church, that on that principle you are, in fact, touching the whole, and upsetting the grounds upon which alone the Establishments of the country—Church and State—can be defended. If it is necessary for religious equality that there shall be no endowments or privileges accorded to the ministers of the Established Church, then I understand the argument. It is the voluntary system pure and simple, and one fairly to be debated and argued; but you cannot justly put forward religious equality when you are only going to apply the principle to a small part of the empire.*

* *Hansard*, vol. 101, col. 505.

But the proposal for 'religious equality' came from the Government, not from Mr. Gladstone. It was Lord Mayo who invented the phrase. Mr. Hardy's apprehension that disestablishment in Ireland must necessarily lead to disestablishment in England, is one form of that most foolish of Parliamentary arguments—dread of the 'thin edge of the wedge.' It amounts to this—that we are to abstain from doing what may be expedient and just to-day, because possibly something else which is inexpedient and unjust may be proposed to-morrow. We are to suppose that to-morrow we shall not be able to distinguish the limits of right and wrong, and that in the conduct of our affairs we are certain to be deluded by false analogies.

The circumstances of the Church in England and in Ireland are altogether different. There, it is not merely the Church of the small minority—that is a circumstance of subordinate importance—but it is looked upon by the mass of the people with feelings of bitter hostility, and is the occasion of most hateful religious strifes. The struggles and feuds between Orangemen and Roman Catholics are a disgrace to our profession of Christianity. The Legislature is obliged to pass Acts prohibiting their party processions, and to prevent them from flaunting their flags and emblems of discord in each others' faces. Can any calm spectator suppose that the cause of religion is promoted by such examples? The most sacred names and the most solemn subjects are profaned, and the profession of religion is prostituted as an occasion of party strife. With the utmost stretch of charity it is impossible to believe that the fury of Orangeism proceeds from pure love to the doctrines of Christ unmixed with worldly passion.

Here in England we have no such examples of sectarian bitterness. A very large proportion of the population is in avowed communion with the Church. Again,

the Nonconformists regard her with feelings very different from those with which the Romanist of Ireland
regards the Protestant Establishment.   A Baptist or
Wesleyan in England may take exceptions to various
parts of the Prayer-book; but, as a general rule, he has
no conscientious scruple against entering a parish church
and joining in the worship.   Dissenters, excepting a
few extreme bigots, allow that the Church has her use,
that the institution, with all the shortcomings attributed
to it, does at least some service to the cause of Christianity.   The benefits of the parochial system—the
advantage of possessing an educated clergyman in every
remote village to superintend the education of the poor,
to direct and promote local charities, to set an example
of respect to religion and morals—are admitted by the
immense majority of intelligent Englishmen.   The claim
of our Church to be considered national is that she is
doing national work, and conferring national benefits.
In Ireland the Church has not that title.   There her
work is sectarian, and her beneficial influence is limited
to a small fraction of the population.

The debate on Mr. Gladstone's motion for a committee
extended over four nights, and was distinguished by several noble specimens of Parliamentary oratory. A long-
expected, long-continued discussion generally enables
both Houses to demonstrate their high rank as debating
assemblies.   Many of the speeches uttered on the present occasion are worthy of careful analysis, but the
bare mention of a few conspicuous speakers must suffice.
General Peel spoke out with his wonted candour and
directness.   He apprehended, from Lord Stanley's
speech, that 'the destruction of the Irish Church might
prove hereafter to be one of those Conservative triumphs
which the right honourable gentleman the First Lord
of the Treasury promised the party '—but was reassured

by the earnestness of the Home Secretary. Mr. Roebuck
argued against Mr. Gladstone's motion, and promised to
vote for it.   Mr. Lowe concluded a speech of extraordinary power thus:—

The Irish Church is founded on injustice.   It is founded on
the dominant rights of the few over the many, and it will not
stand.   You call it a missionary Church.   If so its mission is
unfulfilled.   As a missionary Church it has failed utterly.   Like
some exotic brought from a far country with infinite pains and
useless trouble, it is kept alive with difficulty and expense in an
ungrateful climate and ungenial soil.   The curse of barrenness
is upon it; it bears no leaves and yields no fruit.*

Scarcely one eminent name except that of Sir Roundell Palmer is absent from the list of speakers—Mr.
Bright, Mr. Coleridge, and Mr. Stansfeld on the one
side, Lord Mayo and Sir Stafford Northcote on the
other, sustained the debate with ability, earnestness,
and dignity worthy of the occasion.   But the most
tolerant judgment cannot accord the same merits to
Mr. Disraeli's perfervid harangue.   Lord Stanley had
opened the Conservative defence with an excess of
caution; his leader closed it with an excess of reckless-
ness.   His peroration was a collection of invectives and
personal imputations.   These were the concluding sen-
tences:—

I know very well what are the powers that are now and have
been for some time meeting together and joining to produce
the consequences which some anticipate, and which I hope may
be yet defeated.   No man can have watched what has taken
place in this country during the last ten years without being
prepared, if he be of a thoughtful mind, for the crisis of this
country.   I repeat the expression which I used in my letter to
my Lord Dartmouth, that the crisis of England is now fast
arriving.   High Church Ritualists and the followers of the
Pope have been long in secret combination, and are now in open
confederacy [*Laughter*].   Yes, but it is a fact.   It is confessed

* *Hansard*, vol. 101, col. 748.

by those who attempted to prevent this combination, to mitigate the occurrence, to avoid the conjuncture, which we always felt would be most dangerous to the country. They have combined to destroy that great blessing of conciliation which both parties in the State for the last quarter of a century have laboured to effect. I am perfectly aware of the great difficulties we have to encounter. I know the almost superhuman power of this combination. They have their hand almost upon the realm of England. Under the guise of Liberalism, under the pretence of legislating in the spirit of the age, they are, as they think, about to seize upon the supreme authority of the realm. But this I can say that so long as, by the favour of the Queen, I stand here, I will oppose to the utmost of my ability the attempt they are making. I believe the policy of the right hon. gentleman, who is their representative, if successful will change the character of the country. It will deprive the subjects of Her Majesty of some of their most precious privileges, and it will most dangerously touch even the tenure of the Crown.[*]

The sober pages of Hansard inadequately represent the violent character of this declamation. The passionate tones in which it was uttered, and wild gesticulations by which it was accompanied, were better suited to one of those meetings which Orangemen call their lodges than to a deliberative assembly. Mr. Gladstone contented himself with observing that 'there are portions of the discursive speech of the right hon. gentleman of which, with every effort on my part, I fail to discern the relevancy; and there are other portions of which it does not seem to me a severe judgment to say that they appear to be due to the influence of a heated imagination.'

The motion for going into Committee was carried against the Government by a majority of 56—the numbers being ayes, 328; noes, 272. The House immediately afterwards adjourned for the Easter recess.

It will not be necessary to give any lengthened account of the subsequent debates in the House of Commons upon the Irish Church; for the principal

---

[*] *Hansard,* vol. 191, col. 923.

arguments with reference to Mr. Gladstone's measures have been already noticed. On April 27 he moved the first of three Resolutions which he submitted to the consideration of the Committee of the whole House. It was as follows:—

That it is necessary that the Established Church of Ireland should cease to exist as an Establishment, due regard being had to all personal interests and all ecclesiastical rights of property.

After three nights' debate this Resolution was carried by a majority of 65—the numbers being ayes, 330; noes, 265.

Mr. Disraeli upon the announcement of this result said that the vote at which the Committee had arrived 'altered the relations between Her Majesty's Government and the present House of Commons; it is therefore necessary for us to consider our position:' and he proposed an adjournment of the House for a few days.*

On Monday, May 4, Mr. Disraeli stated in the House of Commons that on the previous Friday he had tendered his resignation to the Queen, and that Her Majesty expressed her pleasure not to accept the resignation of her Ministers, and her readiness to dissolve Parliament as soon as the state of public business would permit. He added:—

Under these circumstances I advised Her Majesty that although the present constituency was no doubt as morally competent to decide upon the question of the disestablishment of the Irish Church as the representatives of that constituency in this House, still it was the opinion of Her Majesty's Ministers that every effort should be made that the appeal, if possible, should be directed to the new constituency. And I expressed to her Majesty that if we had the cordial co-operation of Parliament, I was advised by those who are experienced and skilful in such matters that it would be possible to make arrangements by which that dissolution could take place in the autumn of this year.

* *Hansard*, vol. 101, col. 1079.

Four days later (May 15) the Solicitor-General,
speaking on behalf of the Government, stated that the
register of voters could be completed by October 20,
and that the general election might be held immediately
after that date. But towards the end of the month the
Ministerial ardour for an appeal to the new constituencies had considerably abated. On May 26 Mr. Sandford
asked 'whether Her Majesty's Government intended to
bring forward any measure for shortening the period
before the forthcoming general election?' The First
Lord of the Treasury answered that 'the subject to
which the honourable gentleman refers is now under the
consideration of Her Majesty's Government, and has
been for some time, and I am bound to say that the
difficulties connected with it are greater than we anticipated; but I trust these difficulties may be overcome.'
These words seemed to prelude a change of key. Many
Opposition members, apparently, became apprehensive
that the Government, having got their most important
Bills expedited and large supplies voted, had become
disinclined to keep their promise of an autumnal Session. This misgiving was manifested in the discussion
on May 29, when Mr. Forster inquired what steps
would be taken to facilitate a dissolution in the autumn.
Mr. Disraeli said, ' When I made the declaration I was
assured by those in whom I placed confidence that an
autumn Session might be obtained; and, of course, I
never contemplated one earlier than November.' He
again referred to ' difficulties,' and concluded, ' I must
repeat that no time has been lost, and that the Government are giving the subject careful consideration.'
This reply appeared to Mr. Gladstone so unsatisfactory,
that he made an earnest appeal to the Minister to bring
the question to an early issue, and added the significant
and formidable words :—

I hope when we meet again he will be able to make a distinct statement of his intentions, and if not, looking at all the circumstances and the nature of the constitutional question, and all the precedents bearing upon it, it will become a matter —in default of just action, which I should much regret—for independent members to consider whether they ought not to take some steps to obtain the judgment of Parliament.

Public attention was also directed to the subject by an article in the 'Times' newspaper of June 4, entitled 'The Prospects of a Dissolution,' in which the constitutional power of the House of Commons to compel a resignation of the Ministry, or an appeal to the country, was considered with reference to Parliamentary precedents. In 1841, when the Government of Lord Melbourne was defeated, the Ministers promised an early dissolution and took the supplies for six months only instead of the usual period. The grants being made for only half the year, the autumnal Session became a matter of necessity, and the Ministry effectually put it out of their own power to break their promise of an early appeal to a new Parliament. It was contended that the constitutional method of securing a second Session in 1868 was that suggested by the precedent of 1841.

On the evening of the same day (June 4) in which this article appeared, Mr. Childers, who had pursued an independent investigation of the subject, drew the attention of the House of Commons to the precedent of 1841, and asked the Chancellor of the Exchequer for how many months of the current financial year he proposed to take the votes. The Chancellor of the Exchequer replied that 'as to the time until which it is necessary that supply should be granted, that must depend upon the time when the dissolution is possible, and at present it is impossible to say what is the earliest period at which Parliament can dissolve.' The same evening Mr. Hardy moved for leave to bring in the Registration Bill, of which an account has already been given. One of the principal objects of that Bill was to make arrangements for an autumn Session. The House of Commons had by this time displayed unmistakeably a determination to keep the Cabinet to the promise of an appeal to the country, and it must be added that some at least of the Ministers were equally anxious to redeem their pledge. On the 8th of June the Chancellor of the Exchequer (Mr. Hunt) used the following remarkable language:—

> There is in the Government a longing and burning desire to ask the verdict of a new Parliament and the country on their conduct and policy. The position they have occupied has been almost too much for human nature to bear, and everything that can be done they will do to hasten a dissolution and the assembling of a new Parliament.

This declaration, made with unmistakeable sincerity, satisfied the House, and all objection to grant the supplies thenceforward ceased. The position of the Ministry had indeed by this time become one which men, influenced by the sentiments of honour and self-respect, could hardly endure. Nominally they were at the head of public affairs, but in reality the chief legislator of the country sat on the Opposition benches. Mr. Gladstone passed his Resolutions on the Irish Church, and then his Bill for suspending appointments in that Church, despite the strenuous resistance of the Ministry. His Bill for abolishing compulsory church rates in England was accepted by them, because they knew that resistance would be hopeless. The favourite Conservative scheme of including suburban voters in borough constituencies they had been compelled to abandon at the dictation of the Opposition. The situation of the Cabinet was humiliating to themselves and injurious to the national interests. It was a direct violation of the fundamental principle of constitutional Government—that the Minister of the Crown should possess the confidence of the House of Commons.

At the time when Mr. Disraeli announced the proffer of his resignation, and that the alternative of an early dissolution had been accepted, he added that having disapproved of the first of Mr. Gladstone's Resolutions respecting the Irish Church, he also disapproved of the second and third; but that he had ' no wish whatever to enter into protracted debates and formal divisions on the second and third Resolutions.' *

These Resolutions were as follows:—

2. That, subject to the foregoing considerations, it is expedient to prevent the creation of new personal interests by the exercise of any public patronage, and to confine the operations of the Ecclesiastical Commissioners of Ireland to objects of immediate necessity, or such as involve individual rights, pending the final decision of Parliament.

3. That an humble Address be presented to Her Majesty, humbly to pray that, with a view to preventing by legislation during the present Session the creation of new personal interests through the exercise of any public patronage, Her Majesty would be graciously pleased to place at the disposal of Parliament her interest in the temporalities of the archbishoprics, bishoprics, and other ecclesiastical dignities and benefices in Ireland and the custody thereof.†

These Resolutions were adopted (May 7) together with a fourth Resolution, proposed by Mr. Whitbread and slightly modified by the addition of a few words at the end suggested by Mr. Gladstone:—

4. That when legislative effect shall have been given to the first Resolution of this Committee respecting the Established Church of Ireland, it is right and necessary that the grant to Maynooth and the Regium Donum be discontinued, due regard being had to all personal interests.

To the Address mentioned in the third Resolution, Her Majesty replied that—' Relying on the wisdom of my Parliament, I desire that my interest in the temporalities of the united Church of England and Ireland,

---

* *Hansard*, vol. 191, col. 1707 (May 4, 1868).
† *Hansard*, vol. 191, col. 1010.

in Ireland, may not stand in the way of the consideration by Parliament of any measure relating thereto
which may be introduced in the present Session.' This
reply was communicated to the House of Commons on
May 12. The next day Mr. Gladstone introduced a
Bill to prevent for a limited time new appointments in
the Church of Ireland, and to restrain for the same
period, in certain respects, the proceedings of the Irish
Ecclesiastical Commissioners. The principal objects of
the measure were to suspend for a year appointments
to sees or livings which might become vacant, and to
make consequential temporary arrangements. Though
the Government had not actively opposed the second
and third Resolutions, this suspensory Bill was the subject of a renewed contest. When the second reading
was moved (May 22), Mr. Hardy proposed that the
Bill should be read a second time that day six months.
Another animated debate ensued. Mr. Disraeli thought
that—

The right hon. gentleman has embarked on a most dangerous
policy—that its consequences will be most serious, or may be
most serious, to the country—that it may dim the splendour of
the British Crown.

The House was not deterred by this appalling prospect. The second reading of the Established Church
(Ireland) Bill was carried by a majority of 54, the
numbers being ayes, 312; noes, 258.

About this time the friends of the Irish Establishment began to look to the House of Lords for comfort.
One of the arguments against passing the Bill in the
Lower House was, that it was sure to be rejected in the
Upper. The suggestion that the Commons should refrain
from the exercise of their independent powers in deference to a conjectured resolution of the House of Lords
had at least the merit of novelty.

The Irish Church Bill reached the House of Peers on

June 18, when Lord Grey gave notice of a motion for its rejection; and a like notice was given by the Lord Chancellor. On June 25 Earl Granville moved the second reading. Earl Grey successfully moved the postponement of it for six months. He said that he did not think disestablishment and disendowment 'the best mode of removing the grievance complained of; but rather than that the present state of things should remain, he should be prepared to vote for disestablishment and disendowment.'

Lord Derby's principal argument against the Bill was founded on respect for proprietary rights.

If they were prepared to disregard a prescription of 300 years, the gifts of bygone sovereigns to their Protestant subjects, the donations of pious founders, and the protection of the Protestant faith—if they were prepared to disconnect religion from Government, and were ready to declare that Ireland should be the only State in which Government should not interest itself in religion—if they were ready to do this at the dictation of a would-be Minister, and at the dictation of a dying House of Commons, then he had not a word to say against the passage of this Bill. But he must enter his protest against the doctrine that Parliament is more entitled to deal with the property of the Irish Church in the manner proposed than with the property of any other Corporation, or any private person. He utterly denied the moral competence of Parliament to take any such course. He had talked of a prescription of 300 years, but that did injustice to his argument. The title of the Church property dated from a period long anterior to the Reformation. With the exception of the confiscation of the monastic property at that time, there was only a transfer of property from one Church to another; there was no diversion of it from ecclesiastical to secular uses. . . . . It is said that Parliament may take away what Parliament has given. But, in the first place, he denied that because Parliament has given an estate it can take it away; and, in the second place, he asserted that the Irish Church did not derive its property from Parliament.

There are here two propositions to be considered—*first*, that Parliament is no more entitled to deal with

the property of the Irish Church than with that of any
other corporation or any private person; *secondly*, that
the Irish Church did not derive its property from Parliament.

It will be convenient to examine first the statement
of a matter of history—that the Irish Church did not
derive its property from Parliament. The property of
the Irish Church may be divided broadly into two kinds
—lands and other gifts from individuals—tithes or
equivalent payments enforced by the civil power. With
respect to the gifts of individuals, it must be at once
admitted that they are not derived from Parliament.
But how does the case stand with respect to tithes ?
Let us look at one or two particulars of their history.
Contributions for the support of the clergy were originally voluntary.   Blackstone tells us that compulsory
payment of tithes were established by ' parliamentary
conventions of estates' in two kingdoms of the Hep-
tarchy.   At first tithes were not allotted to particular
priests ; every man might pay his dues to what priest
he pleased, or into the hands of the diocesan, to be distributed among the clergy. The appropriation of these
payments to the parsons of the respective parishes
in England appears to have been settled about the
year 1200.[*]

The exaction of tithes in Ireland was nearly as ancient as in this country.   At a council of the Irish
clergy at Cashel, in 1172, it was decreed ' that all the
faithful should pay tithes of their cattle, fruits, and all
other increase.'[†]

Tithes were originally paid for everything that yielded
an annual or recurring increase, as corn, hay, fruit,
poultry, and the like. In both countries these payments
have ceased to be made in kind. An Act of 1838, to
which reference has already been made, directs that all

---

[*] 'Blackstone's Commentaries,' vol. 2, ch. 2.
[†] ' Burn's Ecclesiastical Law,' tit. Church in Ireland.

tithes, or compositions for tithes, in Ireland, 'shall wholly cease and determine,' and substitutes 'the payment of an annual sum or rent-charge, equal to three-fourths of the annual amount of such tithe composition.' This sum is charged upon the land, and is payable by the person having the first estate of inheritance in such land. *

From these particulars it follows that tithe may be correctly described as a tax of ten per cent. on particular property, imposed first by the decrees of the clergy, afterwards ratified and confirmed by the law of the land. The impost was literally a property-tax of two shillings in the pound, enforced by Parliament, and, before Parliaments were constituted in their existing form, by their equivalent—the supreme power in the State. It is difficult to see how an impost so established can have any greater sanctity than any other property or income-tax. It stands upon a footing altogether different from private endowments. It was not spontaneously dedicated by individual piety to the service of God. It was a State exaction.

The other proposition for which Lord Derby contends — and of course his speech is here selected because it is typical—is that Parliament has no more right to take away the property of the Irish Church than to take that of any other corporation or any private person. He denies the 'moral competence' of Parliament to do such an act. Others have called it an act of 'spoliation,' or of 'confiscation,' or of 'robbing God.' Let us consider for a moment what all this means. It is impossible, strictly speaking, to inflict injustice on a corporation. You may inflict injustice on the members of it, but not on the institution or mere creation of the law. That cannot suffer pain. Therefore, when every vested or subsisting interest

* 1 & 2 Vict. c. 109, s. 7.

has been provided for, the diversion by the State of corporate funds to a new purpose cannot be a dishonest or immoral act. It may be unwise, but it cannot be unjust, if we use words in their exact sense. To deprive a school or hospital of the endowments of private benefactors is, in most cases, extremely impolitic, because (beside various other reasons) the effect of superseding ancient charities is to deter people from making similar bequests hereafter. But the question of expediency and the question of justice are totally distinct. If adequate compensation be made to all who have acquired an actual interest in the school or hospital, there is not, and cannot be, any confiscation. If the transaction involve a wrong, there must be somebody to complain—somebody to suffer. If there is no person *in esse* who can say he has been robbed, how is it possible to contend that a robbery has been committed?

But it is said, not indeed by Lord Derby, but by some of his followers, that there is a peculiar sanctity in tithes or other property dedicated to ecclesiastical purposes. It may be answered, in the first place, that the assertion is dogmatic. What authority is there for the proposition that funds once given for religious objects may not be withdrawn when the objects fail? Secondly, as a matter of historical fact, tithes have not been given exclusively for religious purposes. In, and previously to, the time of Charlemagne they were subject to a well-known division into four parts ; one to maintain the edifice of the church, the second to support the poor, the third the bishops, the fourth the parochial clergy.*   In

---

* Blackstone, vol. 2, ch. 2. From Blackstone's words it might be inferred that this arrangement was originated by Charlemagne. Selden, in his Historie of Tithes (chap. 6, sec. 7) is more precise, and considers the decrees of Charlemagne the earliest of an *imperial* character which made the payment of tithes obligatory. There are much earlier *ecclesiastical* authorities for a quadrupartite division of offerings to the Church. The earliest such authorities which the present writer has been able to discover are two

this quadrupartite appropriation, one-fourth part of the tithe had no more of a religious character than modern Poor Rates have.   Tithes have in many instances, both before and after the Reformation, become the property of the Crown, and hence, as Blackstone observes, 'have sprung all the lay appropriations or secular parsonages which we now see in the kingdom; they having been afterwards granted from time to time by the Crown.'* Selden, in his Historie of Tithes, says 'Common Law (for by that name, as *common* is distinguished from *sacred*, are the ciuill or municipall laws of all nations stiled) hath neuer given way herein to the Canons, but hath allow'd customes, and made them subject to ciuill tithes, infeodations, discharges, compositions, and the like.' In 1735 the Irish House of Commons abolished tithe of pasture, which in the then existing state of Ireland is said to have exempted ninety-six out of every hundred from contributing to the support of the Clergy.   Another example of the diversion of tithes from ecclesiastical

epistles of Pope Simplicius and Pope Gelasius, both of whom were Pontiffs in the latter part of the fifth century, about the time of the separation of the Eastern and Western Churches.   Gelasius says—

Reditus et oblationes fidelium in quatuor partes dividat; quarum unam sibi retineat; alteram clericis pro officiorum suorum sedulitate distribuat; fabricis tertiam; quartam pauperibus et peregrinis habeat fideliter erogandam.

The epistle of Simplicius is almost exactly to the same effect.   (Decretum Gratiani, secunda pars. causa xii. quæst. ii. c. 26, 28.)

The decree of Gelasius is cited in the Capitularies of Charlemagne—capitulare secundum Anni DCCCV.—

Ut decimæ populi dividantur in quatuor partes; id est una pars Episcopo, alia clericis, tertia pauperibus, quarta Ecclesiæ in fabricis applicetur; sicut in decreto Gelasii Papæ continetur.   (Capitularia Regum Francorum. Parisiis, MDCLXXVII p. 428.)

A tripartite division of tithes was at an early period sanctioned in England.   Ecgberht, who was Archbishop of York from 735 to 766, says in his Excerptiones with respect to tithes—

Ad ornamentum ecclesiæ primam eligant partem; secundam autem ad usum pauperum atque peregrinorum per eorum manus misericorditer cum omni humilitate dispensent; tertiam vero sibimet ipsis sacerdotes reservent. (Antient Laws and Institutes of England, printed under the direction of the Record Commission, page 320.)

* Commentaries, vol. 1, p. 386.

purposes was the Act of 1838, by which landowners
were allowed to pay, instead of the former composition,
a rent-charge of *three-fourths* the amount. The remaining fourth was given them, according to the statute
'as an allowance for the facility and security of collection,' or, as some say, as a pecuniary inducement to
withdraw their opposition to that measure.

With these precedents before us, it is very difficult to
contend that tithes have a peculiarly sacred character.
The whole question of maintaining them is one of
policy, to be settled according to the circumstances
of the country with reference to which the question
arises.

Here, in England, we believe that the Church
confers national benefits—benefits in which the whole
community, directly or indirectly, participates. On no
other ground can any public impost be justified than
this, that the people who pay it share in the advantages
which it purchases. Every shilling of the public
revenue ought to be applied to purposes in which the
whole community is directly or indirectly interested.
In Ireland a large number of those who support the
Church derive no benefit from it. This objection is
sometimes answered, by saying that the rent-charge is
paid by the landlord, who is most frequently a Protestant. But though the landlord pays the charge, the
source from which he pays it is the rent of his tenants.
The money must come out of their pockets, for where
else does it come from? Their rents must in some
degree depend on the tithe-charge to which the landlord is liable, for the same reason that the retail price of
sugar depends in some degree on the duty for which
the importer is liable.

After three nights' debate the House of Lords (June
29) rejected the Established Church (Ireland) Bill by
the very large majority of 95; the numbers being for

the second reading 97, against it 192.   This division does not, however, represent the balance of opinion among their lordships upon the larger question of the ultimate disestablishment of the Irish Church.   Many of the speakers—and therefore presumably of those who voted without speaking—opposed the Suspensory Bill, because they considered that it was premature, and that an appeal to the country ought to precede any Parliamentary action with reference to the Irish Church.

The issue whether a State Church should continue to exist in Ireland, was formally committed to the judgment of the nation by the Royal Speech (July 31), which concluded thus:—

I trust that, under the blessing of Divine Providence, the expression of their opinion on those great questions of public policy which have occupied the attention of Parliament and remain undecided, may tend to maintain unimpaired that civil and religious freedom which has been secured to all my subjects by the institutions and settlement of my realm.

Of course this sentence begs the question at issue. It assumes that the 'institutions and settlement' have secured 'civil and religious freedom.'   That is one of the chief matters in controversy, but the Prime Minister who penned this paragraph could not refrain from a parting shot at his adversaries.

CHAPTER VII.

FINANCIAL HISTORY FROM 1865.

THE very word Finance appears repulsive to many readers; and the mere aspect of a collection of figures is commonly regarded as a warning to turn over the pages on which they occur. In this place, however, there will not be any great array of figures; all that will be attempted is a very general account of the financial condition of the country during the last three years, and of the attempts which have been made to promote economy.

The Conservatives came into power in the summer of 1865, on the resignation of Lord Russell. Consequently, the Governments of Lord Derby, and his successor, Mr. Disraeli, have been responsible for three budgets—those produced in 1866, 1867, and 1868.

The Whigs, when they quitted office in 1865, undoubtedly left to their successors a progressively diminishing expenditure. A mere reference to the totals for each year from 1860 establishes this point conclusively. The actual expenditure for the twelve months ending March 31, 1860, and the following years respectively, was :—

Year ending March 31, 1860 £69,502,289   0   0
                        1861 £72,842,059   10   0
                        1862 £72,086,485   3   5
                        1863 £70,352,007   19   2
(including £1,050,000 raised by loan for fortifications).
                        1864 £67,856,286   2   7
(including £800,000 raised by loan for fortifications).
                        1865 £67,082,206   11   1
(including £620,000 raised by loan for fortifications).
                        1866 £66,474,356   13   3
(including £560,000 raised by loan for fortifications).

These are the figures of actual, not estimated, expenditure. They are taken from the proper authentic source—the 'Annual Finance Accounts,' which are official records of the payments of each year.

Mr. Gladstone was Chancellor of the Exchequer from the commencement of Lord Palmerston's second Administration in June 1859 until July 1866. The expenditure of the year 1859-60 was based on estimates prepared under a Conservative Government. In 1861, when the maximum was reached, four millions of the vast sum were due to the Chinese war. From that time until Mr. Gladstone left office the annual cost of Government diminished every year. In five years the annual charge was diminished by about six millions.

Let us now see *how* this great reduction was accomplished. Was it effected by what is termed a 'cheese-paring economy'—by cutting down the small stipends of poor clerks already under-paid, and similar parsimony? Of course, to answer this question exhaustively, we should have to go through every item of the accounts; but it will be sufficient for the present purpose to enumerate some of the largest sums which make up the aggregate reductions in the several years. The following table* shows several of them. The information is obtained by a comparison of the *estimates* of the several years, as they are the most convenient for present purpose. The figures have, however, been generally checked by a reference to the 'finance accounts,' which show actual expenditure; and there is no material difference.

---

* For the figures given in this table and the preceding, the author is indebted to Mr. John Statham of the Exchequer and Audit department, who has carefully extracted them from the documents cited. Mr. Statham's long experience in the affairs of his department justifies entire reliance on his accuracy.

Year	Description of Grant reduced	Amount of Reduction
1861	Civil Services, Class 7 . . .	£345,402
1862	Army	185,705
„	Navy	800,025
„	Revenue Department . .	153,603
1863	Navy	840,283
1864	Army	1,000,113
„	Navy . . .• . . .	1,058,273
„	Civil	157,506
1865	Army	215,349
„	Navy	303,422
1866	Army	874,908
„	Navy	810,979
„	Revenue Department . .	35,332
„	Civil	13,241

This table almost speaks for itself; it shows the general direction of Mr. Gladstone's efforts to reduce expenditure. The first item, about £345,000, in Class 7 of Civil Services is not a net reduction, but arises partly from transfers of charges to other accounts. But a real diminution was effected in this class which, perhaps, offers the greatest facility for jobbery and waste. This Class 7 consists of a large number of miscellaneous items, most of them of the nature of eleemosynary contributions to local institutions, or grants to private persons. Probably many of the objects for which these grants were made were highly meritorious, but they were just those with respect to which a conscientious Finance Minister would exercise the greatest vigilance.

But the great bulk of the reduction effected by Mr. Gladstone during his tenure of office is in the cost of the Army and Navy. In 1862 the grant for the two war services is diminished by nearly a million; in the next year the naval estimates are reduced by 840,000*l.*; next year more than two millions are taken off from the cost of the two services; and finally, another half million is subtracted in 1865, the last year of Mr. Gladstone's management. The decrease between 1861 and 1866 in the annual charge for the Army and Navy was upwards of *four millions two hundred thousand pounds.* No attempt will be made in this place to justify this pruning of the charges of the Horse Guards and Admiralty, for, in a subsequent page, it will be contended that the process ought to be carried much further.

In the five years in question the annual expenditure was reduced by about *six millions sterling*. The change was effected cautiously, and the most adverse critics have not been able to indicate an instance of sacrifice of efficiency to economy.

These reductions are not the most meritorious of Mr. Gladstone's financial achievements. The chief service which he has rendered to the country is by altering the incidence of taxation—by shifting the burden where it was most galling and oppressive—by reforms which opened new markets, facilitated trade, and cheapened commodities used by all classes of the community. These labours constitute his highest claims to public gratitude, though the others—the actual savings of expenditure—must not be overlooked.

We have now to compare these results with the financial statements of his successors in office—Mr. Disraeli and Mr. Ward Hunt. The actual expenditure in the two years for which they are responsible was as follows:—

> Year ending March 31, 1867, £66,780,000
> „   „   1868,   69,242,000

That is to say, on March 31, 1868, Her Majesty's Government had been twenty months in office, and in that time had raised the expenditure of the country from the sixty-six millions of 1866 to sixty-nine millions and a quarter. In the words of Mr. Gladstone in the House of Commons, May 4, 1868, 'they had contrived to throw back the expenditure of the country three years during a tenure of twenty months;'* that

* *Hansard*, vol. 191, col. 1751.

is, had undone Mr. Gladstone's work for the three
years preceding.

This statement was made in the presence of the Conservative Chancellor of the Exchequer, and has never
been challenged. In fact, the figures speak for themselves. Mr. Ward Hunt does not dispute the increase
of three millions, but he argues that it was required
to secure the efficiency of the Army, Navy, and Civil
Service.

The total expenditure of 1867–8 was, in reality,
71,236,242l., but this includes an extraordinary item
of about two millions for the Abyssinian expedition.*
In fairness towards the Conservative Administration,
we must subtract these two millions, in order to arrive
at the ordinary expenses of the last financial year.
With this correction it appears that the sum spent in
that period, exclusive of the cost of the expedition, was
69,242,000l.

With reference to the future, the Chancellor of the
Exchequer, in his financial statement of April 23, 1868,
said that 'the total estimated expenditure of the year
is 70,428,000l.'† In order to provide for the increased
demands of the public purse, he recommended an addition of 2d. in the pound to the Income Tax; but as
only part of the revenue from this source could be collected in the course of the twelve months, he proposed
to anticipate the produce of the impost by temporarily
borrowing a million sterling, to be paid off in the following year. Here again there was a remarkable contrast
with former budgets. For the first time in several years
the Finance Minister recurred to the delusive expedient
of a temporary loan.

Another subject of grave consideration with respect
to the Conservative budgets of 1867 and 1868 was that

---

* These figures are taken from Mr. Ward Hunt's financial statement,
April 23, 1868.   † *Hansard*, vol. 191, p. 1167.

both involved deficits.   The amounts were not large, but they exhibited a manifest departure from the wholesome practice of preceding years, in which income had uniformly and considerably exceeded expenditure.   In the preceding three years of Mr. Gladstone's management, the excess had been, on the average, about two millions and three quarters annually.

On subjects of this kind there are few persons who can speak with higher authority than Mr. Childers. His statements are made with an exactness and caution which have won the confidence of the House of Commons.   On the present occasion he observed—

> For the first time for many years there was a deficit last year, which was succeeded by another and heavier deficit this year. . . . . The position of their finances therefore was that out of the balances in the Exchequer they were to pay 650,000*l.* for Abyssinia, besides deficits on ordinary expenditure for the last two years of 13,000*l.* and 140,000*l.*   During each of the three previous there had been a considerable surplus.
>
> In the year 1864–5 the surplus was £3,851,000
> „   1865–6   „   1,897,000
> „   1865–7   „   2,654,000
>
> These were the last three years of the Administration of the late Government, and they gave an average surplus of 2,800,000*l.* a year.   The two years of the Administration of the present Government gave deficits of 13,300*l.* and 148,000*l.* His right hon. friend the Member for South Lancashire had pointed out that these deficits were due to the enormous increase of the expenditure of the country.*

Mr. Gladstone, in commenting on this budget, compared the *optional* expenditure of successive years— excluding the interest on the National Debt, which must inevitably be paid.   Obviously this is the correct method of comparison.

> I will not trouble the Committee with any question as to the debt and permanent charge to the country, but will confine myself to what may be called the variable or optional charges—

* *Hansard*, vol. 191, col. 1183.

namely, such as are voted in supply, and I take the original estimates of the years 1866-7, 1867-8, and 1868-9.

The estimates of 1866-7 amounted to £38,165,000
,,   1867-8   ,,   39,733,000
,,   1868-9   ,,   41,863,000

Primâ facie there is an increase of 3,700,000*l*., but the right hon. gentleman has observed with perfect propriety that there are deductions to be made from that increase, because some considerable amounts now appear on both sides of the account which formerly appeared on neither side. . . . If the augmentation is, as I should put it, 2,840,000*l*., or as the right hon. gentlemen would put it, 2,700,000*l*.—for I will not quarrel with him as to the difference—that is more than enough to make good my allegation that it is the increase of the permanent charge which requires us to make good this new demand upon the country. And if that be so, I will not go further than to say that it will be our duty very carefully to consider whether this augmentation of permanent charge is really necessary; whether we can justify it in the face of the country; or whether it may not be our duty to make some efforts for bringing the expenditure of the country—I mean the permanent and ordinary expenditure—within more moderate bounds.*

There was one easy answer to such strictures—by imputing personal motives. Mr. Gladstone's objects were factious; he complained of expenditure merely to damage the Conservative Government.

But even if those were his motives, surely the statements were definite and the figures worth consideration. No—answered the Tory press—you may prove anything by figures.

With reasoners whose minds are thus constituted it is hopeless and useless to argue. Their suggestions amount to this—that all criticisms on a budget are out of place. If figures may be made to prove anything, what is the use of having a budget at all? Why not let the Administration spend the public money without rendering any account?

Mr. Ward Hunt, the Chancellor of the Exchequer,

* *Hansard*, vol. 191, col. 1175.

has admitted the substantial accuracy of Mr. Gladstone's criticism on the growth of the estimates. A letter addressed by him to a friend (August 24, 1868), and published in the newspapers, contains an able defence of his management. This letter is written in a fair and candid spirit, and is valuable as a succinct and accurate account of the financial history of the past year. He commences as follows:—

> I do not complain of the statement that the expenditure voted by Parliament has risen 3,000,000*l.* since the change of Government. Speaking in round numbers, that is sufficiently accurate. The difference between the estimates presented to Parliament by the late Government for 1866–7 and by the present Government for 1868–9, after making all necessary corrections for alterations in account and transfer of charges from the Consolidated and other funds, amounts, I believe, to 2,815,654*l.*

The letter proceeds to enumerate the principal items to which this expenditure was due. The bulk of the three millions is accounted for as follows:—

Excess of Army Estimates	£1,360,000
„	Navy „	584,914
„	Civil Service	570,000

The first item includes large sums for increased pay of troops, for raising militia, converting small arms, and heavy ordnance for forts. The second item includes nearly half a million for increased shipbuilding. The third includes large sums for constabulary in Ireland, law expenses, and miscellaneous expenses. But by far the greater part of the augmentation relates to military and naval charges. The Chancellor of the Exchequer says that many of the new expenses were required by the state of the services. But the authorities which he cites are not universally considered indisputable. He refers to demands from the War Office and the Admiralty. Those two departments are not usually credited with

much forbearance towards the public purse.   The War
Office nominally controls the Horse Guards, but is
generally submissive to that department in matters of
expenditure.   At the Horse Guards the idea of economy
is very unfashionable, and the interests of the 'service'
are supreme.   Mr. Hunt's apology for the 1,360,000*l.*
excess of army estimates is that the money was demanded by military authorities, and commissions in
which the military element strongly predominated.
There is no doubt that the demands were made.   The
'service' would have done itself an unusual injustice if
it had not made them.   In the augmented charge of
the Admiralty the only justification is a mere dictum
of Sir John Pakington, to the effect that he found 'the
reserves by no means in a satisfactory condition.'   This
is one of those vague general statements which it is very
easy to make and very difficult to test.   There are scep-
tical people who will doubt whether the *ipse dixit*
of Sir John Pakington is a sufficient warrant for an
additional outlay of half a million.   He has always
shown himself favourable to large military and naval
expenditure; and was one of the most earnest supporters
of Lord Palmerston's policy of fortifying arsenals and
similar extravagancies.   A few years ago almost any
expenditure upon warlike preparations was tolerated.
Frequent warnings of French invasions, regard for the
'balance of power,' and anxiety about our just influence in the councils of Europe, warranted the at-
tacks made by the Admiralty and Horse Guards on the
public purse.   But these appeals to our fears on the
one hand, and our pride on the other, are beginning
to lose their effect.   The Emperor of the French has
postponed indefinitely his invasion, the balance of power
is left to maintain itself without our help, and we
have got rather indifferent to our just influence in the
councils of Europe.   Somewhat late in the day we

have discovered that we have enough to do in managing our own affairs without attending to those of our neighbours.

Statements respecting the necessity of increased military and naval expenditure may be tested by reference to the accounts of the Admiralty and the Horse Guards. Of the military expenditure we know comparatively little. The day has not yet come—though probably it is not remote—when the accounts of the army which with reference to its numbers is the most costly in the world will be thoroughly examined. Respecting the navy our knowledge is for several reasons more ample. Resolute and judicious inquirers, such as Mr. Childers, Mr. Seely, and Mr. Stansfeld, have done much to throw light upon the internal economy of the dockyards, and the services thus rendered form part of the financial history of this country.

Mismanagement of the Admiralty is an ancient grievance. Samuel Pepys, who was Secretary of the Admiralty in the reign of Charles II., gives a very unfavourable account of the condition of the Fleet in 1684. He complains that several newly built ships had been reported by the Navy Board itself to be in danger of sinking at their moorings, and adds—

And this notwithstanding above six hundred thousand pounds (not yet accounted for by the Navy Board) spent in their building and furniture, with above threescore and ten thousand pounds more demanded for completing them, amounting together to 670,000*l.* ; and therein exceeding not only the Navy officers' own estimates, and their master shipwrights' demands, but even the charge which some of them appear'd to have been actually built for, by above one hundred and seventy thousand pounds; and notwithstanding too the flowing in of the monies provided for them by Parliament faster (for the most part) than their occasions of employing it.

He proceeds to state that King James II. on his accession endeavoured to improve the condition of the

Navy, 'but with such unsuccessfulness (after a whole year's proof of their performances), as upon a fresh view of its state taken in January 168⅜, to discover itself still declin'd to a yet more deplorable degree of calamity.' He cites various specific instances of money misapplied, and severely condemns the conduct of the Navy officers, 'whose estimates of the very same date were found sometimes to differ not less than double, nay, even treble, in the charge of the repairs of the very same ship.'*

One or two particulars will suffice to indicate the direction which Admiralty reform has taken of late years, and the occasions which required it. The enormous magnitude of the subject is shown by a simple comparison of the naval expenditure at the present time and thirty-three years ago.

> Total vote for all Naval pur-
> poses in 1835 . . . £4,245,723
> Vote in 1868–9 . . . 11,177,290

But this statement does not represent the whole growth of expenditure. The Post Office Packet Service was formerly included in the naval vote, but is now separate. Again, half a million probably should be added to the naval expenditure for guns and ammunition supplied by the Ordnance department. For the purposes of comparison, it will be nearly correct to say that in the thirty-three years the cost of the navy and naval forces has risen from four millions and a quarter to twelve millions.

Doubtless a great part of this augmentation is due to additions to our naval forces and armaments, but a very large proportion of that expenditure is due to the enormous increase of public dockyards. There are seven of these establishments at home, and fifteen

---

* Memoires relating to the state of the Royal Navy of England for Ten years determin'd December 1688, printed Anno MDCXC.

stations abroad. In the yards of this country there are some forty different manufactories in which nearly everything used in a ship is made from the raw material. Each dockyard maintains an army of skilled and unskilled labourers, and there is obviously room for an immense amount of waste and extravagance. One of the great checks of such extravagance is to compare items of expenditure at the public yards with corresponding charges by private firms. But until very recent times it was almost impossible to ascertain accurately the cost of any particular ship built by the Royal establishments. Mr. Stansfeld, when he became a Lord of the Admiralty in 1863, effected an important improvement in this respect. After a laborious course of inquiries he induced the Admiralty to authorise a fresh system of accounts, by which the cost of materials for individual ships was recorded. ' The chief object sought to be obtained by these regulations was the establishment of a basis of ship-building on sectional arrangements, and the record of cost in accordance therewith, so as to admit of comparison as far as practicable between ship-building expenditure in Her Majesty's dockyards and that incurred in private trade.' * In the autumn of 1864 Mr. Childers, then Civil Lord of the Admiralty, visited the dockyards with the view of continuing the inquiries which Mr. Stansfeld had commenced in the preceding autumn, and the result of these investigations was a great reform and simplification of accounts.† This useful work has been

---

* Navy Dockyard Accounts. Return No. 405 of 1865.

† *Ibid.* The magnitude of these changes can be represented in a very simple manner. It appears by the evidence of Mr. Fellows before the Select Committee on Admiralty Moneys in 1868, that up to 1861 a ship would be represented as costing 100,000*l.*, which in 1861–4 would be represented as costing 120,000*l.*, and after 1864 140,000*l.*—Evidence, p. 307. In other words, the real cost was formerly understated by at least 40 per cent.

It must always be borne in mind that a first step in Admiralty reform is to arrive at a true account of the cost of individual ships. Mr. Fellows has

carried forward by the exertions of another labourer in
the same field, Mr. Seely, who has rendered valuable
public service by his elaborate investigations of Admiralty management and strenuous efforts to promote
economy in that department.   In the course of the last
session a select committee of the House of Commons
was appointed to inquire into the application of the
money voted by Parliament for ships and the admiralty accounts.   The report of this committee, after
noticing the reforms effected between 1859 and 1865,
recommends further alterations which it is believed
will tend in a material degree to check extravagance.
It is suggested that for the future 'each dockyard
should, for the purposes of account, be treated as a separate establishment;' and that each dockyard, and each
manufacturing establishment in it, shall be debited with
its own charges separately.   The Committee sanctioned
a form of accounts proposed by the Chairman, Mr.
Seely, and that form has now been adopted.*   In order
to appreciate the value of these alterations, it must be
explained that hitherto various expenses of the different
yards have been blended together, and consequently it
has been impossible to institute a strict comparison
between them and to determine which establishments
are the most economical.   They escaped responsibility
by sharing it.

for several years devoted himself to an unofficial investigation of Navy
accounts, and his valuable labours have contributed greatly to elucidate
them.   His evidence in this particular instance is fully confirmed by the
following extract from the evidence of the Comptroller and Accountant-
General of the Navy:—

'75. In that year, 1858-9, I see that you only included in the cost of
ships, wages and materials in ships?—Certainly.

'76. From the year 1858-9 to the year 1861-2, you do not even include
foreman's wages?—They did not include establishment charges.

'77. In the year 1861-2 I think you added items to the extent of about
20 per cent. on your previous charges for ships?—Yes.

'78. And in the year 1864-5 you made another addition of 20 per cent.
or thereabouts?—I dare say that is correct.'

* Report from the Select Committee on Admiralty Moneys and Accounts
No. 409 of 1868.

But no mere improvements of accounts will strike the root of the evil. A thorough cure of it will never be effected until the Establishments are reduced both in number and extent. They are too large and too many. They maintain hosts of supernumeraries and idlers. They are supported by strong local and political influence, and the Government will be bold indeed which confronts the powerful opposition which any attempt to disestablish any of the dockyards will inevitably provoke.

The general principles on which the navy is managed at the present time may be inferred from the language of apologists for the existing system. Lord Henry Lennox, Secretary to the Admiralty, is one of these. In a draft report which he proposed to the Committee just mentioned, he deals with a remarkable case in which several selected firms were invited to send in tenders for certain gunboats, and part of the work was given to the firm which made the *highest* tender. The explanation of Lord Henry Lennox is a curiosity in its way:—'We believe that it is an unjust act in any public department to accept to any great extent offers which it knows must involve those who make them in heavy pecuniary loss and thus drive the honest trader out of the market.'* That is, the Admiralty was afraid of getting the gunboats too cheap, and had more regard for the interests of the contractors than they themselves had. Yet these contractors might have been considered able to take care of themselves. They were some of the most eminent ship-building firms in the kingdom, and had been selected by the Admiralty itself as competent to execute the contract.

Here is another specimen of the reasoning of the most chivalrous of Secretaries. It had been discovered that several thousand tons of valuable ballast iron had been

* Report on Admiralty Moneys, xxv.

actually employed instead of paving-stones in one of the
arsenals.   Surely this was disgraceful extravagance and
waste of material ?   Not at all, in the judgment of Lord
Henry Lennox.   He wanted to report that 'though the
Committee do not recommend this use of the ballast
provided it can be profitably disposed of; it has in no
way deteriorated by being applied to this purpose, and
your Committee recommend its removal as soon as a
profitable sale can be effected.' *

But the disclosures before the Admiralty Moneys'
Committee sink into insignificance when compared with
the revelations of a certain Return entitled Navy (Ships
Sold) ordered on the motion of Mr. Seely, and presented
to Parliament in 1867.†   It appears, from this paper,
the Conservative Government being urgently in want
of money directed, in January 1867, that a large number
of ships should be sold with all their stores—that the
ships were sold for half the price put upon them by
the government officers, and despite their remonstrances
—and that the Naval Stores Act, which renders the
mere possession of such stores by private persons in the
manner proposed a criminal offence, was deliberately
violated.‡

First as to the motive—this is stated with remarkable
candour in a document which probably was never intended to meet the public eye.   In a paper submitted
to the Admiralty by the Controller, Vice-Admiral
Robinson, he states plainly that one of the purposes is
' to obtain by their sale a certain sum of money to be

* Report on Admiralty Moneys, xxiii.
† No. 560 of 1867.
‡ The Act 27 & 28 Vict. c. 91 was passed to prevent embezzlement of
Her Majesty's Naval and Victualling Stores.   The mere unauthorised possession of such property by a private person is a criminal offence.   In the
contemplated transaction it would have been impossible for the Admiralty
to have given the purchaser any written authority identifying the stores sold
to him.

paid into the Exchequer, which shall be a set-off against an increase of Navy Estimates.'* That is, the public property was to be sold at any sacrifice in order that the Conservative Government might make their estimates look as small as possible.

Fortunately, there are some public officers bold enough to resist iniquitous schemes of this kind. The Storekeeper-General, the Hon. Robert Dundas, made a report (February 8, 1867) on the Controller's project, which contains the following passage:—

No amount of money approaching the real value of these ships in relation to their cost, will be forthcoming under any conditions of sale.

It will be hardly expedient to invalidate the Naval Store Act on the uncertain speculation that better terms can be obtained by the unreserved sale of the marked copper and mixed metal on conditions, the efficiency of which must practically depend upon the ships being broken up by the original purchasers.†

He proceeds to observe, that the fact that 'the Admiralty had unreservedly sold large stores would be a permanent pretext in future against convictions under the Naval Store Act for illegal possession.' Another officer who was consulted, Mr. Romaine, makes the same objection. He says (February 8, 1867)—

The very stringent powers given to the Department were granted entirely on the understanding that the naval marked stores were not sold . . . I think further that all attempts to obtain convictions of marine store dealers will in future fail, and that all the steps which have been now for some years taken to diminish the robberies of dockyard stores will prove useless.‡

Here were distinct warnings by experienced officers that the transaction would involve a great pecuniary loss, and would be in contravention of an Act of Parlia-

---

* Report on 'Navy (Ships Sold),' p. 11.
† *Ibid.* p. 13.   ‡ *Ibid.* p. 14.

ment.   These remonstrances were effectual ?   Not a
whit.   The Admiralty Board considered the objections
insignificant compared with the urgent demand of the
Tory Government for ready money.   The Controller
replies :—

> I am quite aware of what is said on the ultimate balance of
> account that may be come to, between the Treasurer and
> Storekeeper's vote if the copper is sold to him, but this
> arrangement does not meet *the urgent want of a large pay-*
> *ment into the Treasury during the ensuing financial year*, and
> the argument of the Storekeeper-General throughout is founded
> on a complete disregard of this necessity . . . I am not the
> least deterred from believing in the soundness of the sugges-
> tion I have made by Mr. Romaine's very forcible remarks on
> the difficulties the Naval Store Act puts in the way of what I
> called an unrestricted sale, but which does restrict in a great
> measure the sale of old metal.*

The Board was resolute, and the contemplated sale
was effected, as their own officers predicted, at a great
loss.   The Return of ships sold on this occasion shows
that the prices realised were, in many instances, less
than half the value estimated by the Dockyard officers.†

* Report, 'Navy (Ships Sold),' p. 15.

† For instance, five ships at Sheerness—the 'Orion,' 'Collingwood,'
'Leander,' 'Cressy,' and 'Chesapeake'—were sold to private firms for
34,773*l.*; the Dockyard officers having reported the value for breaking up
to be sums which in the aggregate amount to 70,915*l.*—Return, Navy Ships
Sold, pp. 6, 7.

In numerous instances mentioned in the Return of 'Navy Ships Sold,' the
Admiralty repurchased stores from the vessel for more than they had received from the purchaser for the vessel and its contents; that is, paid for
the *part* more than they had received for the *whole*. In such cases the
purchaser got not only the vessel gratis but a sum of money besides. The
following are selected merely as specimens of these grotesque transactions.

Ships.	Gross amount of money obtained for each ship.	Amount paid to each purchaser by the Admiralty in repurchasing stores returned bearing ⬆
Cuckoo	£600	£1063 16 8
Petrel	630	1142 17 10

In apologising for these transactions, Lord Henry Lennox, the Secretary to the Admiralty, almost excels himself. In his draft report, already mentioned, he says: 'Respecting such sales as took place in England, the discretion of the Admiralty appears to have been seriously hampered by the Naval Stores Act. Your Committee recommend for the consideration of the Government whether a repeal of the Naval Store Act might not be a benefit to the country, by enabling old and obsolete ships to be disposed of by a sale out and out, in the manner indicated by the Controller.' *

These statements do not include a half or a tithe of the abuses discovered in the recent evidence before the Committee on Admiralty Moneys. But enough, probably, has been stated to show that the existing system of naval management cannot long endure. There are sufficient indications that the military administration is at least equally extravagant. That of the Admiralty is exposed to more obloquy, because, from a variety of circumstances, its affairs have been more frequently brought under public observation. But the Horse Guards and War Office probably will not much longer escape Parliamentary investigation and control. We are approaching a period when the two great spending departments, which superintend the Army and Navy, will be subjected to extensive reforms involving a process of reconstruction. This is not a mere party question. Many statesmen who differ widely on other subjects agree as to the necessity of reducing naval and military expenditure. But from politicians of the school to which Lord Henry Lennox belongs, it is quite clear that such improvements are not to be expected. He, like his leader, is ready at all times, and all occasions,

* Report, Admiralty Moneys, p. xxiii.

to demonstrate the perfection of Tory management. It has been the policy of Mr. Disraeli to procure influence and support by profuse expenditure of public money. In this, as in other respects, the political gambler has played his game with skill and boldness; but he has lost it.

THE END.

In One thick Volume. 8vo. Price £1. 4s. cloth,

THE

INSTITUTIONS OF THE ENGLISH GOVERNMENT;

BEING AN ACCOUNT OF THE CONSTITUTION, POWERS, AND

PROCEDURE OF ITS LEGISLATIVE, JUDICIAL, AND

ADMINISTRATIVE DEPARTMENTS,

WITH

COPIOUS REFERENCES TO ANCIENT AND MODERN AUTHORITIES.

CONTENTS AND ARRANGEMENT OF THE WORK.

Book I.—*Legislature.*—Chapter I. Divisions of Government.—II. The Authority of Parliament.—III. The Origin of Parliament.—IV. The Acts of Parliament.—V. Legislative Prerogatives of the Crown.—VI. The Parliamentary Powers of the Crown.—VII. The Constitution of the House of Lords.—VIII. The Constitution of the House of Commons.—IX. Procedure in Parliament.—X. The Privy Council and Cabinet Council.—XI. The Rights of Petition, Public Meetings and the Press.

Book II.—*Judicature.*—Chapter I. Divisions of the Judicature.—II. Origin of the Courts of Law.—III. Judicial Officers.—IV. Procedure in Courts of Justice generally.—V. The Supreme Power of the Law.—VI. The Judicature of Parliament and the Lords.—VII. The Judicature of the Privy Council.—VIII. The Court of Chancery.—IX. The Superior Courts of Common Law.—X. Courts of Criminal Jurisdiction.—XI. Courts of Special Civil Jurisdiction.

Book III.—*Administrative Government.*—Chapter I. Division of Administrative Offices. II. Administrative Prerogatives of the Crown.—III. The Title of the Crown.—IV. Origin and Distribution of Administrative Offices.—V. The Privy Council and its Committees.—VI. The Secretarial Departments.—VII. The Fiscal Administrative Officers.—VIII. Military and Naval Offices.—IX. Local Administrative Government.

General Index—Index of Statutes—Addenda et Corrigenda—Table of Authorities cited—Analysis of the Work.

OPINIONS OF THE PRESS.

'It is a clear, concise, well ordered and well executed exposition of the present state of the British Commonwealth........in nearly everything a model of good workmanship. Mr. Cox's style is graceful and intelligible ; his learning is great and varied, and his skill in setting forth the materials which he has spent many years in collecting, always from original authorities, is highly to be praised.' EXAMINER.

'A better text-book on the English Constitution can hardly be looked for.' EXAMINER (Second Notice).

'The work before us is a bold and ambitious effort of a thoughtful and able man. There are already numerous works which occupy more or less of the ground which Mr. Homersham Cox has selected for his learned researches, but none of them of the same comprehensive and scientific character as his book.' SOLICITORS' JOURNAL.

'Such is the plan of Mr. Cox's work, which has been ably carried into execution by its author. It is written in a clear style, contains a vast amount of constitutional knowledge, and is calculated to give a good idea of the working of our political system ; while merely party questions have been carefully eschewed.' JURIST, Sept. 3, 1864.

'We have for the first time the anatomy and physiology of the body politic displayed by an able demonstrator, and also for the first time, in a complete plan, exhaustive in its scope, well divided and arranged, and for all but technical purposes sufficiently minute in detail. ....In no single book, and scarcely in any one private library, could we, however well skilled in research, find all the information that is collected in this handsome volume of 750 pages.' MORNING HERALD.

'He has made a careful study of every direct or collateral source of information within his reach, has drawn together a mass of valuable information, and has arranged it in a way both scholarly and attractive........Of the three sections into which Mr. Cox's book is divided, that detailing the duties and responsibilities of the legislature is perhaps the most valuable for its summing-up of much reading among varied and contradictory authorities in a little space ; while the account of the administrative government is specially noteworthy for its information on subjects little understood and nowhere properly explained.' READER.

'One part of the matter, also, though not perhaps absolutely new, must have been collected with much difficulty from the obscure receptacles in which alone it is to be found, and it has certainly been set forth by Mr. Cox in a very judicious and forcible way........ It is no less true than singular that till the present work was published no easily accessible account of the Executive Government of England existed in our own language.' SATURDAY REVIEW.

'Das dritte von der Administration handelnde Buch ist wohl der schätzenswertheste Theil des ganzen, sehr umfassenden und wohlgeordneten Werkes, und enthält eine Menge wichtigster Daten aus Originalquellen. Während der Inhalt des Werkes sich einer streng historischen Methode anschliesst, ist der Styl klar und gefällig, ein Vorzug, der bei Schriften dieser Art nicht gar zu häufig ist.' NATIONAL ZEITUNG.

'It contains the largest amount of information on the subjects of which it treats which is anywhere to be obtained within the same compass, and which in fact can only be found elsewhere in a variety of works ; whilst with respect to the administrative institutions which form the subject of one of the divisions of the treatise, the same information is not to be found in any other book........A most admirable compendium ; accurate, full, clear, and exceedingly well arranged.' LAW MAGAZINE.

'Im Jahre 1763 resolvirten namentlich beide Häuser, dass das "privilege of parliament" sich auf die Abfassung und Veröffentlichung von aufrührerischen Schriften nicht beziehe. Andere Privilegien werden von den beiden Häusern als Körperschaften in Anspruch genommen, namentlich Freiheit der Debatte von jeder Controlle durch die Krone (welche Controlle, wie wir seiner Zeit nachgewiesen haben, ursprünglich nicht darauf gerichtet war, wie die einzelnen Mitglieder sich ausdrückten, sondern mit welchen Gegenständen sich das Parlament befasste) und Strafgewalt über die Mitglieder und über andere. Auf diese letztere, die Jurisdiction über Dritte und auf den Conflict mit der Jurisdiction der Gerichte bezieht sich die anzuführende Stelle aus Homersham Cox, " The Institutions of the English Government," London, 1863, einem Werke, das wir allen angelegentlich empfehlen, denen es um eine rechtsverständige und ungefärbte Darstellung dessen, was man englische Verfassung nennt, zu thun ist.' NORDDEUTSCHE ALLGEMEINE ZEITUNG, April 22, 1866.

London: H. SWEET, 3 Chancery Lane, Fleet Street. 1863.

By the same Author.

— ✦ —

8vo. pp. 214, price 8*s*. 6*d*. cloth,

ANTIENT

PARLIAMENTARY ELECTIONS:

A HISTORY SHEWING HOW PARLIAMENTS WERE CONSTITUTED AND REPRESENTATIVES OF THE PEOPLE ELECTED IN ANTIENT TIMES.

CONTENTS:—Chapter 1. The Rural Population of the Middle Ages. 2. Social Order of the Middle Ages. 3. The Saxon County Court. 4. The County Court after the Conquest. 5. The Origin of Parliaments. 6. The County Suffrage after the Fourteenth Century. 7. Procedure at Elections. 8. The Representation of Boroughs. 9. The Borough Electors.

APPENDIX:—Particulars taken from Manuscript Cartularies in the Record Office, shewing the tenures and services of tenants of various manors in the fourteenth and fifteenth centuries.

A few years ago the compilation of a satisfactory history of Antient Parliamentary Elections would have been almost impracticable. Some of the most important documents relating to the subject were but little known, and others entirely unknown. For example, when the elaborate *Report on the Dignity of a Peer* was published in 1820, the writers were not acquainted with the returns for the very first regularly constituted and complete House of Commons ever convened in this country—that which sat in the twenty-third year of the reign of EDWARD I. Those returns have since been published in the magnificent collection of Parliamentary Writs, edited by Sir FRANCIS PALGRAVE. The publication of that, and of the other great works issued by the Record Commission, marks a new era in the study of Constitutional History. But the very magnitude and number of the volumes, and the obscurity of the language in which they are written, render them inaccessible to all but the most diligent and determined inquirers. In another branch of the subject discussed in the present work—the Saxon polity—most important additions to our means of knowledge have been made within the last few years. In order to investigate accurately the original suffrage, either in counties or boroughs, a knowledge of English political institutions before the Conquest is requisite. It was not until 1840 that the *Antient Laws and Institutes of England* during the Anglo-Saxon period were made fully accessible by the publication of a collection of those laws, edited by Mr. THORPE, under the direction of the Commissioners of

Records. Another work, from which the Author has derived even more important assistance, is the *Codex Diplomaticus Aevi Saxonici*, edited by Mr. KEMBLE, which comprises upwards of fourteen hundred documents, many of which are of the greatest value in ascertaining the nature of Saxon Government.

Besides these recent publications, others, long known to inquirers into the antiquities of the English Constitution, have been consulted. The *Hundred Rolls* of the reign of EDWARD I. and his predecessor have been published more than half a century in two very large and closely-printed folio volumes; but the very obscure contracted Latin in which they are written, and the technical expressions with which they abound, render them unintelligible to all but a very few readers. Yet they are a vast mine of constitutional knowledge, and in some respects more interesting than even the *Domesday Book* itself. Copious use has been made of these and other authorities.

In the study of the subject here discussed, a preparatory consideration of the state of society to which our parliamentary institutions adapted themselves is indispensable. In the first place, therefore, the social and legal status of the various agricultural classes in the Middle Ages has been investigated. The close connection of this subject with the county suffrage will be immediately obvious. The third and fourth chapters treat of that much-controverted subject—the constitution of the antient County Courts. The condition of the persons who frequented those assemblies has long been a vexed problem of history; and there is reason to believe that it is now for the first time solved—principally by a most fatiguing and protracted exploration of the *Hundred Rolls*.

The fifth chapter relates to the origin of Parliament, and the development of the representative system in the thirteenth and fourteenth centuries. In this chapter are collected numerous authorities, which appear to answer in the affirmative the much-controverted question whether villans, the most numerous class of county tenantry, were contributory to parliamentary taxes and the wages of knights of the shire. In the next chapter the changes in the county suffrage in the reigns of HENRY IV. and HENRY VI. are traced, and the Author has endeavoured to show the real reasons for the violent innovations of the latter reign, and the disastrous consequences which ensued.

The remaining chapters deal with the method of procedure at elections, and the borough suffrage. The original suffrage of burgesses extended to all the free inhabitant-householders in towns; and all boroughs, without exception, were, at the original institution of the House of Commons, deemed entitled to send representatives to that assembly. The counter-theory—that only towns of royal demesne, and therefore under royal patronage, sent representatives—was supported by Dr. BRADY, and the *Report on the Dignity of a Peer*; but, as is here shown, the evidence of the returns to the first complete Parliament of EDWARD I. and of other antient documents is fatal to this opinion.

The whole book is a connected chain of arguments in support of these three propositions: that, according to the original constitution of Parliament—

1. *The whole body of free inhabitants of counties, including villans, had a right to vote at elections of knights of the shire.*

2. *All cities and boroughs were entitled to send members to Parliament.*

3. *All the householders of cities and boroughs had a right to vote at elections of citizens and burgesses.*

The subject has been regarded entirely in its historical aspects, apart from all reference to existing controversies. The treatise, indeed, shows that the social and political condition of the country at the period here under examination differed materially from that which at present prevails, and that therefore extreme caution is necessary in deducing from the antient history of Parliament lessons of modern application.

From the '*London Review*' (Jan. 18, 1868).

In this volume Mr. Homersham Cox has gone over the course which was partly traversed by Hallam, in that learned and very unreadable portion of his 'Middle Ages' which he devotes to the English Constitution. It differs, however, from the 'Middle Ages,' not only in being infinitely more readable and interesting, but for that completeness which it derives from the researches into the early history of the country, which have been actively pursued for some years past, and without which, as Mr. Cox himself points out, a satisfactory compilation of the history of ancient parliamentary elections would have been almost impracticable. Mr. Cox devotes a good portion of his space to an examination, based upon early records, of the condition of the rural population of this country during the Middle Ages. He points out, and in this he somewhat closely follows Hallam, that serfdom in this country was at no period nearly so extensive as the popular histories would lead us to infer, and that the villeins, who held by copyhold tenure, comprised among them many who were undoubtedly freemen.

The author then enters with some minuteness into the constitution of the county courts, both in the Saxon and Norman periods, and he gives some very interesting particulars which show the important position which these courts then held. The comparatively well-known dispute between Lanfranc, the Archbishop of Canterbury, and Odo, Bishop of Bayeux, concerning certain lands belonging to the Archbishop, and which was determined by a kind of county court assembled on Penenden Heath (where, strange to say, the nomination of candidates for the western division of Kent takes place at the present day), shows that even in the time of the Conqueror the people of the county assembled in their court had power to decide important questions of title to land. We extract from among the ancient documents quoted by Mr. Cox one relating to a county court held in the reign of King Cnut, at Aylston, in Herefordshire, which affords a valuable illustration of the constitution and working of these tribunals:—

'Here is made known in this writing that a shire moot sat at Ægelnorth's stone in the days of King Cnut. There sat Æthelstan bishop and Ranig ealdorman, and Eadwine the ealdorman's son and Leofwine Wulfige's son and Tharkil White; and Tofig Prud came there on the king's errand. And there were Bryning shire reeve and Ægelweard at Frome and Leofrine at Frome and Godric at Stoke and all the thanes in Herefordshire. Then came there to the moot Eadwine Eanwen's son and there raised a claim against his own mother to a portion of land namely at Wellington and Cradley. Then asked the bishop who would answer for his mother?' Then answered Tharkil White and said that he would if the claim were known to him. As the claim was not known to him three thanes were selected from the moot [who should ride] to where she was, and that was at Fauley.'

After giving a curious account of the manner in which the land was adjudged to Leoflæd, the wife of Tharkil, the record concludes thus:—

'Then Tharkil White stood up in the moot and prayed all the thanes to grant to his wife the lands which her kinswoman had given her. And they did so. And Tharkil then rode to Saint Æthelberht's monastery with the leave and witness of all the folk and caused it to be set in a Christ's book.'

Mr. Cox subsequently gives a singular instance of an appeal to the county court even from the king himself, and as a matter of right, not of favour :—

'A charter of the reign of Æthelred, some time before 995, relates to a claim of land brought in the first instance before that king on the application of one claimant Wynfiod, and subsequently, at the instance of the other claimant, Leofwine, referring to the county court. The king having heard Wynfiod, who produced her title, "sent forthwith by the archbishop and by those who were there to witness with him to Leofwine, and made this known to him. Then he would not [comply] unless it were carried to the shire mote. And they did so. Then the king sent by Abbot Ælfere his brief to the mote at Cuckhamslow, and greeted all the witan who were there assembled. That was Æthelsige bishop, and Æscwig bishop, and Ælfric abbot, and all the shire. And prayed and commanded that they should reconcile Wynfiod and Leofwine as justly as might ever seem to them most just.'"

The Saxon tribunals would seem, from the following curious account of a purchase by the Abbey of Ely, to have been largely used as a machinery for the transfer of land. The Abbey had purchased land at Bluntesham from Winothus for thirty pounds :—

'Five pounds were paid to him at Ely, and "the xxv. pounds which remained were paid to him before the King Edgar and his wise men ; which being done, Winothus in their presence delivered Bluntesham to the bishop with a deed." But afterwards the title of Winothus was disputed by one Boge, who asserted a prior title, alleging that the land had descended to him from his grandmother. The narrative proceeds: "After these things there was assembled the whole county of Huntingdon by Beornoth the alderman and by Afwold and by Ælfric. Forthwith there was a very great assembly. Wlfnoth is summoned and brings with him faithful men, namely all the better men (meliores) of vi Hundreds, and Lefsius, now of Ely, produced there the deed of Bluntesham, who being all gathered together they explained the claim and ventilated (ventilaverunt) and discussed the cause ; and the truth of the matter being known they by their judgment took the land from the sons of Bogan. . . . . . Then Wlnoth produced more than a thousand men, that by their oath he might assert his title to that land ; but the sons of Bogan were unwilling to take the oath, and so all determined that Winoth should have Bluntesham, and faithfully promised to be his helpers in this matter and to bear witness what they had done if ever at any time be or any of his heirs had need. And when all this was done Bishop Œlwood gave to Winoth xl shillings and an armlet worth lii marks because he had laboured much in this and was about to go beyond the sea in the service of God."'

It is as the assemblies in which representatives were chosen to serve in Parliament that the county courts have after all most interest for us, and to that branch of his subject and the ancient suffrages in counties and boroughs and the changes wrought in them, Mr. Cox devotes the greater share of his attention. It is remarkable that as late as the reign of Philip and Mary, Parliamentary candidates dissatisfied with the sheriff's decision as to a majority by show of hands had no right to call for a poll. In 1554 an action was brought by Sir Richard Buckley against Rice Thomas, the sheriff of Anglesea, for refusing him a poll at the county election in the first year of Queen Mary's reign, and the three judges before whom the case came agreed that the right did not exist. In the reign of James I. a more enlightened view of the subject was entertained, and it was decided that the sheriff was bound to take the poll. An account of the mode in which an election was conducted at York, a few years afterwards, shows the means taken for polling the electors to have been by no means of the most satisfactory description :—

'The sheriff was charged,—1. That upon his view, without poll, he gave his judgment for Sir Tho. Wentworth and Sir Tho. Fairfax, to be knights: when Sir Jo. Savyle meet voices ; 2ly, That when the poll required, he said it was only of courtesy to grant it ; 3ly, That he began the poll, but having polled about thirty-five, brake it off. . . . That upon Tuesday last he by his counsel alleged that the day of the election after eight of the clock he made proclamation and read the writ at the usual place. That the writ being read, he caused the gates to be shut ; he took a view of the freeholders, and returning, said he thought Sir Tho. Wentworth and Sir Tho. Fairfax were double the voices of Sir Jo. Savyle. That he chose to take the poll at the postern gate, and having polled about thirty-five, heard the fore gate was broken open, and many freeholders gone out upon Sir John Savyle's persuasion that the poll would last many days. That thereupon he brake off the poll.'

Although the reputation which Mr. Homersham Cox's previous work upon the English Constitution has acquired is of itself sufficient to secure for the book before us a large share of public attention, there are in almost every page indications of a research and painstaking labour which are alone sufficient to obtain for it the thorough appreciation of every one interested in the subject.

London: LONGMANS and CO. 1868

By the same Author.

—◆—

Pages 302. 8vo. Price 7s. 6d. cloth.

A HISTORY

OF THE

REFORM BILLS OF 1866 AND 1867.

CONTENTS.

CHAPTER

    I.—Reform Question since 1832.

    II.—The Franchise Bill of 1866.

    III.—The Redistribution of Seats Bill 1806.

    IV.—The Reform Bills of 1866 in Committee.

    V.—Accession of the Conservative Ministry in 1866.

    VI.—The Government Reform Resolutions of 1867.

    VII.—The First Project of a Reform Bill in 1867.

    VIII.—The Reform Bills presented March 1867.

    IX.—The Second Reading of the Reform Bill 1867.

    X.—The Reform Bill of 1867 in Committee: Borough Suffrage.

    XI.—The Reform Bill of 1867 in Committee: Clauses relating to Residence and Payment of Rates.

    XII.—General Enfranchisement of Householders in Boroughs.

    XIII.—The County Suffrage.

    XIV.—The Distribution of Seats.

    XV.—Distinction of Borough and County Franchise: Boundaries.

    XVI.—The Reform Bill of 1867: The Third Reading in the House of Commons.

    XVII.—The Reform Bill of 1867 in the House of Lords.

    XVIII.—The Lords' Amendments of the Reform Bill of 1867.

    XIX.—The Final Stages of the Reform Bill of 1867.

APPENDIX.—Abstract of the Reform Act of 1867, showing the Additions to, and material Variations from, the original Bill of March 1867.

    The original Reform Bill of 1867, showing the Omitted and Altered Clauses.

London: LONGMANS and CO. 1868.

K

39 Paternoster Row, E.C.

London: *January* 1868.

GENERAL LIST OF WORKS

PUBLISHED BY

Messrs. LONGMANS, GREEN, READER, and DYER.

Arts, Manufactures, &c.	12	Miscellaneous and Popular Metaphysical Works	6
Astronomy, Meteorology, Popular Geography, &c.	7	Natural History and Popular Science	7
Biography and Memoirs	3	Poetry and The Drama	18
Chemistry, Medicine, Surgery, and the Allied Sciences	10	Religious and Moral Works	14
Commerce, Navigation, and Mercantile Affairs	19	Rural Sports, &c.	19
Criticism, Philology, &c.	4	Travels, Voyages, &c.	16
Fine Arts and Illustrated Editions	11	Works of Fiction	17
Historical Works	1	Works of Utility and General Information	20
Index	21—24		

Historical Works.

Lord Macaulay's Works. Complete and uniform Library Edition. Edited by his Sister, Lady TREVELYAN. 8 vols. 8vo. with Portrait, price £5 5s. cloth, or £8 8s. bound in tree-calf by Rivière.

The History of England from the Fall of Wolsey to the Death of Elizabeth. By JAMES ANTHONY FROUDE, M.A. late Fellow of Exeter College, Oxford. Vols. I. to X. in 8vo. price £7 2s. cloth.

Vols. I. to IV. the Reign of Henry VIII. Third Edition, 54s.

Vols. V. and VI. the Reigns of Edward VI. and Mary. Third Edition, 28s.

Vols. VII. & VIII. the Reign of Elizabeth, Vols. I. & II. Fourth Edition, 28s.

Vols. IX. and X. the Reign of Elizabeth. Vols. III. and IV. 32s.

The History of England from the Accession of James II. By Lord MACAULAY.

LIBRARY EDITION, 5 vols. 8vo. £4.
CABINET EDITION, 8 vols. post 8vo. 48s.
PEOPLE'S EDITION, 4 vols. crown 8vo. 16s.

Revolutions in English History. By ROBERT VAUGHAN, D.D. 3 vols. 8vo. 30s.

An Essay on the History of the English Government and Constitution, from the Reign of Henry VII. to the Present Time. By JOHN EARL RUSSELL. Fourth Edition, revised. Crown 8vo. 6s.

On Parliamentary Government in England: its Origin, Development, and Practical Operation. By ALPHEUS TODD, Librarian of the Legislative Assembly of Canada. In two volumes. Vol. I. 8vo. 16s.

The History of England during the Reign of George the Third. By the Right Hon. W. N. MASSEY. Cabinet Edition, 4 vols. post 8vo. 24s.

The Constitutional History of England, since the Accession of George III. 1760—1860. By Sir THOMAS ERSKINE MAY, K.C.B. Second Edit. 2 vols. 8vo. 33s.

Brodie's Constitutional History of the British Empire from the Accession of Charles I. to the Restoration. Second Edition. 3 vols. 8vo. 36s.

Historical Studies. I. On Precursors of the French Revolution; II. Studies from the History of the Seventeenth Century; III. Leisure Hours of a Tourist. By HERMAN MERIVALE, M.A. 8vo. 12s. 6d.

The Government of England: its Structure and its Development. By WILLIAM EDWARD HEARN, LL.D. Professor of History and Political Economy in the University of Melbourne. 8vo. 14s.

Plutology; or, the Theory of the Efforts to Satisfy Human Wants. By the same Author. 8vo. 14s.

Lectures on the History of England. By WILLIAM LONGMAN. VOL. I. from the Earliest Times to the Death of King Edward II. with 6 Maps, a coloured Plate, and 53 Woodcuts. 8vo. 15s.

History of Civilization in England and France, Spain and Scotland. By HENRY THOMAS BUCKLE. Fifth Edition of the entire work, with a complete Index. 3 vols. crown 8vo. 24s.

The History of India, from the Earliest Period to the close of Lord Dalhousie's Administration. By JOHN CLARK MARSHMAN. 3 vols. crown 8vo. 22s. 6d.

History of the French in India, from the Founding of Pondichery in 1674 to its Capture in 1761. By Major G. B. MALLESON, Bengal Staff Corps, some time in political charge of the Princes of Mysore and the King of Oudh. 8vo. 16s.

Democracy in America. By ALEXIS DE TOCQUEVILLE. Translated by HENRY REEVE, with an Introductory Notice by the Translator. 2 vols. 8vo. 21s.

The Spanish Conquest in America, and its Relation to the History of Slavery and to the Government of Colonies. By ARTHUR HELPS. 4 vols. 8vo. £3. VOLS. I. & II. 28s. VOLS. III. & IV. 16s. each.

The Oxford Reformers of 1498; being a History of the Fellow-work of John Colet, Erasmus, and Thomas More. By FREDERIC SEEBOHM. 8vo. 12s.

History of the Reformation in Europe in the Time of Calvin. By J. H. MERLE D'AUBIGNÉ, D.D. VOLS. I. and II. 8vo. 28s. VOL. III. 12s. and VOL. IV. price 16s. VOL. V. in the press.

Library History of France, in 5 vols. 8vo. By EYRE EVANS CROWE. VOL. I. 14s. VOL. II. 15s. VOL. III. 18s. VOL. IV. 18s. VOL. V. just ready.

Lectures on the History of France. By the late Sir JAMES STEPHEN, LL.D. 2 vols. 8vo. 24s.

The History of Greece. By C. THIRLWALL, D.D. Lord Bishop of St. David's. 8 vols. fcp. 28s.

The Tale of the Great Persian War, from the Histories of Herodotus. By GEORGE W. COX, M.A. late Scholar of Trin. Coll. Oxon. Fcp. 7s. 6d.

Greek History from Themistocles to Alexander, in a Series of Lives from Plutarch. Revised and arranged by A. H. CLOUGH. Fcp. with 44 Woodcuts, 6s.

Critical History of the Language and Literature of Ancient Greece. By WILLIAM MURE, of Caldwell. 5 vols. 8vo. £3 9s.

History of the Literature of Ancient Greece. By Professor K. O. MÜLLER. Translated by the Right Hon. Sir GEORGE CORNEWALL LEWIS, Bart. and by J. W. DONALDSON, D.D. 3 vols. 8vo. 36s.

History of the City of Rome from its Foundation to the Sixteenth Century of the Christian Era. By THOMAS H. DYER, LL.D. 8vo. with 2 Maps, 15s.

History of the Romans under the Empire. By C. MERIVALE, LL.D. Chaplain to the Speaker. 8 vols. post 8vo. price 48s.

The Fall of the Roman Republic: a Short History of the Last Century of the Commonwealth. By the same Author. 12mo. 7s. 6d.

The Conversion of the Roman Empire; the Boyle Lectures for the year 1864, delivered at the Chapel Royal, Whitehall. By the same. 2nd Edition. 8vo. 8s. 6d.

The Conversion of the Northern Nations; the Boyle Lectures for 1865. By the same Author. 8vo. 8s. 6d.

Critical and Historical Essays contributed to the *Edinburgh Review*. By the Right Hon. Lord MACAULAY.

> LIBRARY EDITION, 3 vols. 8vo. 36s.
> TRAVELLER'S EDITION, in 1 vol. 21s.
> CABINET EDITION, 4 vols. 24s.
> POCKET EDITION, 3 vols. fcp. 21s.
> PEOPLE'S EDITION, 2 vols. crown 8vo. 8s.

The Papal Drama: an Historical Essay, wherein the Story of the Popedom of Rome is narrated from its Origin to the Present Time. By THOMAS H. GILL. 8vo. price 12s.

History of the Rise and Influence of the Spirit of Rationalism in Europe. By W. E. H. LECKY, M.A. Third Edition. 2 vols. 8vo. 25s.

od in History; Or, the Progress of Man's Faith in a Moral Order of the World. By the late Baron BUNSEN. Translated from the German by SUSANNA WINKWORTH; with a Preface by ARTHUR PENRHYN STANLEY, D.D. Dean of Westminster, 8 vols. 8vo. [Nearly ready.

he History of Philosophy, from Thales to Comte. By GEORGE HENRY LEWES. Third Edition, rewritten and enlarged. 2 vols. 8vo. 30s.

gypt's Place in Universal History; an Historical Investigation. By BARON BUNSEN, D.C.L. Translated by C. H. COTTRELL, M.A. with Additions by S. BIRCH, LL.D. 5 vols. 8vo. £8 14s. 6d.

Maunder's Historical Treasury; comprising a General Introductory Outline of Universal History, and a Series of Separate Histories. Fcp. 10s.

Historical and Chronological Encyclopædia, presenting in a brief and convenient form Chronological Notices of all the Great Events of Universal History. By B. B. WOODWARD, F.S.A. Librarian to the Queen. [In the press.

History of the Christian Church, from the Ascension of Christ to the Conversion of Constantine. By E. BURTON, D.D. late Regius Prof. of Divinity in the University of Oxford. Fcp. 3s. 6d.

Sketch of the History of the Church of England to the Revolution of 1688. By the Right Rev. T. V. SHORT, D.D. Bishop of St. Asaph. Crown 8vo. 10s. 6d.

History of the Early Church, from the First Preaching of the Gospel to the Council of Nicæa, A.D. 825. By the Author of 'Amy Herbert.' Fcp. 4s. 6d.

History of Wesleyan Methodism. By GEORGE SMITH, F.A.S. Fourth Edition, with numerous Portraits. 3 vols. crown 8vo. 7s. each.

The English Reformation. By F. C. MASSINGBERD, M.A. Chancellor of Lincoln. Fourth Edit. revised. Fcp. 7s. 6d.

— · —

Biography and Memoirs.

Dictionary of General Biography; containing Concise Memoirs and Notices of the most Eminent Persons of all Countries, from the Earliest Ages to the Present Time. With a Classified and Chronological Index of the Principal Names. Edited by WILLIAM L. R. CATES. 8vo. 21s.

Memoirs of Sir Philip Francis, K.C.B. with Correspondence and Journals. Commenced by the late JOSEPH PARKES; completed and edited by HERMAN MERIVALE, M.A. 2 vols. 8vo. with Portrait and Facsimiles, 80s.

Life of Baron Bunsen, by Baroness BUNSEN. Drawn chiefly from Family Papers. With Two Portraits taken at different periods of the Baron's life, and several Lithographic Views. 2 vols. 8vo. [Nearly ready.

Life and Correspondence of Richard Whately, D.D. late Archbishop of Dublin. By E. JANE WHATELY, Author of 'English Synonymes.' With 2 Portraits. 2 vols. 8vo. 28s. ;

Extracts of the Journals and Correspondence of Miss Berry, from the Year 1783 to 1852. Edited by Lady THERESA LEWIS. Second Edition, with 8 Portraits. 8 vols. 8vo. 42s.

Life of the Duke of Wellington. By the Rev. G. R. GLEIG, M.A. Popular Edition, carefully revised; with copious Additions. Crown 8vo. with Portrait, 5s.

History of my Religious Opinions. By J. H. NEWMAN, D.D. Being the Substance of Apologia pro Vitâ Suâ. Post 8vo. 6s.

Father Mathew: a Biography. By JOHN FRANCIS MAGUIRE, M.P. Popular Edition, with Portrait. Crown 8vo. 3s. 6d.

Rome; its Rulers and its Institutions. By the same Author. New Edition in preparation.

Letters and Life of Francis Bacon, including all his Occasional Works. Collected and edited, with a Commentary, by J. SPEDDING, Trin. Coll. Cantab. Vols. I. and II. 8vo. 24s.

Life of Pastor Fliedner, Founder of the Deaconesses' Institution at Kaiserswerth. Translated from the German, with the sanction of Fliedner's Family. By CATHERINE WINKWORTH. Fcp. 8vo. with Portrait, price 3s. 6d.

The Life of Franz Schubert, translated from the German of KREITZLE VON HELLBORN by ARTHUR DUKE COLERIDGE, M.A. late Fellow of King's College, Cambridge.   [Nearly ready.

Letters of Distinguished Musicians, viz. Gluck, Haydn, P. E. Bach, Weber, and Mendelssohn. Translated from the German by Lady WALLACE, with Three Portraits. Post 8vo. 14s.

Mozart's Letters (1769-1791), translated from the Collection of Dr. LUDWIG NOHL by Lady WALLACE. 2 vols. post 8vo. with Portrait and Facsimile, 18s.

Beethoven's Letters (1790-1826), from the Two Collections of Drs. NOHL and VON KÖCHEL. Translated by Lady WALLACE. 2 vols. post 8vo. Portrait, 18s.

Felix Mendelssohn's Letters from *Italy and Switzerland*, and *Letters from 1838 to 1847*, translated by Lady WALLACE. With Portrait. 2 vols. crown 8vo. 5s. each.

With Maximilian in Mexico From the Note-Book of a Mexican Officer. By MAX. Baron VON ALVENSLEBEN, late Lieutenant in the Imperial Mexican Army. Post 8vo. 7s. 6d.

Memoirs of Sir Henry Havelock, K.C.B. By JOHN CLARK MARSHMAN. Cabinet Edition, with Portrait. Crown 8vo. price 5s

Faraday as a Discoverer: a Memoir. By JOHN TYNDALL, LL.D. F.R.S. Professor of Natural Philosophy in the Royal Institution of Great Britain, and the Royal School of Mines. Crown 8vo.
                                [Nearly ready

Essays in Ecclesiastical Biography. By the Right Hon. Sir J. STEPHEN, LL.D. Cabinet Edition. Crown 8vo. 7s. 6d

Vicissitudes of Families. By Sir BERNARD BURKE, Ulster King of Arms. FIRST, SECOND, and THIRD SERIES. 3 vols. crown 8vo. 12s. 6d. each.

Maunder's Biographical Treasury. Thirteenth Edition, reconstructed and partly rewritten, with above 1,000 additional Memoirs, by W. L. R. CATES. Fcp. 10s. 6d

Criticism, Philosophy, Polity, &c.

On Representative Government. By JOHN STUART MILL, M.P. Third Edition. 8vo. 9s. crown 8vo. 2s.

On Liberty. By the same Author. Third Edition. Post 8vo. 7s. 6d. crown 8vo. 1s. 4d.

Principles of Political Economy. By the same. Sixth Edition. 2 vols. 8vo. 30s. or in 1 vol. crown 8vo. 5s.

A System of Logic, Ratiocinative and Inductive. By the same. Sixth Edition. 2 vols. 8vo. 25s.

Utilitarianism. By the same. 2d Edit. 8vo. 5s.

Dissertations and Discussions. By the same Author. 3 vols. 8vo. 36s.

Examination of Sir W. Hamilton's Philosophy, and of the Principal Philosophical Questions discussed in his Writings. By the same. Third Edition, 8vo. 16s.

Workmen and Wages at Home and Abroad; or, the Effects of Strikes, Combinations, and Trade Unions. By J. WARD, Author of 'The World in its Workshops,' &c. Post 8vo. 7s. 6d.

The Elements of Political Economy. By HENRY DUNNING MACLEOD, M.A. Barrister-at-Law. 8vo. 16s.

A Dictionary of Political Economy; Biographical, Bibliographical, Historical and Practical. By the same Author. VOL. I royal 8vo. 30s.

Lord Bacon's Works, collected and edited by R. L. ELLIS, M.A. J. SPEDDING, M.A. and D. D. HEATH. VOLS. I. to Philosophical Works, 5 vols. 8vo. £4 VOLS. VI. and VII. Literary and Professional Works, 2 vols. £1 16s.

The Institutes of Justinian; with English Introduction, Translation, and Notes. By T. C. SANDARS, M.A. Barrister-at-Law. Third Edition. 8vo. 15s.

The Ethics of Aristotle with Essays and Notes. By Sir A. GRANT, Bart. M.A. LL.D. Director of Public Instruction in the Bombay Presidency. Second Edition, revised and completed. 2 vols. 8vo. price 28s.

Bacon's Essays, with Annotations.
By R. WHATELY, D.D. late Archbishop of
Dublin. Sixth Edition. 8vo. 10s. 6d.

Elements of Logic. By R. WHATELY,
D.D. late Archbishop of Dublin. Ninth
Edition. 8vo. 10s. 6d. crown 8vo. 4s. 6d.

Elements of Rhetoric. By the same
Author. Seventh Edition. 8vo. 10s. 6d.
crown 8vo. 4s. 6d.

English Synonymes. Edited by Archbishop WHATELY. 5th Edition. Fcp. 8s.

An Outline of the Necessary
Laws of Thought; a Treatise on Pure and
Applied Logic. By the Most Rev. W.
THOMSON, D.D. Archbishop of York. Crown
8vo. 5s. 6d.

Analysis of Mr. Mill's System of
Logic. By W. STEBBING, M.A. Second
Edition. 12mo. 3s. 6d.

The Election of Representatives,
Parliamentary and Municipal; a Treatise.
By THOMAS HARE, Barrister-at-Law. Third
Edition, with Additions. Crown 8vo. 6s.

Speeches on Parliamentary Re-
form, delivered in the House of Commons
by the Right Hon. B. DISRAELI (1848-1866).
Edited by MONTAGUE CORRY, B.A. of
Lincoln's Inn, Barrister-at-Law. Second
Edition. 8vo. 12s.

Speeches of the Right Hon. Lord
MACAULAY, corrected by Himself. Library
Edition, 8vo. 12s. People's Edition, crown
8vo. 3s. 6d.

Lord Macaulay's Speeches on
Parliamentary Reform in 1831 and 1832.
16mo. 1s.

Inaugural Address delivered to the
University of St. Andrews. By JOHN
STUART MILL, Rector of the University.
Library Edition, 8vo. 5s. People's Edition,
crown 8vo. 1s.

A Dictionary of the English
Language. By R. G. LATHAM, M.A. M.D.
F.R.S. Founded on the Dictionary of Dr. S.
JOHNSON, as edited by the Rev. H. J. TODD,
with numerous Emendations and Additions.
Publishing in 36 Parts, price 3s. 6d. each,
to form 2 vols. 4to. VOL. I. in Two Parts,
price £3 10s. now ready.

Thesaurus of English Words and
Phrases, classified and arranged so as to
facilitate the Expression of Ideas, and assist
in Literary Composition. By P. M. ROGET,
M.D. New Edition. Crown 8vo. 10s. 6d.

Lectures on the Science of Lan-
guage, delivered at the Royal Institution.
By MAX MÜLLER, M.A. Taylorian Professor
in the University of Oxford. FIRST SERIES,
Fifth Edition, 12s. SECOND SERIES, 18s.

Chapters on Language. By F. W.
FARRAR, M.A. F.R.S. late Fellow of Trin.
Coll. Cambridge. Crown 8vo. 8s. 6d.

The Debater; a Series of Complete
Debates, Outlines of Debates, and Questions
for Discussion. By F. ROWTON. Fcp. 6s.

A Course of English Reading,
adapted to every taste and capacity; or,
How and What to Read. By the Rev. J.
PYCROFT, B.A. Fourth Edition, fcp. 5s.

Manual of English Literature,
Historical and Critical: with a Chapter on
English Metres. By THOMAS ARNOLD, M.A.
Second Edition. Crown 8vo. 7s. 6d.

Southey's Doctor, complete in One
Volume. Edited by the Rev. J.W. WARTER,
B.D. Square crown 8vo. 12s. 6d.

Historical and Critical Commen-
tary on the Old Testament; with a New
Translation. By M. M. KALISCH, Ph.D.
VOL. I. Genesis, 8vo. 18s. or adapted for the
General Reader, 12s. VOL. II. Exodus, 15s.
or adapted for the General Reader, 12s.
VOL. III. Leviticus, PART I. 15s. or adapted
for the General Reader, 8s.

A Hebrew Grammar, with Exercises.
By the same. PART I. Outlines with Exercises, 8vo. 12s. 6d. KEY, 5s. PART II. Ex-
ceptional Forms and Constructions, 12s. 6d.

A Latin-English Dictionary. By
J. T. WHITE, D.D. of Corpus Christi Col-
lege, and J. E. RIDDLE, M.A. of St. Edmund
Hall, Oxford. Imp. 8vo. pp. 2,128, price 42s.

A New Latin-English Dictionary,
abridged from the larger work of White and
Riddle (as above), by J. T. WHITE, D.D.
Joint-Author. 8vo. pp. 1,048, price 18s.

The Junior Scholar's Latin-English
Dictionary, abridged from the larger work
of White and Riddle (as above), by J. T.
WHITE, D.D. Square 12mo. pp. 662, price
7s. 6d.

An English-Greek Lexicon, containing all the Greek Words used by Writers
of good authority. By C. D. YONGE, B.A.
Fifth Edition. 4to. 21s.

Mr. Yonge's New Lexicon, En-
glish and Greek, abridged from his larger
work (as above). Square 12mo. 8s. 6d.

A Greek-English Lexicon. Compiled by H. G. Liddell, D.D. Dean of Christ Church, and R. Scott, D.D. Master of Balliol. Fifth Edition, crown 4to. 31s. 6d.

A Lexicon, Greek and English, abridged from Liddell and Scott's Greek-English Lexicon. Eleventh Edition, square 12mo. 7s. 6d.

A Sanskrit-English Dictionary, The Sanskrit words printed both in the original Devanagari and in Roman letters; with References to the Best Editions of Sanskrit Authors, and with Etymologies and Comparisons of Cognate Words chiefly in Greek, Latin, Gothic, and Anglo-Saxon. Compiled by T. Benfey. 8vo. 52s. 6d.

A Practical Dictionary of the French and English Languages. By Professor Léon Contanseau, many years French Examiner for Military and Civil Appointments, &c. 12th Edition, carefully revised. Post 8vo. 10s. 6d.

Contanseau's Pocket Dictionary, French and English, abridged from the above by the Author. New Edition. 18mo. price 3s. 6d.

New Practical Dictionary of the German Language; German-English, and English-German. By the Rev. W. L. Blackley, M.A., and Dr. Carl Martin Friedländer. Post 8vo. 7s. 6d.

Miscellaneous Works and Popular Metaphysics.

Lessons of Middle Age, with some Account of the Various Cities and Men. By A. K. H. B. Author of 'The Recreations of a Country Parson.' Post 8vo. 9s.

Recreations of a Country Parson. By A. K. H. B. Second Series. Crown 8vo. 3s. 6d.

The Commonplace Philosopher in Town and Country. By the same Author. Crown 8vo. 3s. 6d.

Leisure Hours in Town; Essays Consolatory, Æsthetical, Moral, Social, and Domestic. By the same. Crown 8vo. 3s. 6d.

The Autumn Holidays of a Country Parson. By the same. Crown 8vo. 3s. 6d.

The Graver Thoughts of a Country Parson, Second Series. By the same. Crown 8vo. 3s. 6d.

Critical Essays of a Country Parson, selected from Essays contributed to Fraser's Magazine. By the same. Crown 8vo. 3s. 6d

Sunday Afternoons at the Parish Church of a Scottish University City. By the same. Crown 8vo. 3s. 6d.

Short Studies on Great Subjects. By James Anthony Froude, M.A. late Fellow of Exeter College, Oxford. Second Edition, complete in One Volume. 8vo. price 12s.

Studies in Parliament: a Series of Sketches of Leading Politicians. By R. H. Hutton. (Reprinted from the Pall Mall Gazette.) Crown 8vo. 4s. 6d.

Lord Macaulay's Miscellaneous Writings.

Library Edition, 2 vols. 8vo. Portrait, 21s.

People's Edition, 1 vol. crown 8vo. 4s. 6d.

The Rev. Sydney Smith's Miscellaneous Works; including his Contributions to the Edinburgh Review. People's Edition, 2 vols. crown 8vo. 8s.

Elementary Sketches of Moral Philosophy, delivered at the Royal Institution. By the same Author. Fcp. 6s.

The Wit and Wisdom of the Rev. Sydney Smith: a Selection of the most memorable Passages in his Writings and Conversation. 16mo. 5s.

Epigrams, Ancient and Modern: Humorous, Witty, Satirical, Moral, and Panegyrical. Edited by Rev. John Booth, B.A. Cambridge. Second Edition, revised and enlarged. Fcp. 7s. 6d.

The Folk-Lore of the Northern Counties of England and the Borders. By William Henderson. With an Appendix on Household Stories by the Rev. S. Baring-Gould. Crown 8vo. 9s. 6d.

Christian Schools and Scholars; or, Sketches of Education from the Christian Era to the Council of Trent. By the Author of 'The Three Chancellors,' &c. 2 vols. 8vo. price 30s.

The Pedigree of the English People; an Argument, Historical and Scientific, on the Ethnology of the English. By Thomas Nicholas, M.A. Ph.D. 8vo. 16s.

The English and their Origin: a Prologue to authentic English History. By Luke Owen Pike, M.A. Barrister-at-Law. 8vo. 9s.

Essays selected from Contributions to the *Edinburgh Review*. By HENRY ROGERS. Second Edition. 3 vols. fcp. 21s.

Reason and Faith, their Claims and Conflicts. By the same Author. New Edition, revised and extended. Crown 8vo. 6s. 6d.

The Eclipse of Faith; or, a Visit to a Religious Sceptic. By the same Author. Eleventh Edition. Fcp. 5s.

Defence of the Eclipse of Faith, by its Author. Third Edition. Fcp. 8s. 6d.

Selections from the Correspondence of R. E. H. Greyson. By the same Author. Third Edition. Crown 8vo. 7s. 6d.

Chips from a German Workshop; being Essays on the Science of Religion, and on Mythology, Traditions, end Customs. By MAX MÜLLER, M.A. Fellow of All Souls' College, Oxford. 2 vols. 8vo. 21s.

The Secret of Hegel: being the Hegelian System in Origin, Principle, Form, and Matter. By JAMES HUTCHISON STIRLING. 2 vols. 8vo. 28s.

An Introduction to Mental Philosophy, on the Inductive Method. By J. D. MORELL, M.A. LL.D. 8vo. 12s.

Elements of Psychology, containing the Analysis of the Intellectual Powers. By the same Author. Post 8vo. 7s. 6d.

The Senses and the Intellect. By ALEXANDER BAIN, M.A. Prof. of Logic in the Univ. of Aberdeen. Second Edition. 8vo. 15s.

The Emotions and the Will, by the same Author. Second Edition. 8vo. 15s.

On the Study of Character, including an Estimate of Phrenology. By the same Author. 8vo. 9s.

Time and Space: a Metaphysical Essay. By SHADWORTH H. HODGSON. 8vo. price 16s.

Occasional Essays. By C. W. HOSKYNS, Author of 'Talpa, or the Chronicles of a Clay Farm,' &c. 16mo. 5s. 6d.

The Way to Rest: Results from a Life-search after Religious Truth. By R. VAUGHAN, D.D. Crown 8vo. 7s. 6d.

From Matter to Spirit. By SOPHIA E. DE MORGAN. With a Preface by Professor DE MORGAN. Post 8vo. 8s. 6d.

The Philosophy of Necessity; or, Natural Law as applicable to Mental, Moral, and Social Science. By CHARLES BRAY. Second Edition. 8vo. 9s.

The Education of the Feelings and Affections. By the same Author. Third Edition. 8vo. 8s. 6d.

On Force, its Mental and Moral Correlates. By the same Author. 8vo. 5s.

Astronomy, Meteorology, Popular Geography, &c.

Outlines of Astronomy. By Sir J. F. W. HERSCHEL, Bart. M.A. Ninth Edition, revised; with Plates and Woodcuts. 8vo. 18s.

Saturn and its System. By RICHARD A. PROCTOR, B.A. late Scholar of St. John's Coll. Camb. and King's Coll. London. 8vo. with 14 Plates, 14s.

The Handbook of the Stars. By the same Author. Square fcp. 8vo. with 3 Maps. price 5s.

Celestial Objects for Common Telescopes. By T. W. WEBB, M.A. F.R.A.S. Revised Edition, with Illustrations.
[*Nearly ready.*

A General Dictionary of Geography, Descriptive, Physical, Statistical, and Historical; forming a complete Gazetteer of the World. By A. KEITH JOHNSTON, F.R.S.E. New Edition, revised to July 1867. 8vo. 31s. 6d.

M'Culloch's Dictionary, Geographical, Statistical, and Historical, of the various Countries, Places, and principal Natural Objects in the World. Revised Edition, with the Statistical Information throughout brought up to the latest returns. By FREDERICK MARTIN. 4 vols. 8vo. with coloured Maps, £4 4s.

A Manual of Geography, Physical, Industrial, and Political. By W. HUGHES, F.R.G.S. Prof. of Geog. in King's Coll. and in Queen's Coll. Lond. With 6 Maps. Fcp. 7s. 6d.

The States of the River Plate: their Industries and Commerce, Sheep Farming, Sheep Breeding, Cattle Feeding, and Meat Preserving; the Employment of Capital, Land and Stock and their Values, Labour and its Remuneration. By WILFRID LATHAM, Buenos Ayres. Second Edition. 8vo. 12s.

Hawaii: the Past, Present, and Future of its Island-Kingdom; an Historical Account of the Sandwich Islands. By MANLEY HOPKINS, Hawaiian Consul-General, &c. Second Edition, revised and continued; with Portrait, Map, and 8 other Illustrations. Post 8vo. 12s. 6d.

Maunder's Treasury of Geography, Physical, Historical, Descriptive, and Political. Edited by W. HUGHES, F.R.G.S. With 7 Maps and 16 Plates. Fcp. 10s. 6d.

Physical Geography for Schools and General Readers. By M. F. MAURY, LL.D. Fcp. with 2 Charts, 2s. 6d.

Natural History and Popular Science.

Elementary Treatise on Physics, Experimental and Applied, for the use of Colleges and Schools. Translated and edited from GANOT's 'Eléméns de Physique' (with the Author's sanction) by E. ATKINSON, Ph.D. F.C.S. New Edition, revised and enlarged; with a Coloured Plate and 620 Woodcuts. Post 8vo. 15s.

The Elements of Physics or Natural Philosophy. By NEIL ARNOTT, M.D. F.R.S. Physician Extraordinary to the Queen. Sixth Edition, rewritten and completed. 2 Parts, 8vo. 21s.

Dove's Law of Storms, considered in connexion with the ordinary Movements of the Atmosphere. Translated by R. H. SCOTT, M.A. T.C.D. 8vo. 10s. 6d.

Rooks Classified and Described. By BERNHARD VON COTTA. An English Edition, by P. H. LAWRENCE (with English, German, and French Synonymes), revised by the Author. Post 8vo. 14s.

Sound: a Course of Eight Lectures delivered at the Royal Institution of Great Britain. By Professor JOHN TYNDALL, LL.D. F.R.S. Crown 8vo. with Portrait and Woodcuts, 9s

Heat Considered as a Mode of Motion. By Professor JOHN TYNDALL, LL.D. F.R.S. Third Edition. Crown 8vo. with Woodcuts, 10s. 6d.

Light: its Influence on Life and Health. By FORBES WINSLOW, M.D. D.C.L. Oxon. (Hon.). Fcp. 8vo. 6s.

An Essay on Dew, and several Appearances connected with it. By W. C. WELLS. Edited, with Annotations, by L. P. CASELLA, F.R.A.S. and an Appendix by R. STRACHAN, F.M.S. 8vo. 5s.

A Treatise on Electricity, in Theory and Practice. By A. DE LA RIVE, Prof. in the Academy of Geneva. Translated by C. V. WALKER, F.R.S. 3 vols. 8vo. with Woodcuts, £3 13s.

A Preliminary Discourse on the Study of Natural Philosophy. By Sir JOHN F. W. HERSCHEL Bart. Revised Edition, with Vignette Title. Fcp. 3s. 6d.

The Correlation of Physical Forces. By W. R. GROVE, Q.C. V.P.R.S. Fifth Edition, revised and augmented by a Discourse on Continuity. 8vo. 10s. 6d. The Discourse on Continuity, separately, price 2s. 6d

Manual of Geology. By S. HAUGHTON, M.D. F.R.S. Fellow of Trin. Coll. and Prof. of Geol. in the Univ. of Dublin. Second Edition, with 66 Woodcuts. Fcp. 7s. 6d.

A Guide to Geology. By J. PHILLIPS, M.A. Prof. of Geol. in the Univ. of Oxford. Fifth Edition. Fcp. 4s.

A Glossary of Mineralogy. By H. W. BRISTOW, F.G.S. of the Geological Survey of Great Britain. With 486 Figures. Crown 8vo. 6s.

Van Der Hoeven's Handbook of ZOOLOGY. Translated from the Second Dutch Edition by the Rev. W. CLARK, M.D. F.R.S. 2 vols. 8vo. with 24 Plates of Figures, 60s.

Professor Owen's Lectures on the Comparative Anatomy and Physiology of the Invertebrate Animals. Second Edition, with 235 Woodcuts. 8vo. 21s.

The Comparative Anatomy and Physiology of the Vertebrate Animals. By RICHARD OWEN, F.R.S. D.C.L. 3 vols. 8vo. with upwards of 1,200 Woodcuts. VOLS. I. and II. price 21s. each. VOL. III. (completing the work) is nearly ready.

The First Man and His Place in Creation, considered on the Principles of Common Sense from a Christian Point of View; with an Appendix on the Negro. By GEORGE MOORE, M.D. M.R.C.P.L &c. Post 8vo. 8s. 6d.

ṭe Primitive Inhabitants of Scandinavia: an Essay on Comparative Ethnography, and a contribution to the History of the Developement of Mankind. Containing a description of the Implements, Dwellings, Tombs, and Mode of Living of the Savages in the North of Europe during the Stone Age. By SVEN NILSSON. Translated from the Author's MS. of the Third Edition; with an Introduction by Sir JOHN LUBBOCK. 8vo. with numerous Plates. 　　　　　　　　　　[*Nearly ready.*

ṭhe Lake Dwellings of Switzerland and other Parts of Europe. By Dr. F. KELLER, President of the Antiquarian Association of Zürich. Translated and arranged by J. E. LEE, F.S.A. F.G.S. Author of 'Isca Silurum.' With several Woodcuts and nearly 100 Plates of Figures. Royal 8vo. 31s. 6d.

ṭomes without Hands: a Description of the Habitations of Animals, classed according to their Principle of Construction. By Rev. J. G. WOOD, M.A. F.L.S. With about 140 Vignettes on Wood (20 full size of page). Second Edition. 8vo. 21s.

ṭible Animals; being an Account of the various Birds, Beasts, Fishes, and other Animals mentioned in the Holy Scriptures. By the Rev. J. G. WOOD, M.A. F.L.S. Copiously Illustrated with Original Designs, made under the Author's superintendence and engraved on Wood. In course of publication monthly, to be completed in 20 Parts, price 1s. each, forming One Volume, uniform with 'Homes without Hands.'

ṭhe Harmonies of Nature and Unity of Creation. By Dr. G. HARTWIG, 8vo. with numerous Illustrations, 18s.

ṭhe Sea and its Living Wonders. By the same Author. Third Edition, enlarged. 8vo. with many Illustrations, 21s.

ṭhe Tropical World. By the same Author. With 8 Chromoxylographs and 172 Woodcuts. 8vo. 21s.

ṭhe Polar World: a Popular Account of Nature and Man in the Arctic and Antarctic Regions. By the same Author. 8vo. with numerous Illustrations. 　　[*Nearly ready.*

ṭeylon. By Sir J. EMERSON TENNENT, K.C.S. LL.D. 5th Edition; with Maps, &c. and 90 Wood Engravings. 2 vols. 8vo. £2 10s.

ṭhe Wild Elephant, its Structure and Habits, with the Method of Taking and Training it in Ceylon. By the same Author. Fcp. with 22 Woodcuts, 8s. 6d.

Manual of Corals and Sea Jellies. By J. R. GREENE, B.A. Edited by J. A. GALBRAITH, M.A. and S. HAUGHTON, M.D. Fcp. with 39 Woodcuts, 5s.

Manual of Sponges and Animalcule; with a General Introduction on the Principles of Zoology. By the same Author and Editors. Fcp with 16 Woodcuts. 2s.

Manual of the Metalloids. By J. APJOHN, M.D. F.R.S. and the same Editors. 2nd Edition. Fcp. with 38 Woodcuts, 7s. 6d.

A Familiar History of Birds. By E. STANLEY, D.D. late Lord Bishop of Norwich. Fcp. with Woodcuts, 3s. 6d.

Kirby and Spence's Introduction to Entomology, or Elements of the Natural History of Insects. Crown 8vo. 5s.

Maunder's Treasury of Natural History, or Popular Dictionary of Zoology. Revised and corrected by T. S. COBBOLD, M.D. Fcp. with 900 Woodcuts, 10s.

The Elements of Botany for Families and Schools. Tenth Edition, revised by THOMAS MOORE, F.L.S. Fcp. with 154 Woodcuts, 2s. 6d.

The Treasury of Botany, or Popular Dictionary of the Vegetable Kingdom; with which is Incorporated a Glossary of Botanical Terms. Edited by J. LINDLEY, F.R.S. and T. MOORE, F.L.S. assisted by eminent Contributors. Pp. 1,274, with 274 Woodcuts and 20 Steel Plates. 2 Parts, fcp. 20s.

The British Flora; comprising the Phænogamous or Flowering Plants and the Ferns. By Sir W. J. HOOKER, K.H. and G. A. WALKER-ARNOTT, LL.D. 12mo. with 12 Plates, 14s. or coloured, 21s.

The Rose Amateur's Guide. By THOMAS RIVERS. New Edition. Fcp. 4s.

Loudon's Encyclopædia of Plants; comprising the Specific Character, Description, Culture, History, &c. of all the Plants found in Great Britain. With upwards of 12,000 Woodcuts. 8vo. 42s.

Loudon's Encyclopædia of Trees and Shrubs; containing the Hardy Trees and Shrubs of Great Britain scientifically and popularly described. With 2,000 Woodcuts. 8vo. 50s.

Maunder's Scientific and Literary Treasury; a Popular Encyclopædia of Science, Literature, and Art. New Edition, thoroughly revised and in great part rewritten, with above 1,000 new articles, by J. Y. JOHNSON, CORR. M.Z.S. Fcp. 10s. 6d.

A Dictionary of Science, Literature, and Art. Fourth Edition, re-edited by the late W. T. BRANDE (the Author) and GEORGE W. COX, M.A. 3 vols. medium 8vo. price 63s. cloth.

Essays from the Edinburgh and Quarterly Reviews; with Addresses and other Pieces. By Sir J. F. W. HERSCHEL, Bart. M.A. 8vo. 18s.

Chemistry, Medicine, Surgery, and the Allied Sciences.

A Dictionary of Chemistry and the Allied Branches of other Sciences. By HENRY WATTS, F.C.S. assisted by eminent Contributors. 5 vols. medium 8vo. In course of publication In Parts. VOL. I. 31s. 6d. VOL. II. 26s. VOL. III. 31s. 6d. and VOL. IV. 24s. are now ready.

Handbook of Chemical Analysis, adapted to the Unitary System of Notation. By F. T. CONINGTON, M.A. F.C.S. Post 8vo. 7s. 6d.

Conington's Tables of Qualitative Analysis, to accompany the above, 2s. 6d.

Elements of Chemistry, Theoretical and Practical. By WILLIAM A. MILLER, M.D. LL.D. Professor of Chemistry, King's College, London. 3 vols. 8vo. £3. PART I. CHEMICAL PHYSICS, Revised Edition, 15s. PART II. INORGANIC CHEMISTRY, 21s. PART III. ORGANIC CHEMISTRY, 24s.

A Manual of Chemistry, Descriptive and Theoretical. By WILLIAM ODLING, M.B. F.R.S. PART I. 8vo. 9s. PART II. nearly ready.

A Course of Practical Chemistry, for the use of Medical Students. By the same Author. New Edition, with 70 new Woodcuts. Crown 8vo. 7s. 6d.

Lectures on Animal Chemistry Delivered at the Royal College of Physicians in 1865. By the same Author. Crown 8vo. 4s. 6d.

The Toxicologist's Guide: a New Manual on Poisons, giving the Best Methods to be pursued for the Detection of Poisons By J. HORSLEY, F.C.S. Analytical Chemist. Post 8vo. 8s. 6d.

The Diagnosis, Pathology, and Treatment of Diseases of Women; including the Diagnosis of Pregnancy. By GRAILY HEWITT, M.D. &c. Second Edition, enlarged; with 116 Woodcut Illustrations. 8vo. 21s.

Lectures on the Diseases of Infancy and Childhood. By CHARLES WEST, M.D. &c. 5th Edition, revised and enlarged 8vo. 16s.

Exposition of the Signs and Symptoms of Pregnancy: with other Papers on subjects connected with Midwifery. By W. F. MONTGOMERY, M.A. M.D. M.R.I.A. 8vo. with Illustrations, 25s.

A System of Surgery, Theoretical and Practical, in Treatises by Various Authors. Edited by T. HOLMES, M. Cantab. Assistant-Surgeon to St. George's Hospital. 4 vols. 8vo. £4 18s.

Vol. I. General Pathology, 21s.

Vol. II. Local Injuries: Gun-shot Wounds, Injuries of the Head, Back, Face, Neck, Chest, Abdomen, Pelvis, of the Upper and Lower Extremities, and Diseases of the Eye. 21s.

Vol. III. Operative Surgery. Diseases of the Organs of Circulation, Locomotion &c. 21s.

Vol. IV. Diseases of the Organs of Digestion, of the Genito-Urinary System, and of the Breast, Thyroid Gland, and Skin; with APPENDIX and GENERAL INDEX. 30s.

Lectures on the Principles and Practice of Physic. By THOMAS WATSON, M.D. Physician-Extraordinary to the Queen. New Edition In preparation.

Lectures on Surgical Pathology. By J. PAGET, F.R.S. Surgeon-Extraordinary to the Queen. Edited by W. TURNER, M. New Edition In preparation.

A Treatise on the Continued Fevers of Great Britain. By C. MURCHISON, M.D. Senior Physician to the London Fever Hospital. 8vo. with coloured Plates, 18s.

Outlines of Physiology, Human and Comparative. By JOHN MARSHALL, F.R.C.S. Professor of Surgery in University College, London, and Surgeon to the University College Hospital. 2 vols. crown 8vo. with 122 Woodcuts, 32s.

Anatomy, Descriptive and Surgical. By HENRY GRAY, F.R.S. With 410 Wood Engravings from Dissections. Fourth Edition, by T. HOLMES, M.A. Cantab. Royal 8vo. 28s.

The Cyclopædia of Anatomy and Physiology. Edited by the late R. B. TODD, M.D. F.R.S. Assisted by nearly all the most eminent cultivators of Physiological Science of the present age. 5 vols. 8vo. with 2,853 Woodcuts, £6 6s.

Physiological Anatomy and Physiology of Man. By the late R. B. TODD, M.D. F.R.S. and W. BOWMAN, F.R.S. of King's College. With numerous Illustrations. VOL. II. 8vo. 25s.

VOL. I. New Edition by Dr. LIONEL S. BEALE, F.R.S. in course of publication; PART I. with 8 Plates, 7s. 6d.

Histological Demonstrations; a Guide to the Microscopical Examination of the Animal Tissues in Health and Disease, for the use of the Medical and Veterinary Professions. By G. HARLEY, M.D. F.R.S. Prof. in Univ. Coll. London; and G. T. BROWN, M.R.C.V.S. Professor of Veterinary Medicine, and one of the Inspecting Officers in the Cattle Plague Department of the Privy Council. Post 8vo. with 223 Woodcuts, 12s.

A Dictionary of Practical Medicine. By J. COPLAND, M.D. F.R.S. Abridged from the larger work by the Author, assisted by J. C. COPLAND, M.R.C.S. and throughout brought down to the present state of Medical Science. Pp. 1,560, in 8vo. price 36s.

The Works of Sir B. C. Brodie, Bart. collected and arranged by CHARLES HAWKINS, F.R.C.S.E. 3 vols. 8vo. with Medallion and Facsimile, 48s.

A Manual of Materia Medica and Therapeutics, abridged from Dr. PEREIRA's Elements by F. J. FARRE, M.D. assisted by R. BENTLEY, M.R.C.S. and by R. WARINGTON, F.R.S. 1 vol. 8vo. with 90 Woodcuts, 21s.

Thomson's Conspectus of the British Pharmacopœia. Twenty-fourth Edition, corrected by E. LLOYD BIRKETT, M.D. 18mo. 5s. 6d.

Manual of the Domestic Practice of Medicine. By W. B. KESTEVEN, F.R.C.S.E. Third Edition, thoroughly revised, with Additions. Fcp. 5s.

Sea-Air and Sea-Bathing for Children and Invalids. By WILLIAM STRANGE, M.D. Fcp. 3s.

The Restoration of Health; or, the Application of the Laws of Hygiene to the Recovery of Health: a Manual for the Invalid, and a Guide in the Sick Room. By W. STRANGE, M.D. Fcp. 6s.

Gymnasts and Gymnastics. By JOHN H. HOWARD, late Professor of Gymnastics, Comm. Coll. Rippouden. Second Edition, revised and enlarged, with various Selections from the best Authors, containing 445 Exercises; and illustrated with 135 Woodcuts, including the most Recent Improvements in the different Apparatus now used in the various Clubs, &c. Crown 8vo. 10s. 6d.

The Fine Arts, and *Illustrated Editions.*

Half-Hour Lectures on the History and Practice of the Fine and Ornamental Arts. By W. B. SCOTT. Second Edition. Crown 8vo. with 50 Woodcut Illustrations, 8s. 6d.

An Introduction to the Study of National Music; Comprising Researches into Popular Songs, Traditions, and Customs. By CARL ENGEL. With Frontispiece and numerous Musical Illustrations. 8vo. 16s.

Lectures on the History of Modern Music, delivered at the Royal Institution. By JOHN HULLAH. FIRST COURSE, with Chronological Tables, post 8vo. 6s. 6d. SECOND COURSE, the Transition Period, with 26 Specimens, 8vo. 16s.

The Chorale Book for England; a complete Hymn-Book in accordance with the Services and Festivals of the Church of England: the Hymns translated by Miss C. WINKWORTH; the Tunes arranged by Prof. W. S. BENNETT and OTTO GOLDSCHMIDT. Fcp. 4to. 12s. 6d.

Congregational Edition. Fcp. 2s.

Six Lectures on Harmony. Delivered at the Royal Institution of Great Britain before Easter 1867. By G. A. MACFARREN. 8vo. 10s. 6d.

Sacred Music for Family Use; A Selection of Pieces for One, Two, or more Voices, from the best Composers, Foreign and English. Edited by JOHN HULLAH. 1 vol. music folio, 21s.

The New Testament, illustrated with Wood Engravings after the Early Masters, chiefly of the Italian School. Crown 4to. 63s. cloth, gilt top; or £5 5s. morocco.

Lyra Germanica, the Christian Year. Translated by CATHERINE WINKWORTH; with 125 Illustrations on Wood drawn by J. LEIGHTON, F.S.A. Quarto, 21s.

Lyra Germanica. the Christian Life. Translated by CATHERINE WINKWORTH; with about 200 Woodcut Illustrations by J. LEIGHTON, F.S.A. and other Artists. Quarto, 21s.

The Life of Man Symbolised by the Months of the Year in their Seasons and Phases; with Passages selected from Ancient and Modern Authors. By RICHARD PIGOT. Accompanied by a Series of 25 full-page Illustrations and numerous Marginal Devices, Decorative Initial Letters, and Tailpieces, engraved on Wood from Original Designs by JOHN LEIGHTON, F.S.A. Quarto, 42s.

Cats' and Farlie's Moral Emblems; with Aphorisms, Adages, and Proverbs of all Nations : comprising 121 Illustrations on Wood by J. LEIGHTON, F.S.A. with an appropriate Text by R. PIGOT. Imperial 8vo. 31s. 6d.

Shakspeare's Sentiments and Similes printed in Black and Gold, and illuminated in the Missal style by HENRY NOEL HUMPHREYS. In massive covers, containing the Medallion and Cypher of Shakspeare. Square post 8vo. 21s.

Sacred and Legendary Art. By Mrs. JAMESON. With numerous Etchings and Woodcut Illustrations. 6 vols. square crown 8vo. price £5 15s. 6d. cloth, or £12 12s. bound in morocco by Rivière. To be had also in cloth only, in FOUR SERIES, as follows:—

Legends of the Saints and Martyrs. Fifth Edition, with 19 Etchings and 187 Woodcuts. 2 vols. square crown 8vo. 31s. 6d.

Legends of the Monastic Orders. Third Edition, with 11 Etchings and 88 Woodcuts. 1 vol. square crown 8vo. 21s.

Legends of the Madonna. Third Edition, with 27 Etchings and 165 Woodcuts. 1 vol. square crown 8vo. 21s.

The History of Our Lord, as exemplified in Works of Art. Completed by Lady EASTLAKE. Second Edition, with 13 Etchings and 281 Woodcuts. 2 vols. square crown 8vo. 42s.

Arts, Manufactures, &c.

Drawing from Nature; a Series of Progressive Instructions in Sketching, from Elementary Studies to Finished Views, with Examples from Switzerland and the Pyrenees. By GEORGE BARNARD, Professor of Drawing at Rugby School. With 18 Lithographic Plates and 108 Wood Engravings. Imp. 8vo. 25s. or in Three Parts, royal 8vo. 7s. 6d. each.

Gwilt's Encyclopædia of Architecture. Fifth Edition, with Alterations and considerable Additions, by WYATT PAPWORTH. Additionally illustrated with nearly 400 Wood Engravings by O. JEWITT, and upwards of 100 other new Woodcuts. 8vo. 52s. 6d.

Tuscan Sculptors, their Lives, Works, and Times. With 45 Etchings and 28 Woodcuts from Original Drawings and Photographs. By CHARLES C. PERKINS. 2 vols. imp. 8vo. 63s.

Original Designs for Wood-Carving, with Practical Instructions in the Art. By A. F. B. With 20 Plates of Illustrations engraved on Wood. Quarto, 18s.

The Grammar of Heraldry: containing a Description of all the Principal Charges used in Armory, the Signification of Heraldic Terms, and the Rules to be observed in Blazoning and Marshalling. By JOHN E. CUSSANS. Fcp. with 196 Woodcuts, 4s. 6d.

Hints on Household Taste in Furniture and Decoration. By CHARLES L. EASTLAKE, Architect. With numerous Illustrations engraved on Wood. [*Nearly ready.*

The Engineer's Handbook; explaining the Principles which should guide the young Engineer in the Construction of Machinery. By C. S. LOWNDES. Post 8vo. 5s.

The Elements of Mechanism.
By T. M. GOODEVE, M.A. Prof. of Mechanics at the R.M. Acad. Woolwich. Second Edition, with 217 Woodcuts. Post 8vo. 6s. 6d.

Ure's Dictionary of Arts, Manufactures, and Mines. Sixth Edition, chiefly re-written and greatly enlarged by ROBERT HUNT, F.R.S., assisted by numerous Contributors eminent in Science and the Arts, and familiar with Manufactures. With 2,000 Woodcuts. 3 vols. medium 8vo. £4 14s. 6d.

Treatise on Mills and Millwork.
By W. FAIRBAIRN, C.E. F.R.S. With 18 Plates and 322 Woodcuts. 2 vols. 8vo. 32s.

Useful Information for Engineers. By the same Author. FIRST, SECOND, and THIRD SERIES, with many Plates and Woodcuts. 3 vols. crown 8vo. 10s. 6d. each.

The Application of Cast and Wrought Iron to Building Purposes. By the same Author. Third Edition, with 6 Plates and 118 Woodcuts. 8vo. 16s.

Iron Ship Building, its History and Progress, as comprised in a Series of Experimental Researches on the Laws of Strain; the Strengths, Forms, and other conditions of the Material; and an Inquiry into the Present and Prospective State of the Navy, including the Experimental Results on the Resisting Powers of Armour Plates and Shot at High Velocities. By W. FAIRBAIRN, C.E. F.R.S. With 4 Plates and 130 Woodcuts. 8vo. 18s.

Encyclopædia of Civil Engineering, Historical, Theoretical, and Practical. By E. CRESY, C.E. With above 3,000 Woodcuts. 8vo. 42s.

The Artisan Club's Treatise on the Steam Engine, in its various Applications to Mines, Mills, Steam Navigation, Railways, and Agriculture. By J. BOURNE, C.E. New Edition; with 37 Plates and 546 Woodcuts. 4to. 42s.

A Treatise on the Screw Propeller, Screw Vessels, and Screw Engines, as adapted for purposes of Peace and War; with notices of other Methods of Propulsion, Tables of the Dimensions and Performance of Screw Steamers, and Detailed Specifications of Ships and Engines. By the same Author. Third Edition, with 54 Plates and 287 Woodcuts. Quarto, 63s.

Catechism of the Steam Engine, in its various Applications to Mines, Mills, Steam Navigation, Railways, and Agriculture. By JOHN BOURNE, C.E. New Edition, with 199 Woodcuts. Fcp. 6s.

Handbook of the Steam Engine, by the same Author, forming a KEY to the Catechism of the Steam Engine, with 67 Woodcuts. Fcp. 9s.

A History of the Machine- Wrought Hosiery and Lace Manufactures. By WILLIAM FELKIN, F.L.S. F.S.S. With 3 Steel Plates, 10 Lithographic Plates of Machinery, and 10 Coloured Impressions of Patterns of Lace. Royal 8vo. 21s.

Manual of Practical Assaying, for the use of Metallurgists, Captains of Mines, and Assayers in general; with copious Tables for Ascertaining in Assays of Gold and Silver the precise amount in Ounces, Pennyweights, and Grains of Noble Metal contained in One Ton of Ore from a Given Quantity. By JOHN MITCHELL, F.C.S. 8vo. with 360 Woodcuts, 21s.

The Art of Perfumery; the History and Theory of Odours, and the Methods of Extracting the Aromas of Plants. By Dr. PIESSE, F.C.S. Third Edition, with 53 Woodcuts. Crown 8vo. 10s. 6d.

Chemical, Natural, and Physical Magic, for Juveniles during the Holidays. By the same Author. Third Edition, enlarged with 38 Woodcuts. Fcp. 6s.

Loudon's Encyclopædia of Agriculture: Comprising the Laying-out, Improvement, and Management of Landed Property, and the Cultivation and Economy of the Productions of Agriculture. With 1,100 Woodcuts. 8vo. 31s. 6d.

Loudon's Encyclopædia of Gardening: Comprising the Theory and Practice of Horticulture, Floriculture, Arboriculture, and Landscape Gardening. With 1,000 Woodcuts. 8vo. 31s. 6d.

Loudon's Encyclopædia of Cottage, Farm, and Villa Architecture and Furniture. With more than 2,000 Woodcuts. 8vo. 42s.

Garden Architecture and Landscape Gardening, illustrating the Architectural Embellishment of Gardens; with Remarks on Landscape Gardening in its relation to Architecture. By JOHN ARTHUR HUGHES. 8vo. with 194 Woodcuts, 14s.

Bayldon's Art of Valuing Rents and Tillages, and Claims of Tenants upon Quitting Farms, both at Michaelmas and Lady-Day. Eighth Edition, revised by J. C. MORTON. 8vo. 10s. 6d.

Religious and *Moral Works.*

An Exposition of the 39 Articles, Historical and Doctrinal. By E. Harold Browne, D.D. Lord Bishop of Ely. Seventh Edition. 8vo. 16s.

Examination-Questions on Bishop Browne's Exposition of the Articles. By the Rev. J. Gorle, M.A. Fcp. 3s. 6d.

The Life and Reign of David King of Israel. By George Smith, LL.D. F.A.S. Crown 8vo. 7s. 6d.

The Acts of the Apostles; with a Commentary, and Practical and Devotional Suggestions for Readers and Students of the English Bible. By the Rev. F. C. Cook, M.A., Canon of Exeter, &c. New Edition, 8vo. 12s. 6d.

The Life and Epistles of St. Paul. By W. J. Conybeare, M.A. late Fellow of Trin. Coll. Cantab. and J. S. Howson, D.D. Principal of Liverpool Coll.

Library Edition, with all the Original Illustrations, Maps, Landscapes on Steel, Woodcuts, &c. 2 vols. 4to. 48s.

Intermediate Edition, with a Selection of Maps, Plates, and Woodcuts. 2 vols. square crown 8vo. 31s. 6d.

People's Edition, revised and condensed, with 46 Illustrations and Maps. 2 vols. crown 8vo. 12s.

The Voyage and Shipwreck of St. Paul; with Dissertations on the Ships and Navigation of the Ancients. By James Smith, F.R.S. Crown 8vo. Charts, 10s. 6d.

Evidence of the Truth of the Christian Religion derived from the Literal Fulfilment of Prophecy, particularly as Illustrated by the History of the Jews, and the Discoveries of Recent Travellers. By Alexander Keith, D.D. 37th Edition, with numerous Plates, in square 8vo. 12s. 6d.; also the 39th Edition, in post 8vo. with 5 Plates, 6s.

The History and Destiny of the World and of the Church, according to Scripture. By the same Author. Square 8vo. with 40 Illustrations, 10s.

History of Israel to the Death of Moses. By Heinrich Ewald, Professor of the University of Göttingen. Translated from the German. Edited, with a Preface, by Russell Martineau, M.A. Professor of Hebrew in Manchester New College, London. 8vo. 18s.

A Critical and Grammatical Com-mentary on St. Paul's Epistles. By C. J. Ellicott, D.D. Lord Bishop of Gloucester and Bristol. 8vo.

Galatians, Third Edition, 8s. 6d.
Ephesians, Fourth Edition, 8s. 6d.
Pastoral Epistles, Third Edition, 10s. 6d.
Philippians, Colossians, and Philemon, Third Edition, 10s. 6d.
Thessalonians, Third Edition, 7s. 6d.

Historical Lectures on the Life of Our Lord Jesus Christ; being the Hulsean Lectures for 1859. By the same Author. Fourth Edition. 8vo. 10s. 6d.

The Destiny of the Creature; and other Sermons preached before the University of Cambridge. By the same. Post 8vo. 5s.

The Greek Testament; with Notes, Grammatical and Exegetical. By the Rev. W. Webster, M.A. and the Rev. W. F. Wilkinson, M.A. 2 vols. 8vo. £2 4s.

Vol. I. the Gospels and Acts, 20s.
Vol. II. the Epistles and Apocalypse, 24s.

An Introduction to the Study of the New Testament, Critical, Exegetical, and Theological. By the Rev. S. Davidson, D.D. LL.D. 2 vols. 8vo. [*In the press.*

Rev. T. H. Horne's Introduction to the Critical Study and Knowledge of the Holy Scriptures. Eleventh Edition, corrected, and extended under careful Editorial revision. With 4 Maps and 22 Woodcuts and Facsimiles. 4 vols. 8vo. £3 13s. 6d.

Rev. T. H. Horne's Compendious In-troduction to the Study of the Bible, being an Analysis of the larger work by the same Author. Re-edited by the Rev. John Ayre, M.A. With Maps, &c. Post 8vo. 9s.

The Treasury of Bible Know-ledge; being a Dictionary of the Books, Persons, Places, Events, and other Matters of which mention is made in Holy Scripture; intended to establish its Authority and illustrate its Contents. By Rev. J. Ayre, M.A. With Maps, 15 Plates, and numerous Woodcuts. Fcp. 10s. 6d.

Every-day Scripture Difficulties explained and illustrated. By J. E. Prescott, M.A. Vol. I. *Matthew* and *Mark;* Vol. II. *Luke* and *John.* 2 vols. 8vo. 9s. each.

he Pentateuch and Book of Joshua Critically Examined. By the Right Rev. J. W. COLENSO, D.D. Lord Bishop of Natal. People's Edition, in 1 vol. crown 8vo. 6s. or in 5 Parts, 1s. each.

he Church and the World: Essays on Questions of the Day. By various Writers. Edited by Rev. ORBY SHIPLEY, M.A. FIRST and SECOND SERIES. 2 vols. 8vo. 15s. each. THIRD SERIES preparing for publication.

racts for the Day; a Series of Essays on Theological Subjects. By various Authors. Edited by the Rev. ORBY SHIPLEY, M.A. I. *Priestly Absolution Scriptural*, 9d. II. *Purgatory*, 9d. III. *The Seven Sacraments*, 1s. 6d. IV. *Miracles and Prayer*, 6d. V. *The Real Presence*, 1s. 3d. VI. *Casuistry*, 1s. VII. *Unction of the Sick*, 9d. VIII. *The Rule of Worship*, 9d. IX. *Popular Rationalism*, 9d.

he Formation of Christendom. PART I. By T. W. ALLIES. 8vo. 12s.

hristendom's Divisions; a Philosophical Sketch of the Divisions of the Christian Family in East and West. By EDMUND S. FFOULKES, formerly Fellow and Tutor of Jesus Coll. Oxford. Post 8vo. 7s. 6d.

hristendom's Divisions, Part II. *Greeks and Latins*, being a History of their Dissentions and Overtures for Peace down to the Reformation. By the same Author. Post 8vo. 15s.

he Hidden Wisdom of Christ and the Key of Knowledge; or, History of the Apocrypha. By ERNEST DE BUNSEN. 2 vols. 8vo. 28s.

he Keys of St. Peter; or, the House of Rechab, connected with the History of Symbolism and Idolatry. By the same Author. 8vo. 14s.

he Temporal Mission of the Holy Ghost; or, Reason and Revelation. By Archbishop MANNING, D.D. Second Edition. Crown 8vo. 8s. 6d.

ngland and Christendom. By the same Author. Preceded by an Introduction on the Tendencies of Religion in England, and the Catholic Practice of Prayer for the Restoration of Christian Nations to the Unity of the Church. Post 8vo. 10s. 6d.

ssays on Religion and Literature. Edited by Archbishop MANNING, D.D. FIRST SERIES, 8vo. 10s. 6d. SECOND SERIES, 14s.

Essays and Reviews. By the Rev. W. TEMPLE, D.D. the Rev. R. WILLIAMS, B.D. the Rev. B. POWELL, M.A. the Rev. H. B. WILSON, B.D. C. W. GOODWIN, M.A. the Rev. M. PATTISON, B.D. and the Rev. B. JOWETT, M.A. 12th Edition. Fcp. 5s.

Mosheim's Ecclesiastical History. MURDOCK and SOAMES's Translation and Notes, re-edited by the Rev. W. STUBBS, M.A. 3 vols. 8vo. 45s.

Bishop Jeremy Taylor's Entire Works: With Life by BISHOP HEBER. Revised and corrected by the Rev. C. P. EDEN, 10 vols. £5 5s.

Passing Thoughts on Religion. By the Author of 'Amy Herbert.' New Edition. Fcp. 5s.

Self-examination before Confirmation. By the same Author. 32mo. 1s. 6d.

Readings for a Month Preparatory to Confirmation from Writers of the Early and English Church. By the same. Fcp. 4s.

Readings for Every Day in Lent, compiled from the Writings of Bishop JEREMY TAYLOR. By the same. Fcp. 5s.

Preparation for the Holy Communion; the Devotions chiefly from the works of JEREMY TAYLOR. By the same. 32mo. 3s.

Principles of Education drawn from Nature and Revelation, and Applied to Female Education in the Upper Classes. By the same. 2 vols. fcp. 12s. 6d.

The Wife's Manual; or, Prayers, Thoughts, and Songs on Several Occasions of a Matron's Life. By the Rev. W. CALVERT, M.A. Crown 8vo. 10s. 6d.

Lyra Domestica; Christian Songs for Domestic Edification. Translated from the *Psaltery and Harp* of C. J. P. SPITTA, and from other sources, by RICHARD MASSIE. FIRST and SECOND SERIES, fcp. 4s. 6d. each.

'Spiritual Songs' for the Sundays and Holidays throughout the Year. By J. S. B. MONSELL, LL.D. Vicar of Egham and Rural Dean. Sixth Thousand. Fcp. price 4s. 6d.

The Beatitudes: Abasement before God: Sorrow for Sin; Meekness of Spirit; Desire for Holiness; Gentleness; Purity of Heart; the Peace-makers; Sufferings for Christ. By the same Author. Third Edition, revised. Fcp. 3s. 6d.

His Presence not his Memory, 1855. By the same Author, in memory of his Son. Fifth Edition. 16mo. 1s.

Lyra Germanica, translated from the German by Miss C. WINKWORTH. FIRST SERIES, Hymns for the Sundays and Chief Festivals; SECOND SERIES, the Christian Life. Fcp. 3s. 6d. each SERIES.

Hymns from Lyra Germanica, 18mo. 1s.

Lyra Eucharistica ; Hymns and Verses on the Holy Communion, Ancient and Modern; with other Poems. Edited by the Rev. ORBY SHIPLEY, M.A. Second Edition. Fcp. 7s. 6d.

Lyra Messianica ; Hymns and Verses on the Life of Christ, Ancient and Modern; with other Poems. By the same Editor. Second Edition, enlarged. Fcp. 7s. 6d.

Lyra Mystica ; Hymns and Verses on Sacred Subjects, Ancient and Modern. By the same Editor. Fcp. 7s. 6d.

Lyra Sacra ; Hymns, Ancient and Modern, Odes, and Fragments of Sacred Poetry. Edited by the Rev. B. W. SAVILE, M.A. Third Edition, enlarged. Fcp. 5s.

The Catholic Doctrine of the Atonement; an Historical Inquiry into its Development in the Church: with an Introduction on the Principle of Theological Developments. By H. N. OXENHAM, M.A. 8vo. 8s. 6d.

Endeavours after the Christian Life: Discourses. By JAMES MARTINEAU. Fourth and cheaper Edition, carefully revised; the Two Series complete in One Volume. Post 8vo. 7s. 6d.

Introductory Lessons on the History of Religious Worship; being a Sequel to the 'Lessons on Christian Evidences.' By RICHARD WHATELY, D.D. New Edition. 18mo. 2s. 6d.

Travels, Voyages, &c.

The North-West Peninsula of Iceland; being the Journal of a Tour in Iceland in the Summer of 1862. By C. W. SHEPHERD, M.A. F.Z.S. With a Map and Two Illustrations. Fcp. 8vo. 7s. 6d.

Pictures in Tyrol and Elsewhere. From a Family Sketch-Book. By the Author of 'A Voyage en Zigzag,' &c. Quarto, with numerous Illustrations, 21s.

How we Spent the Summer; or, a Voyage en Zigzag in Switzerland and Tyrol with some Members of the ALPINE CLUB. From the Sketch-Book of one of the Party. Third Edition, re-drawn. In oblong 4to. with about 300 Illustrations, 15s.

Beaten Tracks ; or, Pen and Pencil Sketches in Italy. By the Authoress of 'A Voyage en Zigzag.' With 42 Plates, containing about 200 Sketches from Drawings made on the Spot. 8vo. 16s.

Florence, the New Capital of Italy. By C. R. WELD. With several Engravings on Wood, from Drawings by the Author. Post 8vo. 12s. 6d.

Map of the Chain of Mont Blanc, from an actual Survey in 1863—1864. By A. ADAMS-REILLY, F.R.G.S. M.A.C. Published under the Authority of the Alpine Club. In Chromolithography on extra stout drawing-paper 28in. × 17in. price 10s. or mounted on canvas in a folding case, 12s. 6d.

History of Discovery in our Australasian Colonies, Australia, Tasmania, and New Zealand, from the Earliest Date to the Present Day. By WILLIAM HOWITT. With 3 Maps of the Recent Explorations from Official Sources. 2 vols. 8vo. 20s.

The Capital of the Tycoon: Narrative of a 3 Years' Residence in Japan. By Sir RUTHERFORD ALCOCK, K.C.B. 2 vols. 8vo. with numerous Illustrations, 42s.

The Dolomite Mountains. Excursions through Tyrol, Carinthia, Carniola, and Friuli. By J. GILBERT and G. C. CHURCHILL, F.R.G.S. With numerous Illustrations. Square crown 8vo. 21s.

A Lady's Tour Round Monte Rosa; including Visits to the Italian Valleys. With Map and Illustrations. Post 8vo. 14s.

Guide to the Pyrenees, for the use of Mountaineers. By CHARLES PACKE. With Maps, &c. and Appendix. Fcp. 6s.

The Alpine Guide. By JOHN BALL, M.R.I.A. late President of the Alpine Club. Post 8vo. with Maps and other Illustrations.

Guide to the Eastern Alps. [Just ready.

Guide to the Western Alps, including Mont Blanc, Monte Rosa, Zermatt, &c. price 7s. 6d.

Guide to the Oberland and all Switzerland, excepting the Neighbourhood of Monte Rosa and the Great St. Bernard; with Lombardy and the adjoining portion of Tyrol. 7s. 6d.

The Englishman in India. By CHARLES RAIKES, Esq. C.S.I. formerly Commissioner of Lahore. Post 8vo. 7s. 6d.

The Irish in America. By JOHN FRANCIS MAGUIRE, M.P. for Cork. Post 8vo. 12s. 6d.

The Arch of Titus and the Spoils of the Temple; an Historical and Critical Lecture, with Authentic Illustrations. By WILLIAM KNIGHT, M.A. With 10 Woodcuts from Ancient Remains. 4to. 10s.

Curiosities of London; exhibiting the most Rare and Remarkable Objects of Interest in the Metropolis; with nearly Sixty Years' Personal Recollections. By JOHN TIMBS, F.S.A. New Edition, corrected and enlarged. 8vo. Portrait, 21s.

Narratives of Shipwrecks of the Royal Navy between 1793 and 1857, compiled from Official Documents in the Admiralty by W. O. S. GILLY; with a Preface by W. S. GILLY, D.D. 3d Edition, fcp. 5s.

Visits to Remarkable Places: Old Halls, Battle-Fields, and Scenes Illustrative of Striking Passages in English History and Poetry. By WILLIAM HOWITT. 2 vols. square crown 8vo. with Wood Engravings, 25s.

The Rural Life of England. By the same Author. With Woodcuts by Bewick and Williams. Medium 8vo. 12s. 6d.

A Week at the Land's End. By J. T. BLIGHT; assisted by E. H. RODD, R. Q. COUCH, and J. RALFS. With Map and 96 Woodcuts. Fcp. 6s. 6d.

Works of Fiction.

The Warden: a Novel. By ANTHONY TROLLOPE. Crown 8vo. 2s. 6d.

Barchester Towers: a Sequel to 'The Warden.' By the same Author. Crown 8vo. 3s. 6d.

Stories and Tales by the Author of 'Amy Herbert,' uniform Edition, each Tale or Story complete in a single volume.

AMY HERBERT, 2s. 6d.	KATHARINE ASHTON, 3s. 6d.
GERTRUDE, 2s. 6d.	
EARL'S DAUGHTER, 2s. 6d.	MARGARET PERCIVAL, 5s.
EXPERIENCE OF LIFE, 2s. 6d.	LANETON PARSONAGE, 4s. 6d.
CLEVE HALL, 3s. 6d.	URSULA, 4s. 6d.
IVORS, 3s. 6d.	

A Glimpse of the World. By the Author of 'Amy Herbert.' Fcp. 7s. 6d.

The Journal of a Home Life. By the same Author. Post 8vo. 9s. 6d.

After Life; a Sequel to the 'Journal of a Home Life.' By the same Author. Post 8vo.
[Nearly ready.

Gallus; or, Roman Scenes of the Time of Augustus: with Notes and Excursuses illustrative of the Manners and Customs of the Ancient Romans. From the German of Prof. BECKER. New Edit. Post 8vo. 7s. 6d.

Charicles; a Tale illustrative of Private Life among the Ancient Greeks: with Notes and Excursuses. From the German of Prof. BECKER. New Edition, Post 8vo. 7s. 6d.

Springdale Abbey: Extracts from the Letters and Diaries of an ENGLISH PREACHER. 8vo. 12s.

The Six Sisters of the Valleys: an Historical Romance. By W. BRAMLEY-MOORE, M.A. Incumbent of Gerrard's Cross, Bucks. Fourth Edition, with 14 Illustrations. Crown 8vo. 5s.

Tales from Greek Mythology. By GEORGE W. COX, M.A. late Scholar of Trin. Coll. Oxon. Second Edition. Square 16mo. 3s. 6d.

Tales of the Gods and Heroes. By the same Author. Second Edition. Fcp. 5s.

Tales of Thebes and Argos. By the same Author. Fcp. 4s. 6d.

A Manual of Mythology, in the form of Question and Answer. By the same Author. Fcp. 3s.

Cabinet Edition of Novels and Tales by By G. J. WHITE MELVILLE:—

The Gladiators: a Tale of Rome and Judæa. Crown 8vo. 5s.

Digby Grand, 5s.

Kate Coventry, 5s.

General Bounce, 5s.

Holmby House, 5s.

Good for Nothing, 6s.

The Queen's Maries, 6s.

The Interpreter, a Tale of the War.

Poetry and *The Drama.*

Moore's Poetical Works, Cheapest Editions complete in 1 vol. including the Autobiographical Prefaces and Author's last Notes, which are still copyright. Crown 8vo. ruby type, with Portrait, 6s. or People's Edition, in larger type, 12s. 6d

Moore's Poetical Works, as above, Library Edition, medium 8vo. with Portrait and Vignette, 14s. or in 10 vols. fcp. 8s. 6d. each.

Moore's Lalla Rookh, Tenniel's Edition, with 68 Wood Engravings from Original Drawings and other Illustrations. Fcp. 4to. 21s.

Moore's Irish Melodies, Maclise's Edition, with 161 Steel Plates from Original Drawings. Super-royal 8vo. 31s. 6d.

Miniature Edition of Moore's Irish *Melodies,* with Maclise's Illustrations, (as above) reduced in Lithography. Imp. 16mo. 10s. 6d.

Southey's Poetical Works, with the Author's last Corrections and copyright Additions. Library Edition, in 1 vol. medium 8vo. with Portrait and Vignette, 14s. or in 10 vols. fcp. 8s. 6d. each.

Lays of Ancient Rome; with *Ivry* and the *Armada.* By the Right Hon. Lord Macaulay. 16mo. 4s. 6d.

Lord Macaulay's Lays of Ancient Rome. With 90 Illustrations on Wood, Original and from the Antique, from Drawings by G. Scharf. Fcp. 4to. 21s.

Miniature Edition of Lord Macaulay's Lays of Ancient Rome, with Scharf's Illustrations (as above) reduced in Lithography. Imp. 16mo. 10s. 6d.

Poems. By Jean Ingelow. Twelfth Edition. Fcp. 8vo. 5s.

Poems by Jean Ingelow. A New Edition, with nearly 100 Illustrations by Eminent Artists, engraved on Wood by the Brothers Dalziel. Fcp. 4to. 21s.

A Story of Doom, and other Poems. By Jean Ingelow. Fcp. 5s.

Poetical Works of Letitia Elizabeth Landon (L.E.L.) 2 vols. 16mo. 10s.

Playtime with the Poets : a Selection of the best English Poetry for the use of Children. By a Lady. Crown 8vo. 5s.

Memories of some Contemporary Poets; with Selections from their Writings. By Emily Taylor. Royal 18mo. 5s.

Bowdler's Family Shakspeare; cheaper Genuine Edition, complete in 1 vol. large type, with 36 Woodcut Illustrations, price 14s. or in 6 pocket vols. 3s. 6d. each.

Shakspeare's Sonnets never before Interpreted ; his Private Friends identified; together with a recovered Likeness of Himself. By Gerald Massey. 8vo. 18s.

Arundines Cami, sive Musarum Cantabrigiensium Lusus Canori. Collegit atque edidit H. Drury, M.A. Editio Sexta, curavit H. J. Hodgson, M.A. Crown 8vo. price 7s. 6d.

Horatii Opera, Library Edition, with Copious English Notes, Marginal References and Various Readings. Edited by the Rev. J. E. Yonge, M.A. 8vo. 21s.

Eight Comedies of Aristophanes, viz. the Acharnians, Knights, Clouds, Wasps, Peace, Birds, Frogs, *and* Plutus. Translated into Rhymed Metres by Leonard-Hampson Rudd, M.A. 8vo. 15s.

The Æneid of Virgil Translated into English Verse. By John Conington, M.A. Corpus Professor of Latin in the University of Oxford. Crown 8vo. 9s.

The Iliad of Homer Translated into Blank Verse. By Ichabod Charles Wright, M.A. 2 vols. crown 8vo. 21s.

The Iliad of Homer in English Hexameter Verse. By J. Henry Dart, M.A. of Exeter College, Oxford. Square crown 8vo. 21s.

Dante's Divine Comedy, translated in English Terza Rima by John Dayman, M.A. [With the Italian Text, after *Brunetti,* interpaged.] 8vo. 21s.

The Holy Child. A Poem in Four Cantos; also an Ode to Silence, and other Poems. By S. Jenner, M.A. Fcp. 8vo. 5s.

Poetical Works of John Edmund Reade; with final Revision and Additions. 3 vols. fcp. 18s. or each vol. separately, 6s.

Rural Sports, &c.

Encyclopædia of Rural Sports; a Complete Account, Historical, Practical, and Descriptive, of Hunting, Shooting, Fishing, Racing, &c. By D. P. BLAINE. With above 600 Woodcuts (20 from Designs by JOHN LEECH). 8vo. 42s.

Col. Hawker's Instructions to Young Sportsmen in all that relates to Guns and Shooting. Revised by the Author's Son. Square crown 8vo. with Illustrations. 18s.

The Rifle, its Theory and Prac- tice. By ARTHUR WALKER (79th Highlanders), Staff, Hythe and Fleetwood Schools of Musketry. Second Edition. Crown 8vo. with 125 Woodcuts, 5s.

The Dead Shot, or Sportsman's Complete Guide; a Treatise on the Use of the Gun, Dog-breaking, Pigeon-shooting, &c. By MARKSMAN. Fcp. with Plates, 5s.

A Book on Angling: being a Complete Treatise on the Art of Angling in every branch, including full Illustrated Lists of Salmon Flies. By FRANCIS FRANCIS. Second Edition, with Portrait and 15 other Plates, plain and coloured. Post 8vo. 15s.

Ephemera's Handbook of Ang- ling: Teaching Fly-fishing, Trolling, Bottom-fishing, Salmon-fishing; with the Natural History of River Fish. Fcp. 5s.

The Fly-Fisher's Entomology. By ALFRED RONALDS. With coloured Representations of the Natural and Artificial Insect. Sixth Edition; with 20 coloured Plates. 8vo. 14s.

Youatt on the Horse. Revised and enlarged by W. WATSON, M.R.C.V.S. 8vo. with numerous Woodcuts, 12s. 6d.

Youatt on the Dog. (By the same Author.) 8vo. with numerous Woodcuts, 6s.

The Cricket Field; or, the History and the Science of the Game of Cricket. By JAMES PYCROFT, B.A. 4th Edition. Fcp. 5s.

The Horse-Trainer's and Sports- man's Guide: with Considerations on the Duties of Grooms, on Purchasing Blood Stock, and on Veterinary Examination. By DIGBY COLLINS. Post 8vo. 6s.

Blaine's Veterinary Art: a Treatise on the Anatomy, Physiology, and Curative Treatment of the Diseases of the Horse, Neat Cattle, and Sheep. Seventh Edition, revised and enlarged by C. STEEL. 8vo. with Plates and Woodcuts, 18s.

On Drill and Manœuvres of Cavalry, combined with Horse Artillery. By Major-Gen. MICHAEL W. SMITH, C.B. 8vo. 12s. 6d.

The Horse's Foot, and how to keep it Sound. By W. MILES, Esq. 9th Edition, with Illustrations. Imp. 8vo. 12s. 6d.

A Plain Treatise on Horse-shoeing. By the same Author. Post 8vo. with Illustrations, 2s. 6d.

Stables and Stable Fittings. By the same. Imp. 8vo. with 13 Plates, 15s.

Remarks on Horses' Teeth, addressed to Purchasers. By the same. Post 8vo. 1s. 6d.

The Dog in Health and Disease. By STONEHENGE. With 70 Wood Engravings. New Edition. Square crown 8vo. 10s. 6d.

The Greyhound. By the same Author. Revised Edition, with 24 Portraits of Greyhounds. Square crown 8vo. 21s.

The Ox, his Diseases and their Treatment; with an Essay on Parturition in the Cow. By J. R. DOBSON, M.R.C.V.S. Crown 8vo. with Illustrations, 7s. 6d.

Commerce, Navigation, and Mercantile Affairs.

Banking, Currency, and the Ex- changes: a Practical Treatise. By ARTHUR CRUMP, Bank Manager, formerly of the Bank of England. Post 8vo. 6s.

The Elements of Banking. By HENRY DUNNING MACLEOD, M.A. of Trinity College, Cambridge, and of the Inner Temple, Barrister-at-Law. Post 8vo.
[*Nearly ready.*

The Theory and Practice of Banking. By HENRY DUNNING MACLEOD, M.A. Barrister-at-Law. Second Edition, entirely remodelled. 2 vols. 8vo. 30s.

A Dictionary, Practical, Theo- retical, and Historical, of Commerce and Commercial Navigation. By J. R. M'CULLOCH. New Edition in the press.

Elements of Maritime International Law. By WILLIAM DE BURGH, B.A. of the Inner Temple, Barrister-at-Law. 8vo.

Papers on Maritime Legislation; with a Translation of the German Mercantile Law relating to Maritime Commerce. By ERNST EMIL WENDT. 8vo. 10s. 6d.

Practical Guide for British Shipmasters to United States Ports. By PIERREPONT EDWARDS, Her Britannic Majesty's Vice-Consul at New York. Post 8vo. 8s. 6d.

The Law of Nations Considered as Independent Political Communities. By TRAVERS TWISS, D.C.L. Regius Professor of Civil Law in the University of Oxford. 2 vols. 8vo. 30s. or separately, PART I. Peace, 12s. PART II. War, 18s.

A Nautical Dictionary, defining the Technical Language relative to the Building and Equipment of Sailing Vessels and Steamers, &c. By ARTHUR YOUNG. Second Edition; with Plates and 150 Woodcuts. 8vo. 18s.

Works of Utility and General Information.

Modern Cookery for Private Families, reduced to a System of Easy Practice in a Series of carefully-tested Receipts. By ELIZA ACTON. Newly revised and enlarged; with 8 Plates, Figures, and 150 Woodcuts. Fcp. 6s.

On Food and its Digestion; an Introduction to Dietetics. By W. BRINTON, M.D. Physician to St. Thomas's Hospital, &c. With 48 Woodcuts. Post 8vo. 12s.

Wine, the Vine, and the Cellar. By THOMAS G. SHAW. Second Edition, revised and enlarged, with Frontispiece and 31 Illustrations on Wood. 8vo 16s.

A Practical Treatise on Brewing; with Formulæ for Public Brewers, and Instructions for Private Families. By W. BLACK. Fifth Edition. 8vo. 10s. 6d.

How to Brew Good Beer: a complete Guide to the Art of Brewing Ale, Bitter Ale, Table Ale, Brown Stout, Porter, and Table Beer. By JOHN PITT. Revised Edition. Fcp. 4s. 6d.

The Billiard Book. By Captain CRAWLEY, Author of 'Billiards, its Theory and Practice,' &c With nearly 100 Diagrams on Steel and Wood. 8vo. 21s.

Whist, What to Lead. By CAM. Third Edition. 32mo. 1s.

The Cabinet Lawyer; a Popular Digest of the Laws of England, Civil, Criminal, and Constitutional. 23rd Edition, entirely recomposed, and brought down by the AUTHOR to the close of the Parliamentary Session of 1867. Fcp. 10s. 6d.

The Philosophy of Health; or, an Exposition of the Physiological and Sanitary Conditions conducive to Human Longevity and Happiness. By SOUTHWOOD SMITH, M.D. Eleventh Edition, revised and enlarged; with 113 Woodcuts. 8vo. 7s. 6d.

A Handbook for Readers at the British Museum. By THOMAS NICHOLS. Post 8vo. 6s.

Hints to Mothers on the Management of their Health during the Period of Pregnancy and in the Lying-in Room. By T. BULL, M.D. Fcp. 5s.

The Maternal Management of Children in Health and Disease. By the same Author. Fcp. 5s.

Notes on Hospitals. By FLORENCE NIGHTINGALE. Third Edition, enlarged; with 13 Plans. Post 4to. 18s.

The Executor's Guide. By J. C. HUDSON. Enlarged Edition, revised by the Author, with reference to the latest reported Cases and Acts of Parliament. Fcp. 6s.

The Law relating to Benefit Building Societies; with Practical Observations on the Act and all the Cases decided thereon, also a Form of Rules and Forms of Mortgages. By W. TIDD PRATT, Barrister. 2nd Edition. Fcp. 3s. 6d.

Willich's Popular Tables for Ascertaining the Value of Lifehold, Leasehold, and Church Property, Renewal Fines, &c.; the Public Funds; Annual Average Price and Interest on Consols from 1731 to 1861; Chemical, Geographical, Astronomical, Trigonometrical Tables, &c. Post 8vo. 10s.

Decimal Interest Tables at Twenty-four Different Rates not exceeding Five per Cent. Calculated for the use of Bankers. To which are added Commission Tables at One-eighth and One-fourth per Cent. By J. R. COULTHART. New Edition. 8vo. 15s.

Maunder's Treasury of Knowledge and Library of Reference: comprising an English Dictionary and Grammar, Universal Gazetteer, Classical Dictionary, Chronology, Law Dictionary, Synopsis of the Peerage, useful Tables, &c. Fcp. 10s. 6d.

INDEX.

cton's Modern Cookery 20
Lcock's Residence in Japan.............. 19
llib on Formation of Christianity 15
lpine Guide (The) 18
vensleben's Maximilian in Mexico 4
john's Manual of the Metalloids 9
rnold's Manual of English Literature .. 5
nott's Elements of Physics 8
randines Cami 18
utumn Holidays of a Country Parson ... 4
yre's Treasury of Bible Knowledge...... 14

acon's Essays by Whately 5
——— Life and Letters, by Spedding .. 2
——— Works.............................. 4
ain on the Emotions and Will 7
——— on the Senses and Intellect 7
——— on the Study of Character 7
all's Guide to the Central Alps......... 18
——— Guide to the Western Alps 10
——— Guide to the Eastern Alps 16
annard's Drawing from Nature 12
ayldon's Rents and Tillages 13
eaton Tracks 10
cker's Charicles and Gallus 17
ethoven's Letters 4
enfey's Sanskrit-English Dictionary ... 6
rry's Journals 3
lack's Treatise on Brewing............. 20
lackley and Friedlander's German
and English Dictionary ......·........ 6
laine's Rural Sports 19
——— Veterinary Art 19
light's Week at the Land's End 17
ooth's Epigrams 6
ourne on Screw Propeller 13
———'s Catechism of the Steam Engine.. 13
——— Handbook of Steam Engine 13
——— Treatise on the Steam Engine 13
owdler's Family Shakspeare........... 18
ramley-Moore's Six Sisters of the Valleys 17
rande's Dictionary of Science, Literature,
and Art................................. 18
ray's (C.) Education of the Feelings 7
——— Philosophy of Necessity 7
——— On Force.......................... 7
rinton on Food and Digestion 20
ristow's Glossary of Mineralogy 8
rodie's Constitutional History 1
——— (Sir C. B.) Works................. 11
rowne's Exposition 32 Articles 14
uckle's History of Civilisation 2
ull's Hints to Mothers 20
——— Maternal Management of Children.. 20
unsen's Ancient Egypt 3
——— God in History 3
——— Memoirs 3

Bunsen (E. De) on Apocrypha............ 15
———'s Keys of St. Peter 15
Burke's Vicissitudes of Families 4
Burton's Christian Church 3

Cabinet Lawyer........................ 20
Calvert's Wife's Manual 15
Cates's Biographical Dictionary 3
Cats and Farlie's Moral Emblems 12
Chorale Book for England 11
Christian Schools and Scholars 6
Clough's Lives from Plutarch 2
Colenso (Bishop) on Pentateuch and Book
of Joshua............................... 15
Collins's Horse Trainer's Guide 19
Commonplace Philosopher in Town and
Country 6
Conington's Chemical Analysis 10
——— Translation of Virgil's Æneid 18
Contanseau's Two French and English
Dictionaries 6
Conybeare and Howson's Life and Epistles
of St. Paul 14
Cook's Acts of the Apostles............. 14
Copland's Dictionary of Practical Medicine 11
Coulthart's Decimal Interest Tables 20
Cox's Manual of Mythology............. 17
——— Tales of the Great Persian War ... 2
——— Tales from Greek Mythology ... 17
——— Tales of the Gods and Heroes... 17
——— Tales of Thebes and Argos 17
Crawley's Billiard Book................ 20
Cresy's Encyclopædia of Civil Engineering 13
Critical Essays of a Country Parson...... 6
Crowe's History of France 2
Crump on Banking, &c................... 19
Cussans's Grammar of Heraldry 12

Dart's Iliad of Homer 18
D'Aubigné's History of the Reformation in
the time of Calvin 2
Davidson's Introduction to New Testament 14
Dayman's Dante's Divina Commedia 18
Dead Shot (The), by Marksman 19
De Burgh's Maritime International Law.. 20
De la Rive's Treatise on Electricity 8
De Morgan on Matter and Spirit 7
De Tocqueville's Democracy in America. 2
Disraeli's Speeches on Reform 5
Dobson on the Ox 19
Dove on Storms 6
Dyer's City of Rome 2

Eastlake's Hints on Household Taste 12
Edwards's Shipmaster's Guide 20
Elements of Botany 9

ELLICOTT's Commentary on Ephesians 14
———— Destiny of the Creature 14
———— Lectures on Life of Christ 14
———— Commentary on Galatians 14
———— Pastoral Epist. 14
———— Philippians,&c. 14
———— Thessalonians 14
ENGEL's Introduction to National Music .. 11
Essays and Reviews 15
—— on Religion and Literature, edited by
MANNING, FIRST and SECOND SERIES .. 15
EWALD's History of Israel 14

FAIRBAIRN'S Application of Cast and
Wrought Iron to Building 13
———— Information for Engineers 13
———— Treatise on Mills and Millwork 13
FAIRBAIRN on Iron Shipbuilding 13
FARRAR's Chapters on Language 5
FELKIN on Hosiery & Lace Manufactures.. 13
FFOULKES's Christendom's Divisions 15
FLIEDNER's (Pastor) Life.................. 4
FRANCIS's Fishing Book 19
———— (Sir P.) Memoir and Journal 3
FROUDE's History of England 1
———— Short Studies 6

GANOT's Elementary Physics 8
GILBERT and CHURCHILL's Dolomite Moun-
tains 16
GILL's Papal Drama 2
GILLY's Shipwrecks of the Navy 17
GOODEVE's Elements of Mechanism........ 13
GORLE's Questions on BROWNE's Exposition
of the 39 Articles 14
GRANT's Ethics of Aristotle.............. 4
Graver Thoughts of a Country Parson.... 6
Gray's Anatomy.......................... 11
GREENE's Corals and Sea Jellies 9
———— Sponges and Animalculae....... 9
GROVE on Correlation of Physical Forces .. 8
GWILT's Encyclopædia of Architecture 13

Handbook of Angling, by EPHEMERA...... 19
Hare on Election of Representatives 5
HARLEY and BROWN's Histological Demon-
strations 11
HARTWIG's Harmonies of Nature.......... 9
———— Polar World 9
———— Sea and its Living Wonders.... 9
———— Tropical World 9
HAUGHTON's Manual of Geology 8
HAWKER's Instructions to Young Sports-
men 19
HEARN's Plutology 8
———— on English Government 8
HELPS's Spanish Conquest in America 2
HENDERSON's Folk-Lore 6
HERSCHEL's Essays from Reviews 10
———— Outlines of Astronomy........ 7
———— Preliminary Discourse on the
Study of Natural Philosophy 8
HEWITT on the Diseases of Women 10
HODGSON's Time and Space.............. 7
HOLMES's System of Surgery 10
HOOKER and WALKER-ARNOTT's British
Flora 9
HOPKINS's Hawaii 8
HORNE's Introduction to the Scriptures .. 14
———— Compendium of the Scriptures .. 14

HORSLEY's Manual of Poisons ....
HOSKYNS's Occasional Essays............
How we Spent the Summer............
HOWARD's Gymnastic Exercises ....
HOWITT's Australian Discovery..........
———— Rural Life of England ......
———— Visits to Remarkable Places ....
HUDSON's Executor's Guide ....
HUGHES's Garden Architecture..........
———— (W.) Manual of Geography ....
HULLAH's History of Modern Music ......
———— Transition Musical Lectures ....
———— Sacred Music ....
HUMPHREYS's Sentiments of Shakspeare ..
HUTTON's Studies in Parliament ....
Hymns from Lyra Germanica ....

INGELOW's Poems ....
———— Story of Doom ....
Icelandic Legends, SECOND SERIES ......

JAMESON's Legends of the Saints and Mar-
tyrs ....
———— Legends of the Madonna ......
———— Legends of the Monastic Orders
JAMESON and EASTLAKE's History of Our
Lord ....
JENNER's Holy Child..................
JOHNSTON's Gazetteer, or General Geo-
graphical Dictionary ....

KALISCH's Commentary on the Bible......
———— Hebrew Grammar............
KEITH on Destiny of the World..........
———— Fulfilment of Prophecy......
KELLER's Lake Dwellings of Switzerland ..
KESTEVEN's Domestic Medicine ....
KIRBY and SPENCE's Entomology..........
KNIGHT's Arch of Titus...............

Lady's Tour round Monte Rosa............
LANDON's (L. E. L.) Poetical Works ......
LATHAM's English Dictionary..............
———— River Plate................
LAWRENCE on Rocks..................
LECKY's History of Rationalism ....
Leisure Hours in Town................
Lessons of Middle Age ....
Letters of Distinguished Musicians ......
LEWES's Biographical History of Philosophy
LIDDELL and SCOTT's Greek-English Lexicon
———— Abridged ditto ......
Life of Man Symbolised................
LINDLEY and MOORE's Treasury of Botany
LONGMAN's Lectures on History of England
LOUDON's Encyclopædia of Agriculture ....
———— Gardening ......
———— Plants ....
———— Trees and Shrubs
———— Cottage, Farm, and Villa Architecture
LOWNDES's Engineer's Handbook ....
Lyra Domestica......................
—— Eucharistica....................
—— Germanica 12,
—— Messianica ....
—— Mystica ....
—— Sacra ....
MACAULAY's (Lord) Essays..............

Macaulay's History of England 1
———— Lays of Ancient Rome 18
———— Miscellaneous Writings...... 6
———— Speeches 5
———— Works 1
Macfarren's Lectures on Harmony 11
Macleod's Elements of Political Economy .. 4
———— Dictionary of Political Economy .. 4
———— Elements of Banking........ 19
———— Theory and Practice of Banking 19
McCulloch's Dictionary of Commerce 19
———— Geographical Dictionary 7
Maguire's Irish in America 17
———— Life of Father Mathew 8
———— Rome and its Rulers 3
Malleson's French in India 2
Manning on Holy Ghost 15
———— England and Christendom 16
Marshall's Physiology 10
Marshman's History of India 2
———— Life of Havelock 4
Martineau's Endeavours after the Christian Life 16
Massey on Shakspeare's Sonnets 18
———— 's History of England 1
Massingberd's History of the Reformation 8
Maunder's Biographical Treasury 4
———— Geographical Treasury 8
———— Historical Treasury 3
———— Scientific and Literary Treasury 9
———— Treasury of Knowledge 20
———— Treasury of Natural History .. 9
Maury's Physical Geography.......... 8
May's Constitutional History of England.. 1
Melville's Digby Grand.............. 17
———— General Bounce 17
———— Gladiators 17
———— Good for Nothing 17
———— Holmby House............ 17
———— Interpreter 17
———— Kate Coventry............ 17
———— Queen's Maries 17
Mendelssohn's Letters 4
Merivale's (H.) Historical Studies 1
———— (C.) Fall of the Roman Republic 2
———— Romans under the Empire .. 2
———— Boyle Lectures 2
Miles on Horse's Foot and Horse Shoeing . 19
———— on Horse's Teeth and Stables .. 19
Mill on Liberty 4
———— on Representative Government .. 4
———— on Utilitarianism 4
———— 's Dissertations and Discussions .. 4
———— Political Economy 4
———— System of Logic.......... 4
———— Hamilton's Philosophy 4
———— Inaugural Address at St. Andrew's. 5
Miller's Elements of Chemistry 10
Mitchell's Manual of Assaying 13
Monsell's Beatitudes 15
———— His Presence not his Memory.. 15
———— 'Spiritual Songs' 15
Montgomery on Pregnancy 10
Moore's Irish Melodies.............. 18
———— Lalla Rookh.............. 18
———— Journal and Correspondence .. 6
———— Poetical Works.......... 18
———— (Dr. G.) First Man 8
Morell's Elements of Psychology 7
———— Mental Philosophy 7
Mosheim's Ecclesiastical History 15

Mozart's Letters 4
Müller's (Max) Chips from a German Workshop 7
———— Lectures on the Science of Language 5
———— (K. O.) Literature of Ancient Greece 2
Murchison on Continued Fevers,........ 10
Mure's Language and Literature of Greece 2

New Testament Illustrated with Wood Engravings from the Old Masters 12
Newman's History of his Religious Opinions 8
Nicholas's Pedigree of the English People 6
Nichols's Handbook to British Museum.. 5
Nightingale's Notes on Hospitals 20
Nilsson's Scandinavia 9

Odling's Animal Chemistry 10
———— Course of Practical Chemistry .. 10
———— Manual of Chemistry.......... 10
Original Designs for Wood Carving 18
Owen's Comparative Anatomy and Physiology of Vertebrate Animals 8
Owen's Lectures on the Invertebrata..... 8
Oxenham on Atonement 16

Packe's Guide to the Pyrenees 16
Paget's Lectures on Surgical Pathology .. 10
Pereira's Manual of Materia Medica...... 11
Perkins's Tuscan Sculptors 12
Phillips's Guide to Geology 8
Pictures in Tyrol 16
Piesse's Art of Perfumery 13
———— Chemical, Natural, and Physical Magic 13
Pike's English and their Origin 6
Pitt on Brewing 20
Playtime with the Poets 18
Pratt's Law of Building Societies 20
Prescott's Scripture Difficulties........ 14
Proctor's Handbook of the Stars 7
———— Saturn 7
Pycroft's Course of English Reading 5
———— Cricket Field 19

Raikes's Englishman in India 17
Raymond on Fishing without Cruelty 18
Reade's Poetical Works 18
Recreations of a Country Parson 6
Reilly's Map of Mont Blanc.......... 16
Rivers's Rose Amateur's Guide 9
Rogers's Correspondence of Grayson 7
———— Eclipse of Faith 7
———— Defence of Faith 7
———— Essays from the Edinburgh Review 7
———— Reason and Faith 7
Roget's Thesaurus of English Words and Phrases 5
Ronalds's Fly-Fisher's Entomology 19
Rowton's Debater 5
Rudd's Aristophanes 18
Russell on Government and Constitution 1

Sandars's Justinian's Institutes 4
Schubert's Life, translated by Coleridge 4
Scott's Lectures on the Fine Arts 11
Seebohm's Oxford Reformers of 1498 .. 2
Sewell's After Life 16
———— Glimpse of the World 16
———— History of the Early Church 8
———— Journal of a Home Life 17

SEWELL's Passing Thoughts on Religion   ..   13
———— Preparation for Communion   13
———— Principles of Education   13
———— Readings for Confirmation   13
———— Readings for Lent   13
———— Examination for Confirmation ..   15
———— Stories and Tales   17
SHAW's Work on Wine   20
SHEPHERD's Iceland   16
SHIPLEY's Church and the World   15
———— Tracts for the Day............   15
Short Whist   19
SHORT's Church History   3
SMITH's (SOUTHWOOD) Philosophy of Health   20
———— (J.) Paul's Voyage and Shipwreck   14
———— (G.) Reign of King David........   14
———— Wesleyan Methodism   8
———— (SYDNEY) Miscellaneous Works ..   6
———— Moral Philosophy   6
———— Wit and Wisdom   6
SMITH on Cavalry Drill and Manoeuvres...   19
SOUTHEY's (Doctor)   6
———— Poetical Works............   18
Springdale Abbey....................   17
STANLEY's History of British Birds.......   9
STEBBING's Analysis of MILL's Logic.....   5
STEPHEN's Essays in Ecclesiastical Bio-
graphy   4
———— Lectures on History of France   2
STIRLING's Secret of Hegel.............   7
STONEHENGE on the Dog..............   19
———— on the Greyhound   19
STRANGE on Sea Air   11
———— Restoration of Health   11
Sunday Afternoons at the Parish Church ..   6

TAYLOR's (Jeremy) Works, edited by EDEN   15
———— (E.) Selections from some Con-
temporary Poets   18
TENNENT's Ceylon   9
———— Wild Elephant.............   9
THIRLWALL's History of Greece   2
TIMBS's Curiosities of London   17
THOMSON's (Archbishop) Laws of Thought   5
———— (A. T.) Conspectus   11
TODD (A.) on Parliamentary Government ..   2
———'s Cyclopædia of Anatomy and Physio-
logy   11
———— and BOWMAN's Anatomy and Phy-
siology of Man   11

TROLLOPE's Barchester Towers...........   17
———— Warden   17
TWISS's Law of Nations   20
TYNDALL's Lectures on Heat............   6
———— Lectures on Sound   6
———— Memoir of FARADAY   4

URE's Dictionary of Arts, Manufactures, and
Mines   13

VAN DER HOEVEN's Handbook of Zoology..   8
VAUGHAN's (R.) Revolutions in English
History.........................   1
———— Way to Rest   7

WALKER on the Rifle   19
WARD's Workmen and Wages..........   4
WATSON's Principles and Practice of Physic   10
WATTS's Dictionary of Chemistry..........   10
WEBB's Objects for Common Telescopes....   7
WEBSTER & WILKINSON's Greek Testament   13
WELD's Florence   16
WELLINGTON's Life, by GLEIG   3
WELLS on Dew   8
WENDT's Papers on Maritime Law   20
WEST on Children's Diseases   10
WHATELY's English Synonymes   5
———— Life and Correspondence......   3
———— Logic   5
———— Rhetoric   5
———— on Religious Worship   16
Whist, what to Lead, by CAM..........   20
WHITE and RIDDLE's Latin-English Dic-
tionaries   5
WILLICH's Popular Tables   20
WINSLOW on Light...................   8
WOOD's Bible Animals   9
———— Homes without Hands..........   9
WOODWARD's Historical and Chronological
Encyclopædia.....................   3
WRIGHT's Homer's Iliad   18

YONGE's English-Greek Lexicon   5
———— Abridged ditto.............   5
———— Horace   18
YOUNG's Nautical Dictionary............   20
YOUATT on the Dog   19
———— on the Horse.................   19